The wheels crossed onto the bridge with a double bump and rumbled on the planking. She felt an odd, vertiginous swaying and heard a CRACK as loud as gunfire.

"Whoa," exclaimed Gregory. The van lurched as he braked.

CRACK. Too late. CRACK-CRACK.

The bridge swayed, the planking dropped away in front of them and Janet's stomach lurched as they hung in the air for a moment and then, with a down rush like a roller coaster's first drop, plunged nose first into the ravine.

The crash of metal on rock went on and on, fading and rising and fading as if somebody were playing with the volume dial. At last it died away and the only sound was the rain battering the outside of the van.

Previously published Worldwide Mystery titles by
GRETCHEN SPRAGUE

DEATH IN GOOD COMPANY
MAQUETTE FOR MURDER
MURDER IN A HEAT WAVE

GRETCHEN SPRAGUE

DEATH BY THUNDER

WORLDWIDE®

TORONTO • NEW YORK • LONDON
AMSTERDAM • PARIS • SYDNEY • HAMBURG
STOCKHOLM • ATHENS • TOKYO • MILAN
MADRID • WARSAW • BUDAPEST • AUCKLAND

DEATH BY THUNDER

A Worldwide Mystery/December 2006

First published by St. Martin's Press LLC.

ISBN-13: 978-0-373-26585-5
ISBN-10:   0-373-26585-9

Copyright © 2005 by Elmer Sprague.
All rights reserved. No part of this book may be reproduced
or transmitted in any form or by any means, electronic or
mechanical, including photocopying, recording or by any
information storage and retrieval system, without permission
in writing from the publisher. For information, contact:
St. Martin's Press, 175 Fifth Avenue, New York, NY 10010-7848 U.S.A.

All characters in this book are fictitious, and any resemblance to
actual persons, living or dead, is purely coincidental.

® and TM are trademarks of Harlequin Enterprises Limited.
Trademarks indicated with ® are registered in the United States
Patent and Trademark Office, the Canadian Trade Marks Office
and in other countries.

Printed in U.S.A.

Acknowledgment

Thanks to Patti McCormack Smith, PE, for advice about bridge construction.

PART ONE

November 1987
Paul

ONE

Blasphemy and Trespass

THE SIGN STOOD on the shoulder of Oak Hollow Road, tilted a little on its portable frame:

CAUTION BLASTING
TURN OFF TWO-WAY RADIOS

Paul Willard hurled the van into the tight curves that followed the course of the stream. At the mouth of Henley Lane, he braked hard, wrenched the wheel right, scattered gravel between third-growth stands of black birch. The blast permit was tacked to a tree beside a driveway cut at the top of the first steep rise.

Blasphemers.

Paul slowed, turned right and jounced up the rutted clay track between felled trees and uprooted stumps. A couple of hundred yards up, he left the van skewed behind a parked dump truck and continued on foot, passing a parked backhoe and then Alta's red Mercedes, tucked in next to an oak. Fifty yards farther up, two people in hard hats beside a parked van looked around at the sound of his footsteps; then the shorter one headed down the track toward him.

Alta.

Alta Ferguson, blasphemer-in-chief.

Health-club fit inside a scarlet ski jacket, her strategically faded jeans tucked into work boots, she picked her way down the

ruts toward him as sure-footed as a doe. When they came within
easy earshot, she said, "Hello, Paul." Out of sight behind her, a
drill screamed in rock. Below the brim of her hard hat, the art-
fully natural fine-boned face smiled. "To what do I owe the pleasure, neighbor?"

"Oh—" His bare hands deep in his mackinaw pockets, Paul
bore down on the local drawl he'd been perfecting for twenty
years: two slow syllables—"O-oh—" and a pause, as if to gather
the words. "Neighborly curiosity, I guess." Pause. "You're in an
almighty rush to blast, it looks like."

She smiled as if he'd wished her well. "You know construction. If we don't get the footings in before frost, we'll be held up
until summer."

He knew construction. These days, everybody knew construction.

Five or six snowflakes meandered through the air. Snow! he
shouted silently. *Blow! C'mon, Earth, gimme a blizzard! Gimme
a "B," gimme an "L," gimme an "I"*—

But Earth wasn't to be chivvied; the first week of November
was too early for serious snow. Paul eased into a stroll again,
passing Alta and ambling on up the rutted track to the edge of
the flat, stony hilltop where the van was parked. DELEO CON-
STRUCTION—COMPLETE EXCAVATION SERVICES was lettered on
the door. The man beside it was in the first half of his forties,
stocky and fit, with the alert diplomat's eyes of the independent
contractor.

The drill/screech stopped, leaving Paul's ears ringing. Twenty
yards farther on, a man in protective gear was wrestling a drill
along the base of a treeless mound of bedrock that bulked against
the mottled gray sky.

Paul extended his hand to the man by the van. "Paul Willard."

The man accepted it. "Tony DeLeo."

"The man in charge?"

"Blasting contractor."

Paul nodded sideways toward the bulk of stone. "Big job."

DeLeo's eyes didn't move from Paul's face, but his head rose a millimeter in what might have been the beginning of a nod.

"Yes," Paul acknowledged. "We-ell, I think maybe it'd be a good idea if you held off on the blasting."

"Oh?"

"Until I have a chance to see your insurance coverage."

A couple of beats of silence. "You from the state?"

"In a manner of speaking."

"Paul," said Alta. "Really. He isn't from the state, Tony. He's from dreamsville. He lives down the road and he doesn't want me to build my house where he can see it from his front deck."

"Correction," Paul said. "I'm a citizen, therefore I'm from the state. I'm from the Town of Claysburgh, the County of Putnam, the State of New York—"

"Paul," said Alta.

"—the United States of America, the planet Earth, the planetary system of Sol, the galaxy dubbed Milky Way, the universe, seen and unseen—"

"Paul, get out of the way," said Alta. "We're about to blast."

"Not until I inspect Mr. DeLeo's liability coverage."

"Paul—"

"It's my right under New York law."

"Oh, *God*."

He turned a smile toward her. "I'm a neighboring property owner who might be at risk from the blasting. I have a right to know if I'm covered."

"Oh, my God, everybody's a lawyer. You're not at risk. Your precious fifteen acres are a mile away."

"A mile by the road. A good deal less by crow flight."

"How far do you think a rock can fly?"

"We-ell—" A sideways glance at DeLeo, whose face showed nothing. "When did you last look at a bedrock map?"

"A *bedrock* map? What are you talking about?"

"You didn't think about it? I'm surprised, Alta, an active little builder like you. What I'm concerned with, as a landowner at risk, is that this outcrop here"—he tapped his boot toe on the stone they were standing on—"that you want to blast away to put up your big glass house and your double tennis court and your Olympic swimming pool—"

Alta was smiling.

He stopped.

He started over, tamping down rage with rehearsed pedantry. "This outcrop, as you'd know if you'd paid attention, is part of a faulted granite sheet that underlies the Oak Hollow watershed. As everybody knows who has ever looked at a highway cut, the faults in this granite are full of water. This granite is our aquifer. If you blast here, you've got a chance of shutting down my well, and five or six others besides." He matched Alta's smile. "Then you'd see lawyers."

"My God, you are full of it." Alta moved a couple of steps down the track. "Tony, let's get on with the job. Paul, you can come back down out of range or you can stay up here and get some of that faulted granite on your skull. You want to make Marion a widow?"

Tony DeLeo said, "Just a second, Mrs. Ferguson."

Alta stopped.

DeLeo said, "There's a copy of the policy in the van. I don't have any problem letting him look at it."

"He's bullshitting you, Tony."

"That's okay." DeLeo leaned into the van and pulled a scuffed portfolio from behind the seat. He unzipped it and thumbed through a sheaf of papers, took out four long, densely printed sheets, and held them out to Paul. "If you can make any sense out of it."

Paul nodded and took the papers. He began reading at the top. Over at the stone mound, the drill screamed, drowning the crisp rustle of paper. Presently it stopped; things clattered, and after a few minutes the workman came across to the van lugging the drill. DeLeo went around and opened the back for him. He came back and said, "I think the part you want is on the third page."

Paul looked up and nodded again. He turned slowly to page three and read a turgid paragraph.

Alta said, "Paul, come *on*."

He ignored her and read through to the end. Slowly he folded the policy, then handed it to DeLeo, who tucked it back into the portfolio and said, "All okay?"

"Well—" *(We-ell)* "I don't know." He was running out of stalls.

Alta said, "Oh, shit."

"Mr. DeLeo," Paul said, "just let me show you something." He started past the van toward the drilling site. Behind him, Alta said, "Tony—"

DeLeo said, "Don't worry," and caught up with Paul. Their boots rasped on the stone. Paul stopped for a moment and ran his toe across grooves in the surface. "Ice age glaciation."

"Mm-hm," said DeLeo.

Paul crossed to the base of the stone mound, where a scarp angled steeply down to the floor of the valley called Oak Hollow. The unweathered rock inside the drill holes was salmon pink. "She's blowing away half of this rock so she can have a pool beside the house," he said. "A pool with a view."

"Mm-hm." DeLeo was humoring him. Fine; better indulgence than impatience.

They were overlooking a winding stretch of Oak Hollow Road. Far below, a fuel-oil truck and three cars swung into the curves. "I just want to show you why I'm concerned," he said. "My house is right through that fold, just south of that stand of hemlocks." He moved his head to show the direction, but didn't take his eyes from the road. "It's weathered cedar, so it's hard to see from here."

DeLeo said, "I like a house that fits in."

"Like this one will," said Paul.

DeLeo was silent.

Down on the road, a silver subcompact flashed into view, taking the snaky turns at speed, slowing just before it passed out of sight. Even from up there, Paul could see the right turn signal begin to blink.

He tipped his head toward the uneven face of the mound. "From below, this looks like an animal head. My wife and I call it Big Bear."

"An Indian name?" Still indulging him.

"Just private between us. Earth laid down this stone a billion years ago. It's the oldest visible stone in North America."

"That's what they say."

"It's blasphemy," said Paul.

DeLeo said nothing.

"But just another job."

Silence, then, "I can't get used to a woman using language like she does." He took his hand from the stone. "Okay, let's go."

Alta still stood next to DeLeo's van. "Satisfied, Mr. Citizen of the Universe?"

"Hard to tell." Paul's ears strained.

But it was Alta who was the first to hear it. "Somebody's coming up," she said. Then Paul heard the laboring motor and the crunch of tires on the dry clay, and moments later the silver Civic with the dented right-rear fender came jouncing around the last bend in the track.

"Well, well," said Alta, "it's your wife."

Marion braked behind DeLeo's van, opened the car door, and stepped out. Laugh crinkles were active behind her glasses.

"What brings you up here, Marion?" said Alta. "Tracking down your wandering spouse?"

Marion reached back across the front seat and brought out a manila envelope. "Tracking you down, actually." She undid the clasp, pulled out a bundle of papers stapled into a blue backing sheet, and held them out. "Brought you a little present."

Alta made no move.

Marion stooped, laid the papers at Alta's feet, straightened, and said, "You have been duly served with a court order signed by His Honor Justice Whalen, directing you to appear in New York Supreme Court for the County of Putnam on Friday morning, November sixth, to show cause why your building permit shouldn't be revoked, and staying any further work on this project until all parties may be heard. In other words, Alta, no blasting today unless you want to go to jail for contempt of court."

"Are you *serious?*"

"Read it."

"Fuck it."

Marion smiled. "If that's your taste, but I do suggest you read it first."

"*Fuck* it. You people are out of your minds. Judge Whalen is out of his mind. You cannot possibly have any grounds for a court order. I have, for God's sake, danced around this town's land-use maypole for three fucking years. I have every permit for every goddamn move I need to make. So help me God, I think I even have a permit to take a piss at three a.m. on alternate Thursdays. There can't possibly be any reason to stop this project."

"Well, Judge Whalen thinks there may be," said Marion. "It seems there may be something funny about your building permit. The judge wants to hear about it Friday morning."

"My *building* permit? You can't be serious. So help me God, this isn't law, it's harassment." Alta turned to DeLeo. "Forget the building permit. I've got the blasting permit. Tony, blow that fucking rock."

Nobody moved. Then DeLeo bent and picked up the papers. He flipped through, read something in the middle, looked at the last page for a longer time. Finally he refolded it and held it out. "You'd better have your lawyer look at this, Mrs. Ferguson. I can't do any blasting until this gets cleared up."

"Tony—"

He shook his head. "Sorry, but I've got a license to think about."

Another silence; then Alta wheeled on Paul and Marion. "You two will hear from my lawyer. Now get off my land, both of you. You're trespassing."

TWO

Investigator

THEY HAD FINISHED the lemon chicken from the Korean takeout in Phillips Landing and were about to crack open the fortune cookies when the crunch of tires on gravel tightened Paul's chest muscles. "Expecting anybody?" he said.

Marion shook her head. He pushed back his chair and went out to the front room. Through the uncurtained windows he saw an anonymous sedan pull up on the driveway apron in front of the house. Its headlights went off as he flicked on the outdoor floodlight and opened the front door. A man in corduroys and a leather jacket slammed the door and peered up the steps to the front deck. "Paul Willard?"

"Himself."

"Investigator Noel Riesbach, from the sheriff's office." He reached in a pocket as he climbed the steps, pulled out a leather case, and displayed a shield. "I need to talk to you and your wife for a few minutes. Is it all right if I come in?"

Steadying his breathing, Paul stepped back and let him into the house. Marion had followed him into the front room. "Investigator Riesbach," Paul said. "My wife, Marion."

A nod. "I hope I'm not interrupting your dinner. There's been an accident, and I just need to ask you folks a couple of questions."

Marion went white. "Janet?"

"Who's Janet?" said Riesbach.

Then it wasn't. Color came back to Marion's face as she said,

"My cousin, Janet Upton. She just left for Texas." Janet held the place in their lives of the child they had never had. Twenty-two and in love, running off to Texas to marry Cal Stanton, whom they distrusted, she had not parted with them amicably. "Driving," said Marion. "Alone."

"No," Riesbach said. "No, nothing like that."

So it wasn't Janet. "Why don't we sit down," Marion said and did so, settling at one end of the love seat that flanked the fireplace. Paul joined her; Riesbach took one of the easy chairs facing them. "I understand you were up at Alta Ferguson's building site this afternoon," he said.

"Oh, for heaven's sake." Annoyance sharpened Marion's voice. "Don't tell me she's complaining about trespass. We left as soon as she asked us to."

"No," Riesbach said, "nothing like that. I was just wondering when you were there."

"Early afternoon," Paul said. "Two, two-thirty, maybe. I wasn't looking at the time."

Marion said, "I called you from Four Corners at one forty-five."

"And I left right away. So call it two, maybe a couple of minutes before."

"And how long were you there?"

Paul looked at Marion. "I guess we were gone by a quarter to three."

"About that," she said. "I got to the art center a few minutes after three."

"Did you see anybody at the site?" said Riesbach.

Paul said, "Well, Alta. And the blasting contractor, Tony DeLeo, and one of his workmen. Marion came later."

"Anybody else? On Henley Lane, maybe, or in the woods? Hikers, bird-watchers, something like that?"

"It wasn't that nice a day," said Paul.

"So—"

"No hikers, birders, or something like that. Nobody."

Riesbach looked at Marion. She shook her head. "What did you do after you left?" he asked.

Paul said, "I went down to town hall and served some legal papers."

"On—?"

"On Charlie Emmett in the building inspector's office and LaVon Toomey in the clerk's office. It took maybe five minutes. Then I came home and got to work."

"Doing—?"

"Scouting for downed branches in the woods until it got too dark. Then I came home and worked in my studio until Marion got home."

"It isn't far through the woods to the Ferguson property. Did you go anywhere near the building site?"

Paul shook his head. "I went the other way."

Riesbach's eyes were disconcerting—not their pale shade of blue-gray, but their steadiness. "Anybody see you?" he said.

Paul fought to hold his gaze steady. "Our resident doe and this year's twins. Twenty or thirty gray squirrels. Chickadees. Nobody human. Not that I was aware of, anyway."

"And when you got back, what were you doing in your studio?"

Marion answered that one; Paul talked not at all about work in progress and very little about completed projects. "Art," she said. "He assembles downed wood into sculptures." She didn't add that they were able to live on fifteen acres in the Hudson Highlands because Paul's dealer in New York City sold almost all of those assemblages at high five-figure prices; if Riesbach didn't already know that, he could easily find out.

"I see. What about you?"

"After Alta booted us? I went down to the village, to the art center. I was there until after six, helping hang next week's show. Then I went to Wong Lee and got our supper and came home, where I've been for"—she consulted her watch—"the past forty minutes." Then she asked the question that had been floating in the air, unexpressed, since he drove up their driveway. "Why are you asking us all this?"

Paul tried to keep his breathing quiet.

Riesbach said, "Late this afternoon, Alta Ferguson took a fall off that outcrop above Oak Hollow Road. The one you're suing her about."

Marion said, "You're kidding."

"Mrs. Willard, I don't kid about my work."

"No, I didn't—I mean—" Paul watched her gather her wits. "I'm sorry, I'm just startled. Is she badly injured?"

Riesbach's answer punched Paul in the solar plexus. "She was dead when the EMS got there."

PART TWO

August 1995
Janet

THREE

Straw Man

JANET UPTON WAS peering through the viewfinder of her camera, a few feet off the trail that climbed beside the quarry wall, when the storm hit. For a quarter of an hour, mutters had been swelling to drumrolls and flickers had been intensifying to flashes; now a gust whipped the treetops, the sudden swish and hiss heralding the downpour.

Janet hauled her poncho over the camera on the tripod and ducked under it. The first big drops splatted down. Lightning slashed; the instantaneous crack made her jump. Seconds later the rain hit, a waving scrim that veiled the stony outline of the cliff. She tripped the shutter. The din of the storm drowned the click.

But not the cry. An animal sound, not quite a scream, not quite a shout, it penetrated the rolling boom of thunder and the rush of rain. She jerked upright. The poncho slipped and she twitched it automatically back over the camera. Through the rain that curtained the cliff face, she saw something falling—

Some*one* falling.

Her mind tried to call it something else—a monstrous rag doll, a straw man, a scarecrow—

It struck a ledge, bounced too heavily for rag or straw, and tumbled out of sight down a steep slope of jagged boulders.

She ducked back under the poncho and with shaking hands worked the camera loose from the tripod and stuffed it into the day pack at her feet. The zipper stuck for a moment before she jerked it free and slid it shut. She hoisted the pack and slid her arms into the straps, collapsed the tripod and slung its carrying strap over one shoulder, and fought the wind to flap the poncho over the whole bundle. The hood blew back. After two fruitless tugs, she left it. She couldn't get any wetter; the storm had already drenched her T-shirt and plastered her hair to her head.

The first burst subsided into a steady downpour as she picked her way down. Muddy runoff coursed down the middle of the trail; her boots slid on the wet clay between the stones. Concentrating on her footing, she was surprised when she reached level ground.

She followed the trail around a heap of boulders and a sopping thicket of greenbrier and emerged beside the quarry floor, an expanse of leveled bedrock as big as a football field. Through the blowing curtain of rain, she could just see, halfway down the scree slope at the base of the quarried cliff, a bundle that was not stone.

Her heart hammering, she stood paralyzed for a moment. She knew basic first aid; she had practiced the Heimlich maneuver; she had watched a video of CPR. None of that would be of any use to someone who had fallen a hundred feet onto stone. She had once read a description of a human body after a ten-story fall; even in print, the details had nauseated her.

The trailhead where she had parked was a quarter of a mile away, the village of Phillips Landing another half mile by county road. In Phillips Landing were a police station, a firehouse, an ambulance corps. Earl's convenience store, at the edge of the village, had the nearest telephone.

She started out the trail to the road, running through the rain, the poncho flapping against her legs.

THE AMBULANCE AND a sheriff's patrol car were already parked at the trailhead when she got back, and another siren was whooping in the distance. While she'd been phoning, the storm had blown east into Connecticut and once more the air was still and hot. Her hair and her T-shirt had nearly dried.

She parked in the shade. Now with attention to spare for her own affairs, she took her camera out of the pack, unloaded the exposed film, and saw with relief that no rain had leaked in. She sealed the film and dropped it into her shorts pocket beside the two other rolls she had exposed that afternoon, locked the camera in the trunk, and followed the trail back toward the quarry. Somewhere behind her, the approaching siren peaked and died.

Another hiker was standing where the trail came out at the edge of the quarry floor—a young male, barely past his teens, red haired and husky, his face pale behind a spatter of freckles. Across the quarry, the EMS crew was just arriving at the base of the cliff. A uniformed deputy was kneeling on the scree beside the bundle. The *body*. Another man, a civilian, stood near him.

"There's been an accident," the redhead said. "Somebody fell off the cliff."

"I know," Janet said. "I called it in." She heard footsteps on the trail and wrenched her gaze from the cluster of people at the base of the cliff. Another deputy, female, stocky, sweating in her uniform, emerged from the tree cover. Her gaze moved up to the top of the cliff and down to the bundle—the *body*—and her lips pursed in a soundless whistle. Then she turned back to them and took a notebook from her pocket. The ID badge pinned to her shirt said "Deputy Rosa Torres."

The redheaded kid was named Gregory Ferguson; he lived on Ewing Road. Janet said she was Janet Upton and lived at 4 Oak Ridge Lane.

"You together?" asked Deputy Torres.

The kid shook his head; Janet said, "No."

"Did you see what happened?"

The redhead said, "I heard the sirens, is all. I just got down off the mountain and he"—jerking his head toward the cliff— "the officer was coming in from the road. He told me to stay put."

Looking where he'd gestured, Janet saw that the civilian was coming back, already more than halfway across the stone floor of the quarry. "How about you?" Deputy Torres asked her. "Did you see it?"

"Sort of." Janet shoved her fists into her shorts pockets. "Partly. I was off to the side of that trail beside the cliff. About a third of the way up, I guess. I was shooting the quarry face."

"Shooting?"

"Photographing. I'm a photographer."

The man who'd been beside the body stopped just outside the triangle of Janet, deputy, and redhead. A big day pack slung by one strap over his shoulder was still damp.

Janet said, "I heard a scream. I looked up from the camera and saw somebody falling."

"Did you see how he happened to fall?" said Torres.

"No. He was—I couldn't see the top of the cliff. I just saw the—the middle of his fall, not the top. Or the bottom. I didn't see him land. He hit—" She closed her eyes. The afterimage of that rag-doll plunge was engraved on her retina. "He hit a ledge and—he—bounced."

Deputy Torres said, "Take it easy."

"That's all." She opened her eyes again. "I couldn't see the top and I couldn't see the bottom. I didn't see him start to fall and I didn't see him land. I came on down, and—well, I didn't think there was anything I could do for him. I thought the best thing was to get professionals. I went out to Earl's"—Deputy Torres nodded—"and I called the sheriff. And then I came back."

"Okay." Deputy Torres turned to the man who had been with the officer by the body.

He was mid-thirtyish, with stick-straight sun-bleached brown hair and blue eyes vivid against an outdoor tan. He wasn't quite a stranger, Janet realized after a moment. She had met him in an earlier life. Life-Before-Texas. Besotted with Cal Stanton, she hadn't paid much attention, but although they had both aged nearly eight years, she recognized him as Eric Swanson.

It helped that she already knew Eric Swanson had been leading a group hike on Eagle's Nest today.

He said "Hi" to the redheaded kid, a tightness around his mouth attesting to what the body on the rocks must have looked like.

The redheaded kid said, "Who is it?"

Shock had addled Janet's thoughts; only then did it occur to her that the body at the base of the cliff might be someone from the group hike. Her stomach lurched: she knew—she loved—two people who'd been on that hike.

The man who must be Eric Swanson said, "Broderick Hale."

"Oh, my God," said Janet.

He looked at her then, and Deputy Torres said, "You know him?"

"He's my uncle," said Janet.

FOUR

Who, Where, When

HER UNCLE BY MARRIAGE, not by blood. Uncle Bud—Broderick Hale—had been married to Aunt Irene, who had died three years ago; Aunt Irene had been Janet's father's sister. As a child, Janet had kept her distance from Uncle Bud, who was an awful tease. She had known in a vague sort of way that he was expected to take part in the organized hike, but he was not one of the people for whom she had feared.

Deputy Rosa Torres said, "You weren't with him?"

Janet shook her head, and the man who had to be Eric Swanson said, "He was with me. I was leading a group hike up the mountain." He slipped the strap from his shoulder and set the pack on the ground.

"Your name?" said Torres.

If Janet had needed any further confirmation, yes, he was Eric Swanson. His address was forty miles down the river, in Tarrytown.

"Okay," said Deputy Torres. "What happened?"

Eric Swanson, she was remembering, had been a law student, back in Life-Before-Texas. He must have been an actual lawyer for several years now; the concise but complete way he was laying out the situation certainly sounded lawyerly. He must not spend all his waking hours at his desk or in a courtroom, though; his shorts revealed the hard calf and thigh muscles of a hiker.

The Hudson Land Trust, he said, had sponsored the hike as a lobbying effort for a law that would regulate building on steep slopes. The Claysburgh Town Board—one of whom was Broderick Hale—had been specifically invited; interested citizens were also welcome. Eric was a coleader with Marion Willard.

This much Janet had already known. What she also knew was that this was the second try. Way back before Texas, Marion and her husband, Paul, had been among those lobbying for such controls.

(Marion, Janet's mother's cousin—no real relation to Bud Hale, who was Janet's uncle by marriage on her *father's* side, although in Phillips Landing society the connection did constitute a relationship of some importance—Marion was one of the people for whom Janet had feared. Paul was the other. But it was Uncle Bud who had fallen.)

Anyway.

Twelve or thirteen people had shown up, Eric said. The hike had started from the trailhead at the end of Pine Street, in the village. That route was longer than the trail up the side of the quarry, but not nearly as steep.

"Where are they now?" asked Deputy Torres.

"Marion took most of the group back down the Pine Street trail."

"Excuse me." Deputy Torres withdrew a few steps, turned her back, unhooked her radio from her belt, and spoke into it for a minute or two. When she came back, she said, "Okay."

Okay. "We started around ten. Not everybody was in Outward Bound condition, so we took it slow and I worked in rest stops with chats about this and that, the geology of the Highlands, ecological communities, that sort of thing. We got to the summit around twelve-thirty and had lunch. People brought brown bags, I packed fruit punch for the group, and Marion brought brownies. After about an hour, we saw the storm approaching, so we packed up and headed down."

"Who didn't go back down the Pine Street trail?" asked Deputy Torres.

"I'm not sure of everybody," said Eric. "For starters, a couple of people went off on their own in the middle of things. Paul Willard went off on a side trail before we got to the summit. Paul bushwhacks around in the woods all the time, so I didn't have any worries. And Lowell Lamont—"

"*Lowell?*" said Janet.

Everybody looked at her.

"He's Leora's husband," she said.

"Who's Leora?" said Deputy Torres.

"Uncle Bud's daughter." Janet had been fond—was still fond, in a moderate, adult fashion—of her cousin Leora, who was a year younger and had been a good enough companion on extended-family visits. But she had interrupted. "I'm sorry."

Torres said, "Is that the Lamont of Lamont Electric?"

"Yes." Somebody was going to have to tell Leora. She looked at her watch. She wouldn't have time. She shouldn't even be standing here.

She went on standing there.

"Okay," said Torres to Eric. "Where did Lowell Lamont go?"

"I can't say for sure. As soon as we got to the summit, he made a speech and then he left without waiting for lunch. He started back down the way we'd come up, but there are several side trails after you get off the top."

"What kind of speech did he make?" asked Torres.

"Fairly hostile. People in his line of work generally don't like limitations on construction. Anyway, those two went their separate ways fairly early. After the festivities, apparently some people decided to come down this way in spite of the weather." He looked at the redheaded kid. "I guess you did."

"Yeah—" The redhead's voice cracked and he cleared his throat. "Yes, I did."

"Anybody else?" said Torres.

"I'm not sure," said Eric. "Marion was the sheepdog. I stayed at the top until everybody was off, and then I followed them down until we got to the cutoff that joins this trail."

"You're losing me," said Torres.

"Hold on." Eric knelt beside his pack, unzipped a pocket, and took out a map. He unfolded it and spread it on the ground. The redhead and Deputy Torres squatted on either side of him; Janet looked over his shoulder.

It was the hiker's standby, a U.S. Geological Survey topographic map, with contour lines marking twenty-foot changes in elevation. Eric touched a place where the contour lines were packed so closely together that they nearly touched. "This is the quarry face." A nearby spot at the center of a set of irregular concentric circles: "The summit." His finger moved along a zigzag dotted line. "This trail"—he nodded toward the fringe of trees through which Janet had descended—"switchbacks down beside the cliff. Call it the quarry trail. This"—another dotted line, long and wavy, also starting at the summit but leading off at a different angle—"is the trail from the Pine Street trailhead."

"Got it," said Torres.

"Okay," said Eric. "Now, up here, a couple of hundred yards below the summit, there's a short connector trail that runs around the back of the mountain to link the two downward trails. What you have is a triangle. The summit is the apex, the Pine Street trail and the quarry trail are the two legs, and the one that links them—call it the cutoff trail—is the base."

"Got it."

"As I said, I waited until everybody was off the summit, and then I followed them down to where the cutoff trail branches off. Marion waited there to be sure nobody accidentally took the wrong fork. After everybody was past, I took the cutoff over to where it joins the quarry trail and came down this way. I'd left my van down here so if anybody had decided to come down this way, I could give them a lift back to their cars at Pine Street. Anybody who wanted a ride knew to wait for me down here at the trailhead."

"And some people did come down this way?"

The redhead said, "I did."

"And apparently Councilman Hale did," said Eric.

"Yes, he did," said the redhead.

"You saw him?" said Deputy Torres.

"Not—I didn't see him *fall*. I saw where he was standing."

Torres stood up; the men followed suit. She flexed one leg and said to the redhead, "Okay, your turn."

"Yeah, well, I decided I wanted to see something besides the same trees over again. The real views are over here on the river side. So when they started rounding everybody up, I cut off and found this other trail, what we're calling the quarry trail. I was a little ways down and I heard Mr. Hale talking, over on that little spur that goes over to the top of the cliff. You know the place? There's a little side trail over to a ledge that juts out over the top of the cliff. It's a ways above where the cutoff joins the quarry trail."

"It isn't a constructed trail, it's just a path worn down by foot traffic," said Eric. "There's a warning sign, but people go anyway."

"And Mr. Hale was at that overlook?" said Torres.

"And Mr. Vanstaat."

"Vanstaat?"

"Schuyler Vanstaat. I'm friends with his son, Josh. I heard them, so I turned off on that little spur and I saw them standing there. Mr. Hale was talking about what a fantastic view it was and how we need to protect the scenery."

"You don't say." Eric sounded surprised. "Did he by any chance say he was going to vote for the Steep Slopes law?"

"Yeah, he did. Right then he did. Mr. Vanstaat was giving him an argument and Mr. Hale was, like, laughing at him. Then Mr. Vanstaat came back to the trail and I went over. Like, to take a look?"

"Did you talk with Mr. Hale?"

"Just a couple of minutes. He was laughing about Mr. Vanstaat, about that law. He said Mr. Vanstaat was trying to get him to say he'd vote against it, and he'd been teasing him, saying he thought he'd vote for it after all. Then the lightning was getting too close, so I came back to the trail and came on down."

"And Mr. Hale?" asked Torres.

"He stayed. I said it was getting dangerous, but he just laughed. He was still standing there when I left. The storm hit a few minutes after that. I was already a ways down this trail, the quarry trail, I guess just about where the switchbacks start."

"Ms. Upton says she heard a scream. Did you hear it?"

"Well, I guess maybe I did. I thought it was the wind. The storm just started and it was making a lot of noise, raining like you wouldn't believe, and blowing and thundering."

"How about you?" Torres said to Eric.

"I didn't hear it. If it happened soon after the storm hit, I was still around on the other side of the mountain, on the cutoff. I don't think it would have carried that far."

"Did you see Mr. Vanstaat?"

"Not after I left the summit. The last I remember seeing him was when we were eating lunch. He was lobbying Councilman Hale then too."

Deputy Torres checked back through her notes. Janet checked her watch. Three-twenty. She really, really had to leave soon.

But not quite yet, because Deputy Torres announced that she was going to see what was going on at the Pine Street trailhead, and Marion might still be waiting there, and it was Marion to whom Janet had learned to turn when things spun out of control. It was Marion, forgiving the years of estrangement, who had wangled her the job as director of the Highlands Art Center, which had enabled her finally to get out of Texas, all the way clear, finally, of Cal Stanton. So she followed the little parade up through the village. Deputy Torres's patrol car led; Eric and the redhead followed in Eric's black van; Janet, after a brief dispute with her 1983 clunker's ignition, trailed along behind.

Two patrol cars and five civilian vehicles crowded the parking lay-by at the Pine Street trailhead. One of the cars was Marion's ancient silver subcompact. Deputy Torres was talking to a male deputy beside the patrol cars. Janet parked across the road.

Marion, her pepper-and-salt hair tufted from rain and wind, met her in midpavement with a hug, and exclaimed, "Oh, love, what a thing! Are you all right?"

"I guess," said Janet. "Who's telling Leora?"

"Lowell."

"I thought he left in the middle."

"Oh, my dear. He came straggling out of the woods, mud from head to heels, just as Deputy McDonnell drove up with the news. He'd gone off the trail to you-know-what, and got lost, can you believe it? He'd been bushwhacking in all that rain for hours, and then to hear about Bud the minute he got back to civilization—*not* a nice homecoming. Eric," she called across road, "do you have any idea what's happened to Schuyler Vanstaat? He didn't come down with us, and his car's still here."

"Greg saw him up at the top of the quarry trail just before the storm," said Eric.

"Oh, *dear,* he wouldn't have tried to go down that way by himself, would he? In all that rain and wind?"

"He wasn't there when I got down. Maybe he's walking back through the village."

"Schuyler, walking an extra mile? Uphill? He barely made it up the mountain."

Janet said, "Marion, I've got to go."

Marion looked at her watch. "Oh, heavens! Go, love. I'll be there as soon as—oh, dear, where can Schuyler be?"

FIVE

Opening

THE HIGHLANDS ART CENTER was perched at the top of a steep
lane that wound up from Main Street. The building had been
erected seventy-five years before as a city mogul's country hide-
away. After the crash of 1929, title had passed to a series of owners who had put it to various poorly thought-out and unprofitable
uses. Sixteen years ago, a benefactor had acquired the property
for back taxes and deeded it to the art center with a small trust
fund intended to cover maintenance. The space being only mar-
ginally suitable for the workshops and exhibitions that were the
reason for the art center's existence, a more recent benefactor had
established a fund for renovation. The work had been going on
since early April, falling further behind schedule with every
week. The exhibition space and most of the rest of the ground
floor were finally finished, but the workshop areas on the lower
level were still a shambles of bare studs and dangling wiring. The
show opening today should have been mounted in June.

Five cars and the caterer's truck were parked in the lot. A
Dumpster half full of builder's debris took up another three
spaces. Irritated by its continuing presence, Janet pulled into her
regular space at the end farthest from the building. Like most os-
tensibly level areas in the Highlands, the lot sloped; as director,
Janet felt honor bound to park in the slopiest space and leave the
more nearly level ones for artists and patrons. Her twelve-year-
old Plymouth had gone slack in several of its systems; she made

it a practice whenever parking at the art center to double-check that the stick shift was in reverse and double-yank the hand brake.

She retrieved her camera and tripod from the trunk and crunched across the gravel to the building. The poster beside the door had survived the storm. It informed the public that the opening reception of the Highlands Art Center's Mentor-Mentee Show would be held on Saturday, August 5, which was today, from 4:00 until 6:00 p.m. Janet's watch read 3:46.

Not quite disastrous. She wasn't really needed until the doors officially opened. They had hung the show yesterday; the mentors were on hand to reassure the mentees (or vice versa, depending on temperament); and Helen Ives, the assistant director, was adept at converting emergency into routine. Still, it was bad policy and contrary to Janet's nature to show up at the last minute.

She went around the building on the quiet wood-chip path, unlocked the ground-level door to her private entrance, climbed the stairs, and unlocked the upper door. Financially bruised by her failed marriage, she had accepted the tenancy of the apartment on the second floor as part of her pay. Living above the job had its drawbacks, but since the trustees welcomed her presence as insurance against vandalism, the tenancy was worth twice as much as the fraction of salary it displaced.

A shower, hasty. Coffee, instant, since its function was purely medicinal. Rough-weave cotton skirt, flower-printed tank top, sandals. Eight minutes total.

Finger-combing her cropped dark hair in front of the mirror she noted frown lines between her eyebrows. Thirty seconds to draw a deep breath, exhale, relax her face muscles, and switch her mind to automatic. It was a trick she had mastered about four years into her marriage to Cal Stanton. She retrieved the three rolls of film and her keys from her shorts pocket and dropped them into her skirt pocket, and with ninety-two seconds to spare, went down the inner stairs to the office and through it into the gallery.

Early arrivals were trickling in; visitors would soon outnumber exhibitors and mentors. The exhibitors were high school juniors, five of them, selected last summer to work with local artists—a painter, a sculptor, a printmaker, a photographer, and a potter—laboring for the nine months of the school year to produce an exhibitable body of work. Most of the visitors would be parents, grandparents, and more distant relatives; some would be best friends; several, cronies of the mentors. A few would be local art lovers curious to see what kind of product today's sixteen-year-olds turned out.

Helen Ives spotted her, excused herself from a conversation, and crossed the room. "Looks like a real show, doesn't it?" she said. Her title was administrative assistant to the director; her qualifications were a major in art history earned a quarter of a century ago, a flair for order, an emptying nest, and a store of unused energy; her job description was everything she could put her hands on.

"Worth the wait, I guess," said Janet.

"There'll be complaints about the AC not being on yet."

"They've put up with fans for fifteen years."

"But expectations have been raised. Did you hear about Bud Hale?"

The question jolted Janet out of automatic. She shouldn't be surprised, though; a high percentage of Phillips Landing's population had police scanners, and newsmongering was a popular hobby. "Yes," she said. "Where did you hear?"

"I stopped at Earl's for gas and they said he fell off the cliff in the quarry. Did you hear if he survived?"

"He didn't."

"Oh, that's awful. Where did you hear?"

"I was there. That's why I'm so late."

"You mean *there?* That is awful."

"Good word." Janet drew in a deep breath to quell a quiver that threatened her midsection. "I'd better start circulating."

THERE WAS NO escaping it. Whoever hadn't picked up the calls on a scanner was hearing from someone who had. Janet felt sorry for the mentees, whose moment in the sun was being shadowed by the sensation of the decade. Families and best friends sidled dutifully around the gallery looking at the works, but that task completed, they joined the rest, standing with their backs to the art, wineglasses in hand, tutting over this shocking new imbalance in the town's political structure.

Janet did what she could, circulating, smiling, complimenting strengths and ignoring weaknesses, but she kept encountering people who, aware of her relationship to Councilman Hale, uttered condolences that failed to mask their greed for further sensation. "Thank you, thank you," she repeated, "thank you, yes, it's awful, thank you." Fuzz began to gather behind her eyes. Casting about for a temporary escape route, she remembered the rolls of film in her pocket.

To reach the hallway that led to the darkroom, she had to edge past a stocky red-haired youth in rumpled shorts who was examining the photographs. He turned to make room and amazed her by being the kid from the quarry. She dredged up *Gregory* in the same moment in which his face brightened and he exclaimed, "Oh, hey! Hi!"

They played out the recognition scene, establishing that Janet was there because it was her job and Gregory was there because he had planned to attend anyway and decided not to let someone else's disaster change his plans.

"Do you know the photographer?" Janet asked.

"No," he said, "I just wanted to see what gets in."

"And what do you think?"

He said, "Not bad," but his body language said otherwise. Janet smiled; she too had been underwhelmed by the photography entry. Reading her agreement, Gregory confided, "I was going to have some shots in a show here once, but I had to move."

"In the mentor program?"

"No, just a kids' workshop, but we were going to hang a show. I never got to see it."

"When was that?"

"Oh, years ago. I was a freshman."

"What kind of work did you do?"

"Portraits, mostly. Black and white. A lot of darkroom."

"There's a lot of good work still to be done in black and white," she said. "Are you still shooting?"

"Well, I kind of got away from it when I had to move."

"Do you miss it? I would."

"Well—yeah. I do. I didn't realize it until I saw the announcement for this show. It—like, you know, it sort of took me back. I really had a good time in that workshop."

"We've just renovated the darkroom," Janet said. "Want to have a look?"

"Hey, really?" The offer had been a random cast; somewhat to her surprise, she sensed a nibble. "Yeah, I'd like to."

"Follow me." She led him out of the gallery and down the hall, unlocked the darkroom door, and switched on the light.

"Oh, wow." Gregory went directly to the new enlarger. "A color head."

Janet fished the rolls of film from her pocket, found a pencil beside the light table, and printed "J" on the yellow protective paper of each.

He looked across at her. "You're shooting one twenty?"

Okay, the kid was real; he knew the difference between a 35-millimeter cassette and a roll of medium-format film. "This time out," she said.

"Hasselblad?"

She laughed. Hasselblad was the Mercedes-Benz of medium-format cameras. "I got a Pentax 67 a few years ago." It had been a birthday present from Cal, early in their marriage. She'd jettisoned most of the souvenirs but kept the camera. "It's heavy and noisy, but the optics are good." She opened the little refrigerator beside the sink, laid the film inside, closed it, and jiggled the lure a bit. "How do you like what we've done with the darkroom?"

"It's great," he said. "Any chance a person could rent it for a few hours?"

Good grief, a strike. She kept her voice directorially steady. "Ten dollars an hour and a refundable breakage deposit, and you provide your own paper and chemistry." Now set the hook. "Do you want to reserve some time?"

His face said it was Christmas. "Do you take checks?"

Do bears—never mind. "Yes," she said, "we take checks."

SHE HAD LOCKED the check in the office cash box and was passing through the door from the office into the gallery with him when across the room she spotted the tall, muscular body and abundant iron gray hair of Charlie Emmett, the renovation contractor. He caught her eye and nodded, but the greater part of his attention seemed to be fastened on the redheaded kid with her. Then Gregory said, "So long," and headed out to the parking lot, and someone came up and spoke to Charlie, and Janet went back to hostessing.

IT WAS WHILE SHE WAS resting for a moment beside the sculpture exhibit, which she greatly admired, that a dumpy man edged his way across the room toward her. She was relieved to see the missing Schuyler Vanstaat, obviously no longer missing. He was the father of Kristin Vanstaat, who was the sculpture mentee and, in Janet's opinion, much the best artist of the bunch. At the age of sixteen, the girl already had an eye for proportion and a flair for shaping space in unexpected ways. Kristin, who at that moment was at the caterer's table devouring cheese and crackers with a couple of friends, didn't need the disaster of a lost father.

"Ms. Upton," Vanstaat said, "you're quite a heroine to be here after your stressful adventure."

"I've had better days," she said. "I'm glad to see you. Marion was afraid you might have come to grief on the trail down beside the quarry."

"Oh, my no." A blush spread up his pudgy face and over the top of his bald head. "I know my limitations. I wouldn't attempt that goat path in good weather, much less in a cloudburst. I went only as far as a little overlook that Councilman Hale wanted to show me. I tried to talk him into leaving when I saw the storm coming on, but he's never been an easy man to talk into anything."

"No," she said.

"Now I feel guilty for not having tried harder." He sipped his wine. "A deputy was waiting for me at the trailhead when I got down. I was shocked to hear the news. Marion, bless her heart, had brought a thermos of coffee, which I must admit I sorely needed. They told me I'd gone a mile farther than I needed. It seems there's a cutoff trail that avoids some of the climb back to the top. I never saw it." He turned his head as a tall woman dressed by Lord & Taylor edged through the crowd to them. "Ah, my dear," he said, "I'd like you to meet Janet Upton. The director, you know. My wife, Diane."

The fuzz was gathering behind Janet's eyes again. "Ms. Vanstaat," she said with matching formality, grateful for a respite from the violent death of Uncle Bud, "I'm delighted to meet you. I want to tell you how much I admire Kristin's work. You must be very proud."

Diane Vanstaat's murmured thank-you was routine; it was Kristin's father who once more blushed over the top of his head. "I'm glad to hear you say that. I am frightfully proud and I've been afraid it's just paternal prejudice." He looked past Janet's shoulder. "Well, and here's Charlie Emmett. I didn't know you were an art lover, Charlie."

Diane Vanstaat murmured a perfunctory, "Excuse me," and drifted away.

"I just heard about Bud Hale," Charlie said. His face was set in grim lines. "I saw you talking to him up there."

"Not for long," Vanstaat said. "I didn't see you."

"Guess you weren't looking," said Charlie. "Saw you over at that falling-off place with him, and then you went back and the Ferguson kid turned up. And it was right after that the storm hit. I guess that's when it happened. He must have slipped."

"I really don't know," said Vanstaat. "I'd started back by then."

"Did you go down that trail by the quarry?" Janet said to Charlie. "I didn't see you."

Charlie looked at her as if the wall had spoken. "Where were you?"

"Down the trail," she said. "With my camera. I was on my own, not with the hike."

"Got you. No, I didn't go down that way. I had to take the wife over to Stewart to catch a plane, so I cut back to my car."

The fuzz in Janet's head was solidifying; it would be a headache before long if she didn't do something about it. The fans spotted around the gallery weren't doing much more than pushing the heat around. She looked at her watch. Forty-five minutes to go. There was aspirin in the office. "The place looks good, Charlie," she said. "Please excuse me, I've got to move on."

"LOVE, YOU LOOK exhausted," said Marion. Arriving in medias res, she had immediately redeemed her tardiness by greeting every mentor, mentee, parent, grandparent, aunt, uncle, friend, and contributor with the single-minded enthusiasm that had long ago elevated her to the chair of the board of trustees.

They were standing outside the door catching the early evening breeze that rustled the trees around the parking lot. The caterer had hauled off her debris; the lights were off; the lot was nearly empty. The aspirin had taken the edge off Janet's headache. "I've had better days," she said. "Where's Paul? I wanted him to see Kristin Vanstaat's work."

"He'll come when there aren't crowds. He caught sight of something off the trail he wanted to sketch, and you know how that is. I expect he's home by now. Why don't you come out to dinner?"

The offer should have been tempting; Marion was the kind of cook who without visible effort achieved delicious results, and there was always ease and often delight in their conversation. But the fuzz was solidifying again, and she said, "Marion, I'm wiped. I've got to go and see Leora, and then I just want to blank out. Rain check?"

"Anytime, you know that. Tomorrow?"

"Fine."

"But should you be alone, love? You've had an awful shock."

"Marion," Janet said, "what you've got to realize is, after Cal, it's heaven to be alone."

SIX

Expectations

SURROUNDED BY CASSEROLES, neighbors, and minister, Leora barely had a chance to say hello. It occurred to Janet that she might as well have stayed at home, but as she trudged up the stairs to her apartment, she reminded herself that virtue was its own reward and a clear conscience probably more valuable than a clear evening.

The answering machine was blinking. Her first impulse was to punch Delete; her second was to let the thing blink until morning. But curiosity triumphed and she punched Play. An unfamiliar female identified herself as a reporter for a local newspaper based at the other end of the county. She was covering the death of Councilman Broderick Hale; would Ms. Upton please call her back, at any time up to eleven? She recited a number.

Janet hit Delete and went to bed.

She had been afraid of wakefulness and nightmares, but she fell asleep promptly, slept heavily until half past eight, and woke, remembering nothing of her dreams, to family duties. She must tell her parents—who, to complicate the process, were on an Alaska cruise—and her brother.

Shower; shorts and tank top; coffee. Her brother would be the easy part.

He answered on the second ring. "Hi, Rich," she said.

"Hey, sis, what's new?"

She never needed to wrap things up for Rich. "Uncle Bud's dead."

"You don't say. Heart, stroke, or the wrath of God?"

"Wrath of God, I guess. He fell off the Eagle's Nest quarry in a thunderstorm."

"Oof."

"Very oof. I'll call you when they schedule the funeral."

"No sweat. If I came, I'd dance on his grave, and I wouldn't put the cousins through that."

"Decent of you. Listen, Rich, I have to track down the aged Ps. Do you have a number for their travel agent?"

A pause. Then, "Want me to run your life?"

"Try."

"Don't fuck with their vacation."

"Rich—he's Dad's brother-in-law."

"And the sum, cubed, of Pat Buchanan plus Jesse Helms."

She'd learned that when Rich had come out of the closet. "Yes, but they'll be mad."

"No, they'll think they ought to be mad. Listen, if you're afraid they'll take it out on you, write a letter. Say you tried, but the message didn't get through."

"Lie," she said.

"You've got to start sometime. Put their name on the flowers, that'll satisfy them. No, that's right, you burned your credit cards. I'll order the flowers on my Visa and hit them for reimbursement when they get home."

"Hey—Rich?"

"Speak."

"You can run my life anytime."

HALF AN HOUR LATER, while she was eating toast and raspberry jam and disagreeing with the art reviews in last Friday's *Times*, the telephone rang. She picked up; a male voice said, "May I please speak to Janet Upton?"

Another reporter? She chilled her voice. "Speaking."

"Ms. Upton, this is Finlay Keene. I'm very sorry to be bothering you on a Sunday."

"Do I know you?"

"I don't think we've met. I'm an attorney. You may have seen my office on Main Street." Not a reporter, an ambulance chaser. "Forgive me if this seems intrusive, but I need to know if you're the Janet Upton who was related to Broderick Hale."

"Why?"

"Yes, well, I was Broderick Hale's attorney. If you're the Janet Upton who was related to him, I have something to discuss with you."

She laid the remains of her toast back on the plate, sucked raspberry jam from her fingers, and took a fresh grip on the handset. "He was my uncle. What's up?"

"Would you mind telling me the exact relationship?"

"Broderick Hale was married to my father's sister, Irene Upton. She died about three years ago. My father's name is Joseph Upton, and he and my mother live in Hartford. That enough?"

"Excellent. Thank you. Janet—if I may—"

"Sure, Finlay."

"Janet, I wouldn't be calling on a Sunday, but I have to be out of town next week, and there's something in Broderick Hale's will that involves you. I think you're entitled to know about it as soon as possible. Would you be able to drop into my office sometime this morning?"

Will? Involving her? "How about ten minutes?" she said.

FINLAY KEENE'S OFFICE consisted of two rooms and an anteroom that he shared with a real estate brokerage. A window beside his desk looked out on an unexpected little brick-walled rose garden, invisible from Main Street. Keene himself was square faced and white haired and wearing a suit—a lightweight suit, to be sure, but a suit all the same, on an August morning that was heading for a humid ninety-five. Janet was wearing her summer uniform of skirt, tank top, and sandals, and the air-conditioning was raising goose bumps on her arms.

Actually, it was probably more than the air-conditioning.

Finlay Keene said, "I gather this comes as a surprise to you."

"Surprise" came nowhere near covering it. "I'm—" She fell back on a favorite word of her grandmother's. "I'm flabbergasted." So flabbergasted, in fact, that all that had really registered was something about a hundred acres and a partnership. "Would you please run the whole thing by me again? Slowly?"

"Yes, of course." He sat back and folded his hands on top of a bundle of papers on his desk blotter. "In late 1986, your uncle entered into a partnership agreement with a contractor named Charles Emmett—"

"I know Charlie," she said. "He's doing the art center renovation."

"Yes. Well. The initial purpose of the partnership was the purchase of a hundred-acre tract of land, and that purpose was achieved."

"They bought the land."

"Yes. Now the partnership agreement provides for ownership in common without right of survivorship. In plain English, that means that upon Broderick Hale's death, his share of the partnership became part of his estate instead of automatically going to his partner. His will—Bud Hale's will—provides that if the partnership is still in existence at the time of his death, the estate's profit from any sale of the partnership holdings shall pass to you."

"Why me?"

"Affection and esteem, presumably."

"But he has three kids. And grandchildren."

"You don't have to worry about them, Janet. For the most part, Bud was a prudent investor. They're all very well taken care of."

"Does Leora know?"

"Yes, I've talked with her about the estate."

"Does she mind?"

"She gave me no indication of minding."

"What about Charlie? What does he think about having me for a partner?"

"The estate is the partner. You're simply the legatee of Bud's share of the profits."

"If the land gets sold, I get half."

"Somewhat more, actually. Bud had been carrying the mortgage payments for some years. The estate—and ultimately you, as the legatee—will recover those payments from the proceeds."

"Who picks up the tab now?"

"Fortunately, it's no longer an issue. You'll be pleased to know that there's a buyer for the property." He unclasped his hands and patted the papers in front of him. "The closing is scheduled for Monday, a week from tomorrow. As executor of your uncle's estate, I am, of course, empowered to execute his part of the transaction. You're welcome to attend, of course."

And she would attend. By golly, would she ever. She rubbed her hands along her upper arms. "They bought this land in 1986 and they're only selling it now? What took so long?"

Keene took off his bifocals and swung them by the earpiece. "As I said, for the most part, Bud was a prudent investor. But we're all entitled to one or two mistakes, and this purchase didn't work out quite the way they expected. The land was part of the Bradford estate—maybe you've heard of it?"

Maybe she had.

"By the time the last resident Bradford died, the heirs were scattered. They didn't want the land, they wanted cash, and the sooner the better. It was the peak of the land boom. Bud and Charlie picked up this little piece of the estate at what looked at the time like a bargain price. They applied to the planning board for subdivision approval, they had a buyer under contract, and they stood to turn a good profit. But as I'm sure you know, in October of eighty-seven the market crashed. The buyer lost his financing and had to back out, and then the economy went into recession and people stopped buying land."

"So when Uncle Bud put me in his will, it was to leave me a white elephant?"

"Well, until a couple of months ago, I suppose it might have looked a little like that. He did take one sensible precaution. His will sets up a fund sufficient to cover taxes and mortgage payments for six months. But fortunately, the property is going to turn over a long time before that." He swung his glasses. "The fact is, if Bud had lived ten days longer, the land would be in other hands and the partnership would have been dissolved."

"No money."

"Not for you." He put his glasses back on, extracted a few pages from the pile, and slid them across the desk. "I've made copies of the will, the partnership agreement, and the contract of sale. As I said, you don't have to take any action, although you're quite welcome to attend the closing. Bud's share of the proceeds will go into the estate, and when probate is complete, will pass to you. If you need funds before that, any number of lenders would be happy to accommodate you with a loan on your expectations."

It wasn't until then that she thought to ask. "How much money is involved?"

He took his glasses off and swung them again. "Well, I haven't crunched all the figures yet, but, after taxes, expenses, that sort of thing"—he chewed on his lower lip for a moment—"your share will probably work out in the neighborhood of about five hundred thousand."

For a moment, her mind refused to process the number. Five hundred *thousand?* That's half a *million.* Half a million *dollars.*

It was definitely more than the air-conditioning that was raising goose bumps.

SEVEN

Responsibility

ON THE WAY HOME, Janet stopped to buy the *Times*. The newspaper whose reporter she had spurned was beside it on the rack. Councilman Hale's death dominated the front page. Standing on the sidewalk, she scanned it and found nothing in the report that she hadn't already known; nor could she have added anything if she had called the reporter back. She trudged back home, washed her jam-smeared plate and knife, tossed the comforter over the futon on the bedroom floor, then lingered over coffee—the real thing this morning—and skimmed the *Times* until it was time to go down and open the art center.

The work at hand, proofreading the draft of a fund-raising letter, was more tedious than usual.

Half a million dollars.

The years of juggling Cal's intemperate credit-card charges had developed in Janet a capacity for mental arithmetic that would have bemused her fourth-grade teacher. Five hundred thousand dollars invested at, say, 5 percent, would come to—hmmm—twenty-five thousand dollars a year. Minus taxes, of course. Almost enough to live on. Very close to enough if she could wangle grants to cover materials. She could spend her time developing her eye instead of proofreading fund-raisers.

She was surprised by the degree of discomfort the prospect caused her.

THE OFFICE WINDOWS looked out on the parking lot. She had finished proofreading and started drafting the fall workshop schedule when Charlie Emmett's blue pickup pulled in. He climbed out and ambled to the door, leaned a heavy shoulder against the frame, pushed a lumber-company cap to the back of his head, and said, "Howdy, pard." All he needed was a straw to chew on.

"Did you know?" she said.

"Just found out. You know Bud."

"He was an awful tease."

"One way to put it. Anybody with any sense would get away from that edge when that rain hit, but you know Bud. Scared hell out of me when I heard he was dead. We've been taking a beating on that land for going on eight years now. Don't need anything bollixing up the sale."

"Don't look at me," she said. "The estate's your partner. Finlay says he has the authority to sign the papers."

"Right, that's what he told me." Charlie removed his shoulder from the door frame. "Well, okay, just wanted to check in. Take it easy."

KRISTIN VANSTAAT TURNED UP around noon. Wrinkled shorts and a baggy T-shirt emphasized the dumpy build she had inherited from her father. "I got an idea last night," she said. "Is there any work space that isn't a mess?"

"There was one free table in the ceramics workshop the last time I looked." Janet got up and opened the key cabinet on the wall. "Just don't leave any of your stuff out or they'll pitch a fit. There should be room in the front closet. And bring back the key when you're done."

Kristin saluted and went off toward the basement stairs.

AT FOUR O'CLOCK, Janet punched in the Lamonts' number. Leora answered, her soft voice as always making Janet feel she was sounding crude and abrupt. "Lee," she said, "I just found out about your dad's will."

"You mean how he left you that land?" A *fluffy* voice, like her hair.

"It makes me nervous," Janet said. "Everything ought to go to you kids."

"Oh, Jannie"—only Leora ever called her *Jannie*—"don't feel like that."

"Lee, do you know how much that land is worth?"

"It doesn't matter. Jannie, he was *rich.* I didn't even know. I mean, I knew he was okay for money, but not how much."

"Well, I'm glad you feel that way. It just makes me nervous. Listen, I hate to bother you—"

"It's no bother, it's good to have something else to think about."

"Good. What it is, I'm kind of going around in circles. I've been dropped into the middle of this situation and I don't feel like I know enough about it."

"Well, I don't know how much I could help. Daddy never talked to me about business."

"That isn't what I mean. I guess I don't really know what I mean. It's because it involves land, I guess. If it were stocks and bonds, I think I'd feel fine, but land seems different. It's like something alive. It has a history. It—" She heard herself floundering. She was sure of her feeling but at a loss to put it into words. She tried again. "It's, like, if I'm profiting from it, I have a responsibility to it."

"I guess." Leora's voice was uncertain.

She gave up. "Anyway, I thought maybe your dad had more information about it. Maybe in that old sunroom he used for an office?"

"Well—I guess that's where it'd be, if there is anything."

"What I was thinking, would it be an awful intrusion if I had a look? Maybe I could even help you sort things out."

"I guess—sure, that'd be okay. When do you want to go?"

"Tonight? I'm out of here at six." Uncle Bud's house was on the way to Paul and Marion's; there should be time for at least a quick look.

"Well, I'll be giving the girls their supper," said Leora, "but I can give you the key, if you don't mind going by yourself."

Actually, she'd prefer going by herself. "Fine," she said, keeping her voice neutral.

"And Jannie"—Leora's voice dropped a tone—"it'd be better if we don't tell Lowell. He's sort of…"

Kristin appeared at the office door. Janet waved her in. Leora's voice had trailed away. *Sort of? As in Sort of mad that his cousin-in-law was in line for some of the loot?* She said, "Can you give me the key without letting him know?"

"Oh, yes, he isn't here. Every Sunday, they've got this softball league? I told him he'd be better off getting out and working off some steam, you know what I mean? They go out for a couple of beers afterward. He doesn't usually get back until seven-thirty or eight."

"I'll get the key back to you before that."

"No hurry. It's an extra, to the side door? From the carport?"

"Sounds good. Lee, thanks a bunch." A *bunch?* Amazed by what a few minutes with Leora could do to her vocabulary, she hung up and looked at Kristin.

"Ceramics took over that whole closet," Kristin said. "I don't have anyplace to put my stuff."

"I told them they could have three shelves."

"Well, there's twenty of them and only one of me, so I guess they thought they should have it all."

Janet had never cared much for ceramics—neither the process, nor, by and large, the product—but the ceramics classes brought in more fees than the rest of the workshops combined. And after all, there were those—her ex-husband, for one—who disdained photography as not quite art. "I'll look around," she said. "Can you manage for a day or two?"

Kristin grinned. "I'll move the pots closer together."

"Just don't break anything." Not that it wouldn't serve those trespassers right to lose a pot or two, but she limited herself to answering Kristin's grin.

EIGHT

Games

BRODERICK HALE'S PLACE was on Oak Hollow Road, about a quarter of a mile past the big outcrop that Paul and Marion called Big Bear. Janet had always thought it looked more like a raccoon. You couldn't see much of it from the road; the prime view was from Marion and Paul's place, half a mile farther along. When Janet left for Texas, they'd been in the middle of a battle to save it from somebody who wanted to level it and build a house. They'd won their lawsuit and the big raccoon was still there.

She turned into Uncle Bud's driveway, drove a twisting up-hill quarter of a mile through the woods, and parked in the car-port—a late addition to a house that had been there for a hundred years. Her family had spent several Christmases at that house, and from time to time, she and Rich had visited during summer vacation for two or three weeks at a time. It didn't seem like the house of a rich man. Janet had always thought of it as Aunt Irene's house.

But Aunt Irene had been dead for three years. Janet hadn't come back for the funeral; now, turning the key in the lock, she felt the past weighing on her shoulders like a too heavy coat.

The door from the carport opened into the kitchen, where the refrigerator stood open and empty. The Ethan Allen dining-room suite and the willow-pattern dishes in the hutch were the same as always. In the living room, a leather recliner had replaced the big easy chair in which, on long-ago Saturday mornings, seven-year-old Janet and six-year-old Leora had snuggled together to watch cartoons. The wallpaper was new.

Uncle Bud's office was an enclosed sunporch off the end of the living room. In Janet's childhood, admission had been by invitation only. The door was closed now; opening it still felt like trespassing.

She gave herself a mental shake. This attack of nerves, she was sure, was brought on by the extreme degree of distress in which she'd found Leora. Her fair, fluffy cousin seemed to be holding herself together by a desperate effort of will; if it weren't for her two little girls, Janet suspected that Leora would simply crawl under the covers and cry. The reaction seemed extreme, but Bud Hale had not been Janet's father. And thank goodness for that.

In the office, late sunlight glanced off the golden grain of the oak rolltop desk. On a few prized occasions, Uncle Bud had let her come in and roll the top up and down. Her fingertips remembered the soft, rumbling slide as the wooden slats moved in the waxed channels. The oak filing cabinet still stood next to the desk, and once more she noted with pleasure how the grain of the desk drawers mirrored the grain of the file drawers. Across the room, the big old library table still stood against the wall; now it held a computer and a printer.

The filing cabinet was stuffed with folders. One of them, pulled out at random, contained a ten-year-old legal document; somebody named Alta Ferguson had been suing Uncle Bud over a boundary dispute. The name seemed familiar; after a moment, Janet recalled that Alta Ferguson was the builder who'd been planning to blast Big Bear. The blue-backed complaint was the only thing in the folder; maybe they'd settled out of court.

She shoved it back, went on reading file tabs, and finally, four drawers down, found an accordion file labeled "Bradford." She rolled up the rolltop and plunked the file on the desk. It held, among other papers, duplicates of the documents Finlay Keene had given her. More interesting was a separate folder labeled "Grassy Acres Subdivision Application"; in it, along with a stapled bundle of filled-in forms, were several table-top-size maps.

She carried them out to the dining room and unfolded them on the table. One showed the proposed lot lines and suggested locations for houses, wells, septic fields, and driveways. They'd planned to divide the hundred acres into nine lots. More interesting was the second map, which showed contour lines. They were widely spaced; her property was essentially flat. In the corner of that map was an inset showing the location of the property. It was several miles north of the village of Phillips Landing, just over the line, in the next county.

She refolded the maps and stuffed the file back in the file cabinet. Her curiosity still largely unsated, she turned to the computer.

It too gave no evidence of Uncle Bud's wealth. It was even older than the one somebody had donated to the art center—so primitive, in fact, that it lacked a hard drive. All the software was on five-and-a-quarter-inch floppies, stored next to the computer along with the file disks. She thumbed through the storage box. One of the file disks was labeled "Stuff"; the rest were labeled by year, starting with 1986. She found an old WordPerfect and an older DOS and booted up the computer.

The 1986 and 1987 disks contained files entitled "Bradford," but they were nothing more than Uncle Bud's answers to the letters in the paper file and added nothing to what she already knew. She refiled them, slipped the Stuff disk into the drive, and ordered up List Files.

Nine files were entitled CHRISTMS.85 through CHRISTMS.95 and turned out to be the annual letters that had been stuffed into Christmas cards. A dozen had titles like SPRING and ONRIVER and LEAF-DAN.CES. Twelve more were identified only by numbers—01 through 12. She brought up SPRING and got her first real surprise.

It was a poem, headed "SPRING by Broderick Hale."

She read it through. It wasn't good, but one or two lines weren't totally inept. She pulled up the rest of the titled files. All poems, all by Broderick Hale.

It crossed her mind that there was an awful lot she had never known about Uncle Bud.

She wanted these poems. Rich's comments were not to be missed, but she wanted them for kinder reasons as well.

She was looking for the Print command when she heard a vehicle on the driveway. Shading her eyes from the sun, she peered out the window and saw a black van pull up in front of the carport. LAMONT ELECTRIC was painted on the side. The softball game must have ended early, or Lowell had skipped the beer.

She switched off the computer with fingers that shook a little, and slipped the WordPerfect and DOS disks back into the storage box. The Stuff disk she tucked into her shoulder bag. By the time Lowell's key turned in the front door, she was in the living room with the office door closed behind her.

"Oh, it's you," he said. "I wondered whose rustbucket that was."

Janet had met Lowell during Life-Before-Texas, when he'd been dating Leora. He did not lack a certain obvious physical attraction, but in the absence of mental grace, Janet was more repelled than turned on by heavy biceps, tightly curling black hair, and thickly lashed brown eyes. He'd been nice enough to Leora, though, thereby earning himself a degree of goodwill. When she thought about it, which was seldom, Janet wondered whether the niceness had survived seven years of marriage.

He didn't seem inclined to niceness at the moment. His stance—feet apart, hands on hips, fingertips tucked in the pockets of his grass-stained shorts—was just over the line that divided assertive from belligerent. "What the hell are you doing here?" he demanded. He hadn't showered since the softball game, and he hadn't forgone the beer.

"Hi, Lowell," she said. "Just leaving."

"How'd you get in?"

She'd better keep Leora out of it. "I'm an heir," she said. Let him think Finlay Keene had given her a key.

It was, however, not the most fortunate choice of dodges. "Not of this house, you aren't," he said.

He was between her and the front door; she'd have to pass him to get to the side door in the kitchen, as well. There was essentially no place to retreat to; retreat, however, had seldom served her well. It had, for instance, only goaded Cal to further aggression. So she attacked. "Come on, Lowell," she said, "I'll bet you aren't an heir at all. What are *you* doing here?"

She surprised him into an answer. "I'm picking up a suit to bury my father-in-law in," he said. "Doing my wife a favor. Any problem with that?"

"None at all. I'll leave you to it." She took a sideways step to get around him.

It wasn't going to be quite that easy, though. His mouth curving into a grin, he sidestepped to stay in front of her, thrust his pelvis forward, and said, "What's in it for me?"

Oh, shit. The Willards were the nearest neighbors, and their house was out of earshot, more than a quarter of a mile away. But an odd uncertainty in his eyes led her to guess that the obnoxiousness was masking some deeper issue. She tried a response she'd learned in Texas: she lowered her eyelids, tilted her head, smiled, and said, "Lowell, this isn't the time or the place. Be a prince, let me out."

She'd surprised him again. He hesitated; then, his grin widening, he performed a cursory bump and grind and stepped aside. She passed him and went out through the open front door, her spine prickling a little as she turned her back to head for the carport. He didn't follow, but as she opened her car door, he called after her, "Let me know when you're ready, princess."

In your dreams, Cousin-in-Law. Not looking back, she slammed the door, punched down the locks, and then realized that the van was blocking her way out.

Shit. She wasn't about to ask Lowell Lamont to move his damn van.

But there'd been another way out when she'd been here as a child. The carport was open at both ends—no more, really, than a sort of arcade over a passage from the front of the house to the rear. When she was a child, it had led alongside the backyard to a rough road through the woods, one of the old logging roads whose traces still crisscrossed the Highlands. She and Rich had explored it often with the cousins. It passed through what was now a wildlife sanctuary and came out on a little traveled road that led to other roads that led, ultimately, to the village.

Janet put her car in gear and drove ahead, out of the carport and past the backyard. Beyond a toolshed and a deer-fenced garden plot where tomatoes hung heavy on staked vines, she found the opening where the track entered the woods. It seemed to have been used fairly recently; probably by a four-wheel, but under the circumstances, she was ready to give it a shot.

It wasn't long before she was doubting the wisdom of bushwhacking in a twelve-year-old Plymouth. In several places, the road had degenerated into a pair of tire tracks pinched by shrubby undergrowth that scraped against the sides of the car. On steep grades, storm-water runoff had scoured the tracks down to stony rubble. But she was stuck with it. Even if she'd been up for another encounter with Lowell, it was too narrow for turning around and too contorted for backing out.

Presently a weathered placard announced that she was entering Audubon Society land. The track through the sanctuary was no worse and no better.

God, she was sick of men and their games.

She breathed in deeply, shouted, "I'm sick of you all!" and felt better. If her car bogged down, she'd leave it and walk out to that road at the end. After all, she was an heiress; if she felt like it, she could leave the car sitting out here in the woods forever; borrow on her expectations and buy a Jeep.

She rounded a bend and drove out of the trees into slanting sunlight. A narrow road, dusty in the brightness, crossed in front of her.

Her sense of direction had failed her. Was it a right turn or a left that would take her to Marion and Paul's house?

Well, if one direction is wrong, the other isn't. She turned right, and after about half a mile, found herself driving beside a deep ravine and knew where she was. Right was wrong; in this direction, the road connected with a U.S. highway that ran north out of the Highlands and into the next county.

Pinched between the ravine on one side and a high bank on the other, the road wasn't wide enough to turn around in, but before long she came to a driveway cut that led to a bridge that crossed the ravine. She turned in and braked. It was a very deep ravine; from inside the car, she couldn't see the bottom.

As she reversed and headed back the way she had come, an unexpected flick of panic tightened her chest. She had never before suffered from a fear of heights. Uncle Bud's fall must have gone deeper into her psyche than she had realized.

NINE

Whole Ecosystems

AN UNFAMILIAR CAR was parked in front of Paul and Marion's house. Janet pulled up beside it and secured brake and gearshift against the slope. Across the valley, Big Bear still looked like a raccoon.

Marion was in the kitchen, the telephone to her ear. Janet followed her pointing finger to the refrigerator, where she found a pitcher of iced tea on the top shelf and a bowl of pasta salad on the shelf beneath. While Marion was interspersing silences with "Mm" and "Well," Janet filled a glass from the pitcher, went out to the back deck, and settled on a recliner facing the woods.

Inside the house, Marion said, "Patty, I've got to go now…. Yes, I will think about it, but whatever comes of it, thanks for thinking of me." The phone clicked. The refrigerator opened and closed, and Marion came out onto the deck with her own glass. "Sorry, love. Politics."

"Anything I'd understand?"

"The Green League thinks I should be appointed to finish out Bud's term." The loosely organized group called by its members the Green League had been called by others "a bunch of tree-hugging ecofreaks." Marion regarded it as a compliment.

"You don't sound convinced," said Janet.

"Oh, I'd love to be on the Town Board, but this isn't the way. The Board makes the interim appointment itself, and the survivors are already split two to two on every issue from here to eternity."

Back in the woods, footsteps rustled. Paul, in his summer uniform of cutoff jeans and a once navy polo shirt faded white at the seams, came into view on the path from the studio. The man with him, in pressed khaki pants and a muted short-sleeved shirt, was medium in every respect; five minutes after parting from him, it would be hard to remember his face. They took the branch of the path that led to the front of the house.

"Good," Marion said, "he's going."

"Who is he?"

"Investigator Noel Riesbach from the sheriff's office. He's investigating—what did he call it? 'Yesterday's occurrence.'"

"Uncle Bud?"

Out front, a car door slammed and a motor started. Marion said, "Isn't that pathetic? Bud Hale falls off a cliff and smashes every organ in his body and it's an 'occurrence.'"

Inside the house, the refrigerator opened and closed; after a moment, Paul came out with the iced-tea pitcher in one hand and a glass in the other. "Hi, babe," he said. He filled his glass, set the pitcher on a table, and sat down. "Guess what's the topic for today."

Janet would rather talk about something else, but the "occurrence" wasn't to be avoided. "Uncle Bud."

"In particular, did he fall or was he pushed."

"Pushed?" The notion hadn't entered her mind.

"I knew it," said Marion.

"They think somebody *pushed* him?" Janet's head felt as if it were filled with helium.

"We-ell—" Paul drained his glass and set it on the deck rail. "I don't know that what Riesbach thinks is necessarily what *they* think. I don't even know that 'think' is the word you want. But that seemed to be the general idea of this particular go-round. You know what they say: 'If at first you blow it, take another breath.'"

"Paul—" Janet took another breath herself. "What are you talking about?"

"Didn't you know?" said Marion. "No, maybe not. We weren't exactly communicating at the time. When Alta Ferguson fell off Big Bear, this wretched man Riesbach took a notion that Paul pushed her."

Alta Ferguson, the vandal of Big Bear. "Wait a minute. She fell?"

"Oh, yes. Didn't you know?"

Janet shook her head.

"Well, then," said Paul, "you missed a great example of poetic justice. She fell off Big Bear and broke her neck."

"I never heard. And they thought you *pushed* her?"

"Not *they*," said Paul. "Riesbach. If 'thought' is the word."

"But why?"

"Big Bear."

"I thought your lawsuit took care of that."

"Oh, no," said Marion. "All we got was a temporary order that held up everything until the judge could hear the whole case. According to Eric, there were at least five reasons why we should lose."

Eric. That's how she'd known about him; he'd been helping with the Big Bear lawsuit.

"It was a Hail Mary," said Paul. "*If* we'd won, she'd have had to go back to the drawing board, and *if* Steep Slopes had passed, she wouldn't have got another building permit. But it never came to that. You have to admit, it's kind of hard to miss Riesbach's point. But dammit, he's way off base with this notion about Bud. I didn't want Bud to die. Even if I hadn't sort of liked the old SOB, which I did, he was the swing vote on Son of Steep Slopes."

"Was he going to vote for it?"

"Nobody knows," said Marion.

"It was the only chance," said Paul. "Now those turkeys will deadlock it until after the election."

"Can you elect somebody who'll vote for it?"

"Yup. Marion."

Marion said, "I'm running?"

"Thought you knew."

"First I've heard. Patty Dougherty wants me to try for the appointment to finish out the term."

"That's a fool's quest. They'll never agree. Wait and take it to the voters."

"We'll talk about this later." Marion got up and poured herself another glassful of iced tea. "You know, I've been thinking, Bud's falling like that must be terrible for the Ferguson boy. He looked as white as a sheet. It must have brought it all back."

"The Ferguson boy?" said Janet.

"Oh dear, I've got to stop that. It isn't his fault Alta was his mother. What *is* his name? I keep blocking it out."

The Ferguson boy? Alta's son? "Gregory," said Janet. "I hadn't made the connection."

"Gregory Ferguson's emotional state is not our problem," Paul said. "What about you, babe? How are you doing?"

Her head was full of helium, that's how she was doing. She said, "Do you know anything about the Bradford estate?"

"Oh, dear," said Marion.

"You do know something about the Bradford estate."

"You might say," said Paul.

"The Bradfords," said Marion, "were one of those old families that owned hundreds and hundreds of acres for hundreds and hundreds of years. Whole ecosystems, only in those days nobody thought in those terms. Eventually it all came down to a bunch of Californians who didn't have the slightest interest in the Highlands. When the land boom hit in the early eighties, they broke it up and sold it off to the developers. All perfectly within the law, but it would have made such a wonderful park."

"Oh."

"Why're you asking?" said Paul.

She told them why.

"Good heavens," said Marion. "Good heavens."

"It makes me nervous."

"Oh, dear," said Marion, "I wish I hadn't said all that."

"No, it already made me nervous. I didn't ever do anything to earn it. I didn't even like Uncle Bud very much. And now, destroying ecosystems—it feels like blood money."

"Listen," said Paul, "at this point, the damage has been done, and I'd a lot rather that half million went to you than most people I can think of."

"You're trying to make me feel better."

"You bet."

"It still makes me nervous."

"Okay, be nervous."

"Actually, Finlay Keene makes me nervous."

"He's okay," said Paul.

"Well, yes, but I know what she means," said Marion. "Love, why don't you get a lawyer of your own?"

"Good idea," said Paul.

"Eric," said Marion.

"Better idea."

"You met him," said Marion. "He was leading the hike. He does a lot of work for the land trust, but he has a private practice. I'll get you his phone number."

TEN

Wiring

THE DAY WAS WARMING toward the predicted ninety degrees when Janet carried Uncle Bud's Stuff disk down to the office at nine o'clock the next morning. Charlie Emmett's big blue pickup was parked in the lot; Charlie was trundling a wheelbarrow full of broken Sheetrock out a back door and up an improvised ramp to the Dumpster. She propped the office door open to catch whatever air might be moving and heard Charlie encouraging himself with a grunted, "*Up* she goes—and *over* she goes—and *in* she goes." He caught sight of her as he maneuvered the wheelbarrow back down the ramp and, predictably, called, "Hey, pard."

Not for the first time, Janet thought that if he'd only take on some help for this scut work, he wouldn't be so far behind schedule. But then he'd have had to increase his bid to cover the help's pay, and might have lost the contract. The contract had been entered into long before she had arrived; if she ever had to deal with a contractor again, she'd insist on a penalty-for-lateness clause. She waved and went back to her desk.

There was an hour to spare before she had to open the gallery. She switched on the computer, inserted the Stuff disk, and printed the poems. Then she ordered up the file labeled 01.

The screen flashed Enter Password. Well, well; 01 was a locked file.

She tried 02. Enter Password. 03: Enter Password.

All the numbered files were locked.

Curious; Uncle Bud hadn't locked the poems, which one might have expected him to do. What might these files be? And what might he have used for passwords?

Not that Uncle Bud's secrets were any of her business.

Maybe Leora would know. Maybe she'd ask when she returned the disk to Leora. And maybe Leora would tell her—softly and fluffily—that it was none of her business.

But maybe it was her business. Maybe there was something in those locked files that would ease her mind about that blood-money land Uncle Bud had seen fit to leave her. She had to give the disk back to Leora, but she hated to let go of the mystery until she'd had a shot at solving it.

Then it occurred to her that, even though she could neither retrieve nor print the locked files, she could copy them. She found a blank disk in the supply cupboard and told the computer to copy Stuff onto it. While the computer clicked and beeped, she scribbled "IOU one 5 1/4 diskette" on a memo pad, initialed it, and slipped it into the petty-cash box. When the screen flashed Copy Complete, she carried the disks and the poems up to her apartment, put the original Stuff disk in her shoulder bag, and tucked the copy and the poems under a pile of underwear in her dresser.

Then she dialed Leora's number. The answering machine picked up and that was when she remembered that Leora was the part-time secretary to the methodist church. She said, "Lee, it's Janet. I'm at work. Give me a call when you can."

On the way back down to the office, it occurred to her that she was developing an obsession about this legacy.

AT TEN, SHE UNLOCKED the gallery doors and a baker's dozen of seven- to ten-year-olds swarmed in for a story-telling-in-pictures workshop. At ten-thirty, a red van pulled into the lot and discharged Gregory Ferguson. He wasn't pale this morning; he was flushed with the heat. He displayed a shopping bag and said, "Sorry I'm late. You wouldn't believe how hard it is to find black-and-white darkroom supplies."

Janet said, "I believe," and got up to take the darkroom key from the cabinet on the wall. She unlocked the darkroom door, turned on the air conditioner, and left him to it.

A little after twelve, the Lamont electric van pulled into the lot and Lowell climbed out. After an alarmed moment, Janet remembered that Charlie had, of necessity, subcontracted the electrical work. Lowell climbed down and crossed to the back door, by the Dumpster, and presently appeared at the inside office door, where he leaned his shoulder against the door frame, grinned, and said, "Hey, Jan, you didn't have to go bushwhacking out of there last night. Why the hell didn't you ask me to move the truck?"

Oh, lord, men and their games. "If you don't remember why," she said, "you were drunker than I thought."

"Oh, come on, I was just kidding around," he said. "You didn't used to be so uptight." She said nothing; after a moment, he removed his shoulder from the door frame and said, "Well, just to let you know, I'll be turning off the power in a few minutes."

Of course, that's what electricians did. "I thought you were coming next week," she said. She'd been about to look through some slides submitted by an artist who wanted to mount a show, but the slide viewer worked off the office current. The computer would be down; the typewriter was electric. Naturally, the one time something happened ahead of schedule, it was a nuisance.

"Another job fell through," he said. "That a problem?"

She wasn't about to send away a workman prepared to work. "How long will it be off?"

"Hard to say. I have to string all new wire down there. That old wiring's a hazard. You could have had a fire anytime."

At least Mondays were quiet. Helen, having worked the show on Saturday, had the day off; the children's workshop had ended; there was plenty of daylight in the gallery in case anybody dropped in to look at the art; and there must be something she could do with a pencil.

The darkroom.

Enlarger, timers, safelight—everything worked off the building current. The air conditioner. In that windowless room, the heat would be intolerable with the air conditioner off. She pushed back her chair and said, "Somebody's working in the darkroom. I've got to warn him."

Lowell stepped out of her way (no kidding around on the job, apparently) and followed her into the back hallway, where they met Charlie coming up the basement stairs. "We're cutting the juice," Charlie said. "That going to be okay?"

"So long as this job finally gets done." She knocked on the darkroom door.

Gregory shouted, "It's okay, come on in," and she opened the door. The white light was on; he was standing at the sink rinsing out a developing tank. "Hey, hi, Charlie," he said. "What's up?"

"You know each other?" she said.

"Oh, yeah, like, forever. I used to hang out with Kevin all the time. How's he doing?"

"Okay," Charlie said.

"Great. What's the party?"

Lowell said, "We're turning off the power."

"It wasn't supposed to happen today," Janet said. "You can make up your time some other day."

"No problem, I'm done," he said. "I've got to get to work anyway."

"Where you working?" asked Charlie.

"Computer City, up at North Valley Mall."

"Late shift, huh?"

"One to nine." As he spoke, the refrigerator kicked on with a rumble and a buzz.

The refrigerator. She hadn't got around to developing Saturday's film. It was still in the refrigerator, and the room was going to get hot, and the refrigerator was going to go off. This refrigerator, at least. "Will my apartment be off too?" she asked.

"Whole building," said Lowell.

No help there, then. Well, refrigerators were insulated. Nobody would be opening this one, so it should stay cool for a while. The freezer, starting colder, would stay cool longer. She opened the refrigerator and took out the three rolls of film.

Gregory said, "Is that still Saturday's or something new?"

"Saturday's." She opened the freezer, put the film in, and closed it.

"Could I see what you've got when it's printed?"

"Sure," she said, "for what it's worth." It was hard to explain to the laity, but he might understand. "I was just doing studies, sort of like a painter's preparatory sketches. Exploring how the light works." Exploring? *Floundering* was more like it; trying to find her own eye now that she was free of Cal's carping. "How the rain affects the light. It isn't like Texas."

"For sure," said Gregory. "I'd like to see what you got."

"Saturday?" said Charlie. "You were taking pictures in all that rain?"

"Not for long," she said.

"Can I see them too? I want to see how you can take pictures in the rain."

SINCE THE OFFICE was useless, she might as well spend this enforced break looking for a place to store Kristin's sculpture materials. During the months of renovation, all sorts of stuff had been moved, from room to room, from gallery to studio, from closet to corner, in a hurry, by volunteers. Whenever Janet wanted something that she herself had not labeled and shelved, she felt like an archaeologist on a dig. She got a flashlight from her apartment and prowled.

Eventually she found a closet crammed with dusty cartons whose contents seemed to be obsolete. Cleared, it should hold

Kristin's materials. She washed her hands and went out to the gallery to straighten paintings that had slipped askew, and to look again at Kristin's carvings.

WHEN LEORA RETURNED her call just after five, Lowell's truck was still in the lot. Janet said, "Hold on a minute," and got up to close both office doors. Lowering her voice, she said, "Lee, I borrowed a computer disk from your dad's office last night, and I'd just as soon return it when Lowell isn't around."

"He said he saw you. You didn't tell him you were taking anything, did you?"

"Of course not. Can I bring it over tomorrow? Maybe to the church?"

"No, come on out, I'm home tomorrow."

"Morning okay? Nine-thirty or ten?"

"Anytime. The girls get me up early."

THE POWER STAYED OFF all evening, frustrating Janet's desire to develop the film. Okay, tomorrow, after work.

Her two-burner stove top, naturally, was electric. It was too hot to cook anyway, but eating out—even just buying a deli sandwich—was a luxury she'd resolved to forgo until she'd cleared the credit-card debt her marriage had saddled her with. Which would be after Uncle Bud's probate.

She cracked her own refrigerator door open just long enough to snatch a lettuce leaf, a tomato, and a jar of mayonnaise, then remembered that she couldn't make toast. The untoasted L and T was soggy.

After probate she could eat out. Three meals a day if she felt like it. Suppose she spent fifty dollars a day in restaurants (she'd never be able to eat that much, but just suppose), she could eat out every day for—she picked up a pencil and figured-for twenty-seven years and a bit. She could eat every meal out until she was fifty-seven.

The first day she'd have steak. No, lobster. No, the first day she'd have steak and the second day she'd have lobster and the third day—

How long did probate take? Months? Probably years. She wouldn't borrow against her expectations; she wasn't ever going to borrow again, but after probate, why not drive up to Cape Cod for the lobster? How far was Cape Cod? Never mind; she'd drive until she was tired, and when she got tired, she'd stop at the most luxurious motel she could find. She'd work out in the gym, swim in the pool, sleep on a mattress, not a futon. And the next day she'd drive on to Cape Cod and eat lobster.

First, though, she'd buy a new car. And move into a new apartment. Maybe buy a house. A little house, but with room for a darkroom. The money would run out before she was fifty-seven, so what?

She swallowed the last of the sandwich, licked mayonnaise from her fingers, washed her plate and knife, and propped them in the dish rack.

Steak? Lobster? Luxury suites? She might as well be talking about unicorns and fairy godmothers.

Except that there was the unicorn, out in plain sight on the back of the table, disguised as a partnership agreement and a contract of sale and a will. The fairy godmother was a rich, teasing, dead uncle.

And Marion and Paul were right; she'd better have a real-world lawyer to make sure she got a proper harness on this unicorn.

Her inner video screen lighted up with the image of Eric Swanson's long, tanned, hard-muscled legs.

Stop that.

Marion had given her his office number, and of course there was no point in calling his office at eight o'clock at night. On the other hand, at eight o'clock at night, a machine would probably answer, and by talking to a machine she could keep the matter impersonal for as long as possible. On the other hand—

up to three hands by now, she noticed—lawyers work insane hours, and even at eight o'clock at night, she might have to talk to him—

She was behaving like a fifteen-year-old.

She talked to a machine.

ELEVEN

Slackness in the Systems

THE POWER WAS STILL off when Janet woke up, but at eight o'-clock, while she was brushing her teeth and gazing out the bathroom window, she saw the Lamont Electric van pull up beside Charlie's truck.

At nine-fifteen, Eric Swanson returned her call—Eric Swanson himself, no secretary announcing that Mr. Swanson was calling and putting her on hold. How, he asked, was she doing after Saturday's calamity?

She explained.

Interesting. Okay, he'd be glad to take a look. Nine-thirty tomorrow?

Nine-thirty would be fine. And his fee?

Oh, for a read-through and comments, call it a favor to Paul and Marion Willard. He owed them a dozen or two.

She didn't argue. Pleased at having banished the fifteen-year-old, she thanked him and hung up.

Ten minutes later, the refrigerator clicked and began to hum. Could something really be finished? She buckled her sandals and went down to the office and, seeing Lowell climbing into his van, flung open the office door, arresting him with one foot still on the step. "Are you done?" she demanded.

"All set." A try at a grin. "No more excuse for goofing off." He started to climb into the truck, turned back, and said, "Say— Jan?" He looked—could it be?—flustered. Now what? "I guess—" He ran a hand through his black curls. "I guess I better do a little apologizing."

After a moment to assure herself that he'd really said what she thought she'd heard, she said, "Wouldn't hurt."

"Yeah. Well—sorry. I was out of line."

"Right. You were." But after a couple of beats, she was able to see her way clear to saying, "Okay, apology accepted."

He wiped his palm down the side of his work pants and held out his hand. "Friends?"

Oh, why not. She accepted the handshake and said, "Friends," and he released her hand and climbed back into the van and gunned it out of the lot—grateful, no doubt, that she hadn't reported his kidding around to Leora.

Amazing.

The darkroom lights went on when she flicked the switch; the refrigerator was humming; the LED on the timer glowed red. She transferred the film from the freezer back into the refrigerator, mixed up the necessary chemistry, and went out to the lot. Leora lived just outside the village limits, two uphill miles away. If her day had been free, Janet would have welcomed the walk, but Leora had been showing signs of turning into her mother and it might be hard to get away promptly. She drove.

IT WAS NECESSARY to turn down a second breakfast; accepting a glass of iced tea, however, proved an adequate exercise of her guestly responsibilities. Leora's two daughters were sitting at the kitchen table, absorbed in something cartoonish on the wall-mounted TV. Their gene pool was obvious: Lana, the six-year-old, was short and round and had Leora's blue eyes and blond fluff of hair; Lisa, age three, was already nearly as big as her sister, with Lowell's tight black curls and dark eyes. "Look, girls," Leora cried, "here's Cousin Jannie!" Her voice seemed unnaturally shrill.

"Hi, kids," said Janet. The little one took her eyes from the wrote poems to her when they were engaged but I didn't know he was still doing it."

"Sweet" wouldn't have been Janet's word, but never mind. "I wanted you to see it."

"Oh, thank you. I don't know when I'd ever have got around to looking in his computer files. Jannie, this is wonderful. I'll bet I can find something for Reverend Gray to read at the funeral."

In *public?* No, really, never mind. "When is the funeral?" she thought to ask.

"Oh, didn't I—I thought—I'm sorry. It's Wednesday. Tomorrow. Two o'clock."

She should be back from her appointment with Eric in plenty of time. "I'll be there," she said.

Leora had gone back to the list of files. "What are these ones with numbers?" She clicked the mouse on 01. The screen said Enter Password. "It's locked."

"All the numbered ones are locked," said Janet. "Do you have any idea what he might have used for passwords?"

"Oh, gosh. His birthday?" Leora entered April 29, 1934. The screen said Enter Password. 4-29-34: Enter Password. 4/29/34: Enter Password. "Maybe Mom's..." Enter Password. "Oh, fudge. How are we going to find out what's in here?"

"Maybe we aren't supposed to." Janet looked at her watch.

Leora swiveled to face her. "Jannie, don't go." Tears welled again; she said, "No, I know you have to—" She drew in a shuddering breath. "Jannie, I'm scared."

Something was wrong. "Scared of what?"

"I have dreams. I wake up at night and—it's so awful."

Yes. Yes, it was; and Leora hadn't even seen that rain-veiled scarecrow—the rag doll that was her daddy—bouncing off the rocks. But—scared? "What are you scared of?"

"Did—did he really just slip or did—somebody—"

Oh, lord, had that damn what's-his-name, that sheriff's investigator, that Riesbach—had Riesbach been at her? Janet summoned firmness. "No," she said. "No, Lee, he just slipped." Bad enough, but not as bad as that damn Riesbach's fantasy. "I was out there by the quarry. It was raining and blowing like you wouldn't believe. The wind blew him off balance, he slipped, that's all."

"You saw?"

If only she had; but she must not start turning wishes into truths. "I didn't see how he fell, but it's the only thing that makes sense. Everybody had left and he was standing there by himself. Showing off to himself, I'll bet. You know how your dad was."

"He was getting awfully hard of hearing. Somebody could have snuck up." The round little jaw was set. "I'm scared, Jannie."

"Scared of what?"

"What if—" Another of those shuddering breaths. "What if it was Lowell? Daddy wouldn't have expected—Lowell wouldn't even have to sneak—"

Lowell? "Lee—" Oh, God, this was a job for a shrink. She had no idea how to be a shrink. "Lee, that's crazy. Lowell left hours before he fell."

"But nobody knows where he went."

"But, Lee—" Janet broke off; she'd been about to say, "Why on earth?" but that might be a stupid question.

Money.

If Bud Hale, essentially as a joke, could leave a mere niece nearly half a million, his children's inheritance must run to several times that. People did dreadful things for less than that.

But no. Lowell was a reputable electrician in demand in six counties, and Leora would have inherited her share in good time. Why risk a murder charge just to advance a wife's windfall by a few years?

Murder. *Lowell?* "Are you guys in trouble for money?" she asked.

Leora shook her head.

"Then why?"

"He was afraid—"

"Afraid of what?" Janet prompted after a silence.

"Daddy—"

"Lee." No longer able to contain her irritation, Janet made no effort to blunt the edge in her voice. "Lee, will you for Pete's sake stop gasping and fumbling? I'm not going to fill in the blanks. Say what you have to say or I'm going to walk out the door and go to work. Daddy what?"

Shock therapy. Apparently it worked. Leora swiveled to face the computer screen again. Her voice flat, she said, "Lowell was afraid Daddy'd find out I'm a lesbian."

Janet didn't know what she had expected, but it wasn't that. She nearly said, "Is that all?," remembered who *Daddy* was, and said instead, "God, Lee, and you got married?"

Leora swiveled back to face her. "I didn't know. Not really. I mean, I didn't like the way guys came on, but I thought I'd get used to it, you know, when I really fell in love. And Lowell was pretty decent about it, you know what I mean, and he is good looking, and even back then he was making good money."

Lowell, decent about sexual resistance? Well, he had apologized. "God."

"Jannie, don't keep swearing. What else was there to do? I'm no big liberated career woman. I can take dictation and run the computer, but that's just good for a second income. It isn't so bad, really, and I have the girls and I wouldn't give that up for anything. It was okay, really, except that Lowell found out. Just the other day. There's this woman—" The dam breached, Leora blushed. "She gave a talk at Ladies Aid. On quilting. I mean, how womanly can you get? It was three years ago, more than three, almost four, and there was something about her—she isn't really pretty, she's really kind of plain, but I couldn't take my eyes off her. I say I didn't know, but I must have, because afterward, after her talk, I went up and told her about that old crazy quilt of Grandma's, and she said she'd love to see it, and I invited her out to the house—I'd just left Lana at day care, it was only going to be another hour or so—and she just loved the quilt, and we got to talking and—it was like she knew everything I'd been feeling for—forever."

"And Lowell caught you."

"Not then. She lives—no, I'm not going to tell you anything. She started coming up when I put Lana down for her nap—but then her naps got shorter and shorter and it got so complicated, arranging play groups, and then there was Lisa, and I had to juggle both their schedules. I got careless about watching the time, and just the other day she stayed too long and Lowell caught us."

"What did he do?"

"Not—nothing, really. He cursed us out, and after she left, he went out and got drunk and stayed out all night."

And after all, Janet felt a bit of pity for her obnoxious cousin-in-law. No wonder he'd been acting so erratically. She said, "Four years. And you stayed with him."

"What was I going to do? Secretarial doesn't pay anything."

"But now"—helium in her head again—"with your inheritance, you could afford to move out."

"He'd take the girls away from me."

"He couldn't do that. How would he take care of them?"

"His mother. You know what happens. Especially around here. They say the mother's a pervert and they give the children to the father and let his mother take care of them." Was this fluffy little Leora talking? "I wouldn't put the girls through that kind of fight in a million years, even if I thought I could win. And he is their daddy. They need him. And they need me. They'd be lost without both of us."

"God, Lee."

"It was okay, you know. I think he's got a girlfriend. He doesn't bother me much, you know what I mean, except when he's had too many beers. Only—" She drew in a shuddering breath. "You know what it's like here, everybody knows everything about everybody. I shouldn't ever have gotten started with her. If Daddy'd ever found out, he'd have disowned me."

"Oh, come on. Your dad loved you."

"That makes it worse. Maybe Mom could have talked him out of it, but now that she's dead, he'd have disowned me. You know how he is. Was."

Was she dreaming? Could any of this be happening? "And you actually think Lowell would kill your father to keep him from finding out you're gay?"

"Jannie, why do you think he married me? It sure wasn't because I was so good in bed. And he left the hike early and nobody knows where he was when Daddy fell. The sheriff talked to him twice. He said he got lost on the mountain in all that rain, but he knows the woods. He goes hunting up there. I don't think they believe him."

She was awake; this was really happening. "My God, Lee."

"The only thing is, they know the business is doing well, so me getting Daddy's money now instead of later doesn't seem like that much of a motive. They don't know about the rest of it, but I know what Daddy'd have done if he found out, and so did Lowell."

JANET TOOK AN unsatisfactory leave, drove back to the art center with only half her mind on what she was doing, and parked in her usual spot at the far end.

God, what a mess. No wonder Lowell had been acting rattled. Friends? The handshake tingled in her nerve endings. She wiped her right palm on her skirt, recognized an echo of Lowell's gesture, and slammed the car door harder than she'd meant to.

Charlie Emmett's pickup was standing next to the building in a patch of shade; when the door slammed, Charlie's shaggy iron gray head rose above the side panel. He'd been napping in the truck bed. Sleeping on the job; what a surprise. "Sorry I woke you," she called.

He chose to ignore the sarcasm. He yawned and got to his feet and said, "About time somebody did." He climbed down over the tailgate. "It's those damn late shows. The wife's visiting her mother, and I can't seem to find the Off button on my own."

She was debating whether to escalate her response when she heard gravel crunch behind her. In the same instant, Charlie shouted, "Hey, watch it!," and she turned and saw her car inching forward.

She grabbed the door handle, but her weight wasn't enough to stop the slow roll and she had to take a stumbling step to keep up. She forced the handle down, wrenched the door open, and grabbed the steering wheel. The door frame shoved at her back, nearly knocking her off her feet, but she kept her grip and heaved herself into the driver's seat. With her left leg still dangling out the half-closed door, her right foot groped for the brake pedal, found it, and stamped; and the car stopped.

Her heart was hammering. The front bumper was only a yard or so short of the rail that guarded the steep drop-off to the railroad tracks and the river. With her right foot still heavy on the brake, she pulled her left leg in, closed the door, jerked the hand brake another eighth of an inch, and put her hand on the stick shift. It was in neutral. Her habit was to leave the car in gear as a backup in case the hand brake slipped, but maybe, distracted by the mess at the Lamonts' house, she'd been careless.

Or more likely, because the habit was long established and strong, it had slipped into neutral on its own. She contorted herself to fish the keys out of her pocket, where she had dropped them automatically. She started the car, released the brake, depressed the clutch, jammed the gear lever into reverse, and backed once more into her parking slot. This time she set the brake and the gearshift with extra attention and was gentler when she closed the door.

"You need a brake job," Charlie said.

She shoved her shaking hands into her skirt pockets. "Transmission too. It looks like it popped into neutral."

"Well, it won't be long before you can get that Jag."

"Jeep," she said. Winter in the Highlands called for four-wheel drive.

Charlie grinned. "Anything your heart desires."

Anything. Steak; lobster; Jeeps; unicorns. Did they make Jeeps with horns in the middle of their foreheads? Did they make Jeeps with foreheads? "I can't seem to get my mind around it," she said. "You know, I haven't even seen the land?"

"You want to see it? I'll take you out. You doing anything after work?"

The moment for chastising Charlie had come and gone. "How long will it take?"

"Twenty minutes to get there. After that, it depends on how much you want to go tramping around."

"It's too hot to tramp around."

"You got a deal."

THE ROAD TO THE unicorn pasture led north, through valleys and around hills, past driveways that led, presumably, to houses hidden in the forest. Eventually the road emerged onto a plain, and presently Charlie pulled into a turnoff and stopped, facing a padlocked chain that denied access to a narrow grass-grown roadway. The land beyond the chain was low and flat, overgrown with black-birch thickets and brush. The map in Uncle Bud's file had prepared her for the flatness, but not for the dreariness. "This is it?" she said.

"This is it."

"No view."

"The estate sold off the hill land first."

"Who'd be interested in flat land without a view?"

"Farmers."

"Are there still farmers around here?"

"Horse people."

"Are there that many horse people these days?"

"Never took a poll." Charlie grinned sideways at her. "But if somebody wants to play, I'll sell him the chips."

TWELVE

Black; Horses

BEFORE DRIVING OFF with Charlie, Janet had turned on the dark-room air conditioner and taken her film from the refrigerator. By the time he dropped her off again, the darkroom had cooled and the film had warmed.

She turned off the lights and, working by touch, unwound the first roll of film from its spool, threaded it onto the developing reel, and loaded it into the light-tight tank. With the lights on again, she poured the developer into the tank, watched the timer, agitated the tank at thirty-second intervals. When the timer buzzed, she drained the tank, ran in fresh water, rinsed, drained—

Usually the rhythm was soothing. This time, her mind wouldn't shut up.

Leora—
Did he fall or was he pushed?
Lowell?
God, what a mess.

The timer buzzed, jerking her back from inattention.

When the final rinse was finished, she unscrewed the lid and lifted out the reel, dunked it in the Photo-Flo bath, unwound the film, and stripped the water from it between her fingers. Ready for that first intriguing peek at the negative images, she held the strip to the light.

There were no images. The developed film was black from end to end.

Damn, *damn*, *DAMN*.

She fished the envelopes that had held the chemical powders from the trash and verified that she had used the right chemistry.

Had she goofed during that spell of woolgathering?

No, that couldn't be the problem. Nothing in the development process could have produced this disaster. Only an exposure of the whole film to light could produce this all-over blackness.

She reviewed the history of the film. She'd bought it fresh on Saturday morning. Loading and unloading her camera had been routine. A light leak in the camera or in the developing tank would show up only in dark streaks at the edges. And even if she had misread her light meter and overexposed her shots, there would still be some sort of image, and there would be clear spaces between the frames.

X rays? No photographer trusted airport security, but she hadn't been on a plane in years. She hadn't gone to the dentist with the film in her pocket; she hadn't been to the dentist in years, either.

The refrigerator? She had been storing film in the darkroom refrigerator for two months without trouble. But until yesterday, not in the freezer. Could there be some sort of radiation in the freezer? It seemed wildly unlikely, and anyway, it would take a big dose of radiation to blacken the film so absolutely.

A fault in the film itself? Kodak's quality control was reliable, but she supposed there was an outside chance that something might have happened during transportation, or at the store.

But all those notions were far-fetched; they were her mind's effort to avoid the obvious explanation—which was that somebody had unrolled the film in the light and then rolled it up again.

She had been working with a medium-format camera that used 120 film, which came on old-fashioned spools, not the light-tight cassettes used for 35-millimeter film. It would take a special instrument to open a 35-millimeter cassette without bending the lid, but when one unloaded an exposed roll of 120 from the camera, one simply folded the tab end of the protective paper under and stuck it down with an adhesive strip of paper. How hard would it be to peel off that strip, unroll the film in the light, then roll it back up and reapply the adhesive strip?

She hung the ruined negative strip in the drying cabinet, next to Greg's, and picked up one of the undeveloped rolls.

Yes.

Half an inch from the end, the adhesive strip was torn across, as if somebody had started to peel it off and miscalculated the strength of the glue bond. The torn ends had been rematched; working in the dark, she wouldn't have noticed, but examining the roll in white light, she could see the ragged edges. She fished the curled-up yellow protective paper from the first roll out of the trash can and looked at the end.

Same thing—two torn places on that strip. The strip on the third roll, still undeveloped, hadn't torn, but she could see scuff marks where it had been scraped loose.

She dried the tank and the reel, turned out the lights, and developed the second roll, attending to each second of the process.

It was black. She hung it in the drying cabinet. Half an hour later, the third roll matched the other two.

After a moment of unpleasant rumination, she worked her hands into a pair of latex gloves from a box under the sink and stuffed the yellow protective paper and spools into a plastic trash bag. She cleaned up the darkroom and locked it behind her, and carried the bag up to her apartment and shoved it into the back of her bedroom closet. Stripping off the gloves, she wondered why she'd bothered with them; her fingerprints would be all over everything anyway.

It took her a long time to fall asleep. Before starting for Tarrytown in the morning, she put on gloves, retrieved the dry negative strips from the darkroom, put them in a bag, and stowed it in the closet with the other one. The rush-hour drive was not restful.

What had happened to those films?

Wrong question. She knew what had happened: somebody had exposed them to light. The right question was *why?*

The only reason she could think of—aside from the sick joy of vandalism, which she guessed couldn't really be ruled out— was that there had been something on one of those films that somebody didn't want her to see.

Did he fall or was he pushed?

Well, face it; suppose he'd been pushed. So what? None of her shots would show the push, because where he had fallen from wasn't visible from where she'd been shooting.

But suppose the vandal didn't know that. Maybe he—she?— knew she'd been shooting near the quarry and only guessed that her shots might incriminate him. Her? Suppose the film had been destroyed, so to speak, on spec.

A good many people knew she'd been shooting near the quarry, but X would also have to be somebody with access to the art center darkroom.

Who qualified?

Helen; but Helen hadn't been on the mountain when Uncle Bud had fallen. Gregory Ferguson, obviously. Charlie Emmett; for the duration of the renovation, Charlie had almost a full set of keys.

Lowell? Oh, lord, Charlie could have loaned the keys to Lowell.

A horn blared, jerking her attention back to the road. She was cruising in the left lane at sixty—the fastest her car would go without shimmying, but ten miles an hour below the preferred (though illegal) speed.

She speeded up until she reached a clear stretch in the right lane, pulled over, and eased back to sixty. Along with that long overdue transmission and brake work, she needed a front-end alignment.

Maybe she shouldn't wait for probate; maybe, contrary to all her resolve, she should borrow on her expectations and buy that four-wheel-drive unicorn.

WHILE ERIC SWANSON EXAMINED her documents in his large and amply windowed office, Janet sipped gratefully from a mug he had filled from a Mr. Coffee on a shelf in the corner. She had time to observe that his attractiveness depended as much on the suggestion of good humor in the crinkles around his eyes as on the lines and masses that made up his face and body. Not that there was anything wrong with the lines and masses. And he returned his own calls and made his own coffee.

What she hadn't noticed at the quarry on Saturday was that he wore a wedding band.

He looked up, a smile deepening the crinkles. "Well, it isn't your ordinary sort of legacy, but everything seems straightforward enough." He began bundling the papers together. "If I have my geography right, that land isn't exactly scenic. Do you know what the buyers intend to do with it?"

"Charlie says horse farms."

"Mm."

Did she hear a hint of disapproval? "Is that bad?"

His hesitation was of the briefest. "No. Not really."

"But?"

"Be warned, you're talking to a fanatic. No, there's nothing necessarily bad about horse farms. They can contaminate surface water, but most localities have ordinances governing stable construction and waste disposal. Enforcement can be another story, of course, but that's not your problem. There are those who maintain that horse urine poses a threat to groundwater, but I think that's about ninety-nine percent hysteria. Although if it's the land I'm thinking of, it *is* over a sand-and-gravel aquifer."

"That's bad?"

"It's vulnerable. If pollutants get into that kind of aquifer, they spread in all directions. It's sand and gravel that underlies Long Island, and they've had a lot of problems with well contamination."

"From horses?"

"Industrial toxins is more the kind of thing. Underground gasoline tanks, fuel oil, pesticides. I really wouldn't worry about horses."

"And if I did worry, would there be anything I could do about it?"

"No. The contract of sale binds the executor to close the deal."

"Okay, I won't worry about horses. What about unicorns?"

For a couple of seconds, she thought she'd stumped him, but then he laughed. "You don't believe all this."

"Even when I do, I don't."

"I can understand that."

"I mean, why me?"

"Stuff happens."

"Is that a legal term?" She reached across the desk for her papers. "Maybe the land trust should buy the place and protect that sand-and-gravel aquifer from horse urine."

"If the trust was interested in that land, you'd have to find another lawyer, because I'd have a conflict of interest."

IT WAS WELL AFTER ELEVEN when Janet got back to the office. Helen looked up from the computer and said, "Go away, it's your day off."

Janet went over to the key cabinet on the wall. All the keys were hanging on their hooks. "Did you give the darkroom key to anybody in the last week?" she asked.

"Isn't it there? I let Greg in for his session a while ago, but I swear I put it back."

"It's here. I meant earlier."

"*Not I* said the little red hen. Something wrong?"

"Something happened to my film."

"Stolen?"

"Spoiled." She described the havoc.

"Oh, not nice," said Helen. "He's in there now, if you want to ask him."

"IT'S OKAY, COME IN!" Gregory shouted when she knocked.

The white light was on, and in spite of the exhaust fan, the room smelled of fixer. Gregory was taking eight-by-ten sheets from a print washer, squeegeeing excess water from them, and laying them on a drying rack. "I'll be done in a minute," he said.

"No hurry," she said. "I just had a question for you. You know those three rolls of one-twenty film I put in the freezer on Monday?"

"Sure, the ones you shot on Saturday."

"Did you by any chance handle them?"

"No, I didn't. I never even opened the freezer. Why, did something happen?"

She told him.

"That's weird," he said. "All that work. That's awful."

"Did anybody else come into the darkroom while you were working?"

"Just when you and the others came to say the power was going to go off." He laid the last print on the rack and uncorked the hose that drained the washer. "You think somebody tampered with them?"

"It sure looks like it."

He pulled down a handful of paper towels and wiped the sink. "Why would anybody do something like that?"

"Beats me." She leaned over the drying rack. He'd been making contact prints—pages covered with postage-stamp-size images. Portraits. "Looks like you have some nice lighting," she said.

"Thanks. It's people I work with at the mall." He pitched the soaked paper towels in the trash, switched off the air conditioner, and picked up his backpack.

Out in the hot hall, they met Charlie Emmett coming up the basement stairs, mopping his face with a red bandanna. Predictably, he said, "Hey, pard."

"I was just going to look for you," said Janet. "I have a weird question."

"Yeah?"

"Is there any way the freezer in that refrigerator in the darkroom could give out some sort of radiation?"

"You mean like one of those old watch dials? Glow in the dark?"

"Actually, I don't know what I'm talking about."

"Never heard of such a thing. Why?"

"You remember I put some film in the freezer to stay cold, the day you turned the power off?"

"Right, your experiments."

"Well, something overexposed that film, so when I developed it, it came out black."

Charlie scratched his head.

"It looks like somebody unrolled the film in the light and then rolled it back up again," she said.

Gregory said, "Like the time Kevin exposed the film in that old box camera he was playing around with."

"Right, that old Brownie that belonged to my mom."

"Remember that?" said Gregory. "He unrolled the film to see what it was like and then he rolled it up and put it back and took all the pictures, and nothing came out. He thought the camera was broken."

"I remember some hassle about that camera," said Charlie. "Is that what it was?"

"It looks like that's the sort of thing that happened to my film," Janet said. "Have you loaned the darkroom key to anybody?"

"Not me. The thing is, though, as many people've been coming in and out over the years, there're probably keys all over town."

"That's a point."

"Listen," said Gregory, "I've got to get to work. That's really gross about your negs. The light's never the same when you go back."

"Stuff happens," said Janet. "See you Monday."

"Yeah, take it easy," said Charlie. When Gregory had gone, he said, "How about we change the locks while we're doing everything else?"

"Can we stay within the budget?"

"I'll get you a price. Hey, when we sell the land, you can give the place new locks. Deductible."

Sell the land. Yes. "Charlie—did you know that horse farms can pollute the water supply?"

"No," he said, "I can't say as I did. What about it?"

"Does it make you nervous, selling to somebody who might ruin the water supply?"

"No, I can't say as it does. There are laws."

"If they're enforced."

A breath *sheesh*ed out through Charlie's teeth. "What's your problem, partner? You think their money's dirty?"

Not a bad way of putting it. "The thing is, Charlie, I didn't do anything to earn all that money, but coming from land the way it is—it's kind of like being appointed a guardian, you know?"

"No," he said, "I don't know."

She shouldn't have started this, but some perversity of character kept her talking. "I don't mean I wouldn't love to have the money. But I was living without it before Uncle Bud died, so it isn't like I'd be losing anything—"

"*Hey!* Hold it!"

She stopped.

"Just hold it, little gal. Maybe you didn't do anything to earn it, but I put a bundle into that property. If this sale falls through, that fund Bud set up to cover the mortgage is going to run out, and *I* sure as Billy-be-durned don't have the income to keep on paying the bank. That six months runs out, then what happens?

Foreclosure, that's what, and everything Bud and I put into that land is down the tubes."

"Charlie—"

"You're single, you can live in two rooms in an attic. I've got a wife and a family to feed."

"Charlie!"

He stopped.

"Charlie, calm down. It's out of my hands anyway. Finlay Keene is the executor, and he's the one who's going to sell it. I'm just—it just makes me nervous, that's all. That's all I was saying."

"Get over it," he said, and turned back to the cellar stairs.

THIRTEEN

Turtle on Its Back

THE FUNERAL—CLOSED-COFFIN—was over. What remained of Councilman Broderick Hale now lay six feet under in the Phillips Landing cemetery, next to what remained of Aunt Irene; back in the church basement, a hundred voices had accomplished the modulation from respectful hush to normal resonance, and Janet had renewed acquaintance with her other two Hale cousins, Leora's older brothers. They had flown in that morning, one from Houston and the other from a Marine posting in some global hot spot, and were due to fly out again on the weekend.

Watching Lowell enact his assigned role of supportive husband to bereaved daughter, Janet found herself wondering if she had dreamed yesterday's conversation with Leora.

As soon as was decent, Marion and Paul took her out to their place to wind down. They were catching the sluggish breeze on the back deck when Paul, horizontal in a recliner, said, "Where'd Reverend Gray find that poem? If that's the word I want."

"Uncle Bud wrote it."

Jaw sagging, hand to forehead, Paul mimed shock.

"He wrote a bunch," she said. "I found them on a disk in his study. I guess Lee thought he didn't want people to know, so she told Reverend Gray not to say."

"If that was a fair sample," said Paul, "I can't say I blame him."

"Paul," said Marion, herself a published poet, "we just buried him. There's a twenty-four-hour embargo on home truths."

shirt and laced on sneakers and carried her camera bag out to the parking lot. The storm had left the morning washed clean of humidity. The wet gravel glittered; a feathering jet trail was the only mark on the porcelain blue sky.

The broken rail, one end still attached to its post, led the eye to a swath of torn-up weeds and shrubs. Thirty feet below, the car rested upside down against a big old oak. It looked like a giant turtle turned on its back and, for a moment, Janet felt a ridiculous wave of pity for its helplessness.

She started photographing at the top, concentrating on the lines and masses of fence rail, stone, and plowed-up earth. Then she lay on her stomach at the edge of the drop-off, propping her tripod on the downgrade with each leg at a different length, and framed the car's undercarriage with a ragged fringe of weeds. After that, she slung the camera bag over her shoulder, eased her legs over the edge, and inched her way down, the folded-up tripod doing duty as an alpenstock. Twice her feet slipped on wet leaves and dumped her on her rump. The fallen leaves did little to cushion the rock; her butt would probably be black and blue within the hour.

Nobody was going to be looking at her butt, though, and she supposed that was some consolation.

Close up, she abandoned any thought of repairs. The roof was caved in to the seat back and the side that had hit the tree was buckled almost into a right angle. The doors were still locked, and were in any case jammed beyond opening.

As far as she could tell, peering through the cracked windows at the upside-down interior, the hand brake was set. She must have failed to give it that last jerk it had been needing lately. She couldn't figure out what position the gearshift was in, but for the car to have moved, it had to have slipped into neutral, just as it had the other day.

She should have gone to Aamco. Shoulda woulda coulda. Stuff happens.

She tried a few shots of the car, but her concentration had frayed. She stowed the camera and scrambled back up. Charlie Emmett was climbing out of his pickup when she crawled over the edge. He sauntered over, looked down the slope, and whistled. "Brake slip again?"

"Same as the other day, I guess." She brushed wet debris from herself. "It happened during the thunderstorm. Maybe one of those close hits jarred it."

He nodded at the camera case. "Getting ready to sue somebody?"

"Oh, come on, Charlie. Who would I sue, God? It's my fault I didn't take it to the shop."

"Just taking pictures for the family album?"

"Call it art."

"Whatever you say. You aren't going to try to patch her up, are you?"

"No chance. Uncle Bud's buying me new wheels."

"There you go. Get that Jag."

Jeep. She didn't bother correcting him. "Charlie," she said, "we've got to replace that fence. I didn't realize it was so flimsy."

"Visual barrier's what they call it," said Charlie. "I never could see the point myself. The planning board wouldn't let you get away with that now."

"I should hope not. What if somebody'd been in the car? We've got to put up a real guardrail."

"Right. I'll cost it out for you."

FOURTEEN

Black II

BACK IN HER APARTMENT, Janet showered, tossed her muddy jeans over the shower rod to dry, and dressed in skirt and clean shirt. She walked down the road to Main Street and bought the Times and a local daily, went back up to her apartment, made toast. Uncle Bud's death was no longer news. At a few minutes before ten, she went down the inside stairs to the office.

In the middle of her desk was a black, zippered portfolio, the kind artists carry small works in. A Post-it stuck to the top said, "This was in that closet Helen said I could use, and I think you should look at it. Love, Kristin." Beside the portfolio was a note printed in Magic Marker on the back of an obsolete flyer: *Have you ordered copy paper? That mailing has to go out Friday and I'm into the last ream. XXX, Helen*

Oh, lord, she'd forgotten. She pushed the portfolio to the back of her desk, flipped her Rolodex, and called their supplier. Phillips Landing was fifteen miles in the wrong direction; delivery wouldn't be until next Thursday.

A week's delay would be too long. She started to say she'd pick it up herself, remembered with a jolt that she no longer had a car, and said, "I'll get back to you."

It wouldn't do to ask Helen; she attended a reading circle at the library on Thursday evenings, and in any case, she already worked harder, longer, and more effectively than her rate of pay warranted. Janet picked up the phone, punched in the Willards'

number, and got the answering machine. While she was waiting through the message, Gregory Ferguson, backpack dangling from one shoulder, came in from the parking lot. The beep beeped; she nodded to Gregory and said into the phone, "Hi, Marion, it's Janet on Thursday morning with a big favor to ask. My car committed suicide last night. No human casualties, but I have to go up to Office-Rite for a load of copy paper. If you—"

Gregory was waving his arms.

"Hold it," she said into the phone.

He said, "Which Office-Rite?"

Holding the phone away from her mouth, she said, "North Valley Mall."

"I can pick it up."

Into the phone, she said, "I'll call you back," and hung up.

Gregory said, "I work at the computer store up there. I get off at nine, but I could pick up your stuff and stow it in my van on my break."

"You can't sign our corporate Visa," she said.

"Oh. Well, if you could get up there some way, you could sign and I could bring you back with the paper. I think the county runs a bus." He reached across her desk for the phone book.

The county ran a bus. The last trip of the day left the Phillips Landing IGA parking lot at six p.m. and arrived at the North Valley Mall at half past.

Two and a half hours to kill. In a mall. Malls gave her a headache.

But this bird was in the hand, and God knew what bush Paul and Marion had flown to. "Thanks," she said. She'd take her camera. "This isn't your day for the darkroom, is it?"

With his redhead's flush, he said, "I just wondered if it'd be okay if I hung out and did some paperwork. I have to take it back to Town Hall, and it's kind of a long way around to go home and come back."

She pushed back her chair. "Nobody's using the studio."

The studio was a good-size north-windowed back room, not scheduled for use until afternoon. A big folding table, open, stood against one wall. Gregory said, "Great," and slid the backpack off his shoulder.

Back in the office, Helen had arrived. Her first words were, "What happened out there?"

Out there? Oh. "My car jumped off a cliff."

"A lot of that going around," Helen said. "Were you in it?"

"Do I look like it?"

"You're walking a little funny."

"Oh, that. I went down to check out the damage and fell on my ass. Do you know any towing companies?"

"What the junkers'd give you wouldn't cover the towing," Helen said. "Why not just leave it there?"

Next to the art center? It'd look like one of those places where they put up a "No Dumping" sign after it was too late. Janet could just hear the trustees. "Sure," she said. "Call it art."

"You're getting it," said Helen.

"Build some steps down to the wreckage—"

"The Work."

"The Work, right. Stone steps down to The Work and a walkway around it. Post signs—'Please Do Not Touch the Artwork.'"

"Or 'Please Touch.'"

"The board would have a fit and our liability coverage would go out of sight."

"Write a grant proposal." Helen looked out the window. "Who's that?"

In the parking lot, a man Janet didn't recognize was getting out of a car. "Our insurance agent," she said, "coming to tell us how much the new coverage will cost." He was not only a stranger; he was black. Brown, really, sort of milky cocoa colored. This was remarkable, since the Afro-American population of Phillips Landing was so tiny as to be essentially invisible. None ever came to the art center—not to the shows, not to the

fund-raisers, not to the workshops. Could the mentor-mentee show, in some way as yet unknown, be breaking ground? And, she wondered sourly, would such a development strengthen or weaken her position as director?

He locked his car, walked over to the orange tape Charlie had strung across the gap in the fence, and looked down; then he crossed to the open office door and knocked on the frame.

His African-textured hair was conservatively barbered; he wore khaki slacks and a tan polo shirt that blended nicely with his skin; his age was somewhere in the mid-thirties. Only in Phillips Landing's racial monoculture was he likely to attract notice. "I'm looking for Janet Upton," he said.

"You've found her," Janet said. "And this is Helen Ives."

He nodded; Helen said, "Hello." He reached into a back pocket, pulled out a thin leather case, and flipped it open to reveal a gold shield. Janet's heart bumped. "Investigator Zachary Youngblood, from the sheriff's office," he said. He slipped the case back into his pocket and nodded toward the lot. "What happened?"

That couldn't be what he'd come about, but she said, "My car slipped its gear in the middle of the night." No cute answers when a sheriff's investigator is doing the asking. "Am I supposed to report it? Nobody got hurt and no other car was involved."

"Technically, yes, you are supposed to report it," he said.

"Okay. I'm reporting it."

He pulled no triplicate forms from his pocket; it wasn't what he'd come about. He said, "Do you have a minute or two?"

"Sure." She managed to keep her voice steady for the single word. She waved at the chair beside her desk.

He glanced at Helen. "Somewhere private?"

Her heart thumping, Janet did a mental survey. *Not* her apartment; her apartment was her haven. Most of the cellar was a mess. Gregory was in the studio. The gallery? It wouldn't be open to the public until eleven. She took him past the photographs and paintings and Kristin's carvings to a window seat that looked over

treetops to the hills that edged the far side of the river. Its padding was thin; she eased sideways to spare her bruised buttock.

"What I'm here about," said Investigator Youngblood, "is Mr. Hale's death."

Surprise. But no bright remarks; she just said, "Yes."

"Just a couple of things I want to get straightened out. You were doing some photography near the scene."

Not a subject to quiet her heartbeat. "Yes."

"I'd like to see the results."

She drew in a deep breath and let it out. He did nothing to fill the silence. She said, "So would I."

"What do you mean?"

She got to her feet. She'd have to take him up to her apartment after all. "I'd better show you," she said.

Helen looked up but said nothing as Janet led Youngblood back through the office to the inner stairs. She left the doors open, downstairs and up. It crossed her mind that this cop—this sheriff's *investigator*—was the first man to enter her apartment since Paul Willard had hauled the last of her boxes up the stairs on the ninth of June.

She fished the plastic bags out of the back of her closet and handed them to him.

"What's this?" he said.

"This is what was supposed to be my photographs."

He raised his eyebrows. She explained. He opened the bag with the blackened negatives and looked in without touching the contents. He bunched it together again and retwisted the twist tie.

"It can't have been anything I did during the processing," she said. "I think they were tampered with before I started working on them." She described the condition of the adhesive strips and the protective paper. "You'll see when you look at them."

"Who had access to the film?" he said.

"For starters," she said, "me."

A little smile, soon extinguished. "I'd worked that out."

"I didn't do this. Those images were my work."

He had taken out a notebook. "Noted," he said.

"It had to be while the film was in the darkroom. I bought the film Saturday morning and I shot up all three rolls that afternoon. They were with me, in the camera or in my pocket or locked in my car trunk, until I put them in the refrigerator. That was Saturday afternoon." She drew a breath and said, "Gregory Ferguson rents darkroom time. He was working here Monday. Actually, he's here now, in the studio." .

"Did he know the film was there?"

"Yes. So did Charlie Emmett and Lowell Lamont." She explained the renovation and the power cut and moving the film into the freezer. "That was Monday."

"Anybody else?"

Against her will, she'd been thinking about it. "I can't say for sure. We keep the darkroom locked, but there's a key cabinet on the office wall and that's usually open during business hours. If Helen and I were both out of the office, I guess somebody could go in and take a key."

"Does that happen a lot? That nobody's in the office?"

"Not a whole lot. Mainly when one of us has her day off. People come in to look at the art and whoever's here goes out to the gallery to talk to them."

"Could somebody get from the office to the darkroom without your seeing them?"

She paused to think. "I suppose so, if we were back here in this alcove, or downstairs looking in on one of the workshops or checking on the renovation."

"Has anybody had a day off since you put the film in the darkroom?"

"Well, I was off yesterday, but I'd already found out the negs were ruined the night before." She had to close her eyes and count back. "Helen—let's see. Helen had Monday off. That's the day they turned off the power and I moved the film to the freezer."

"Do you have a record of everyone who was in the building between the time you put the film in the refrigerator and the time you developed it?"

"Everybody? No. The opening was going on when I put it in and several people dropped in to see the work on Sunday. There's a guest book, but not everybody signs it. Monday and Tuesday there were workshops. Helen has the attendance sheets for those."

"I'd like copies of the workshop lists and the guest book. And now, if you'd show me where the studio is, I'll have a word with Mr. Ferguson, and then I'll have a look at the darkroom."

FIFTEEN

Elephant; Horses II

CRADLING HER CAMERA CASE on her lap, Janet ordered herself not to think about it. But it was like that childhood tease, *Don't think about elephants:* once they're mentioned, you're doomed. What you have to do, you finally learn, is substitute something else for the elephant. She rummaged around the warehouse of her mind for something else to think about, but the elephant turned up everywhere she looked.

She had taken Investigator Youngblood to the studio and introduced him to Gregory, who had been poring over big sheets of paper spread out on the table. Back in the office, she'd answered Helen's raised eyebrows with a shrug. Presently Youngblood came back, had her sign a receipt for the plastic bags filled with the ruins of her film, and carried them out to his car. But he didn't drive off; he returned carrying a triplicate form and a bag that looked like a doctor's satchel in a Norman Rockwell illustration. He entered the details of her car's demise on the form, detached a copy for her, tucked the others into the breast pocket of his shirt, and said, "Is it okay if I have a look at the darkroom now?"

Janet thought she had a right to demand a search warrant, but what would be the point? She took the darkroom key out of the cabinet, led him down the hall, and unlocked the door.

The satchel contained fingerprint-lifting equipment. "You can stay if you want to," he said, so she did. She pointed out the box

of latex gloves under the sink and said he was welcome to take one. He did, bagging it in plastic and tucking it into the doctor's kit.

The dusting and lifting were slower than on a cop show and lacked the comic relief of a wisecracking partner. When Youngblood was finished, he asked permission to take her fingerprints, which she granted. When that was done, she washed her hands at the darkroom sink, and after that Youngblood thanked her, went back to his car, and drove away.

So HERE WAS THE ELEPHANT on the bus with her, sitting on her lap disguised as a camera bag. Youngblood was going to find her fingerprints on the refrigerator, and on the film and the protective paper and probably even on the spools. Would he find anybody else's? If so, whose?

Think about something else, she ordered herself. *You're a photographer; switch on your vision.* She ordered herself to attend to the local businesses, hacked out of second-growth forest, that lined the road. They were passing a little off-road plaza: a diner, a real estate office, a unisex hairdresser, a warehousey sort of building selling beer and soda by the case, a no-name gas station. A little wetland full of tall, feathery reeds. A distributor of precast concrete, a construction-machinery rental service, a gas station with attached car wash. A couple of hundred feet of scrub: LAND FOR SALE, COMMERCIAL. Beyond it, freestanding and tidy, Lamont Electric—

The damn elephant was back on her lap.

Lamont. Lowell; Leora; two little girls who didn't deserve to be pitched into disaster—

Oh, all *right.* If the blasted animal insisted on pestering her, she might as well pay attention. She looked the elephant square in the trunk; and the longer she looked at it, the more insubstantial it became, until presently it began to resemble a fairy-tale elephant. Babar or some caricature of that sort.

As a child, she remembered, Leora had been constantly ter-

rorized by imagined menaces: trolls, ogres, wolves, witches, wicked stepmothers. Aunt Irene had tried to censor the fairy tales, but that just made room for space aliens and serial killers. On summer visits, Janet had finally opted to sleep by herself on a cot on the screened-in back porch, to avoid being kept awake by the night-light in Leora's room.

So surely this panic about Lowell was just another of Leora's bogymen. Already on edge from having to confront her sexual orientation (what a clunky mouthful), she was once more imagining ogres in the closet.

It was true that nobody knew where Lowell had gone after he left the hike, but according to Eric, he had headed back down the Pine Street trail, which led in the opposite direction from the quarry. Several people had seen Uncle Bud just before the storm started, and Schuyler Vanstaat and Gregory Ferguson had seen each other, and Charlie Emmett said he'd seen both of them. None of them had said anything about seeing Lowell. And even if Lowell had wanted his father-in-law dead, he couldn't have known that Bud Hale was going to stand at the top of the quarry cliff in a thunderstorm. And while you might wonder how an experienced deer hunter could get lost in the woods, you had to remember that he'd recently received a serious emotional shock; his mind might very well not have been focused on where he was going. Certainly his erratic behavior to Janet could well be the out-of-control actions of a rattled man. Yes, maybe Lowell could have got at the film in the freezer, but—

The film.

Once more a live elephant began to take form inside the cartoon lines. Because the destruction of the film hadn't just happened. Somebody had done it.

It might be somebody who felt some sort of malice—toward her in particular, or toward the practice of photography in general. Cal, for instance, had a malicious streak and didn't think much of camera work. But he was in Texas, and she didn't know of anyone else who might be holding such a grudge.

The elephant said, *Forget malice;* the elephant said it had to be somebody who thought the film might hold an incriminating image. And that meant—didn't it?—somebody who had wanted Uncle Bud dead.

Gregory Ferguson, actually, had had the best shot at the film, and of them all, Gregory would know how best to ruin the images. But why? She couldn't imagine why Gregory Ferguson would have wanted Uncle Bud dead.

The bus slowed and lurched into a vast parking lot and stopped at the main entrance to the North Valley Mall. Janet slid the camera bag strap over her shoulder and stood up.

THUNDERSTORMS SEEMED TO BE occurring almost daily. Another began building while she worked. She was struggling to capture the interplay between the slanting rays of the setting sun and the artificial light bouncing off the ranks of cars when clouds began to pile in. The pale daylight faded, distant flickers became middle-distant flashes and then overhead streaks, mumbles became thuds, then cracks. The wind kicked up and drove dust into her eyes. She retreated indoors just as the first big drops splatted down, and killed the time until nine o'clock with a cup of coffee.

She had arranged for the copy paper to be left under an overhang just outside the Office-Rite pickup door, and had stopped in the computer store to tell Gregory to meet her beside the cartons. By the time he arrived, lightning was blazing across the black sky, thunder was drumming, rain was slashing down, and the parking lot was awash. A yellow poncho flapping around his knees, he ran for his van. He backed it under the edge of the overhang, climbed out, and opened the rear hatch.

Janet climbed into the cargo space to receive the cartons as he heaved them in. A narrow foam pad, such as one might place on the ground under a sleeping bag, lay lengthwise on the right-hand side. She tucked her camera bag between the end of the pad and the back of the passenger seat. The cartons were heavy but

Gregory was a husky kid and handled them without effort. At his direction, she kept them off the pad, instead stowing them three deep behind the driver's seat.

When they were loaded, Janet clambered over the gearbox into the passenger seat and buckled her seat belt. Gregory shook water from the poncho, threw it in on top of the cartons, and dashed for the cab. He slammed the door and started the engine and the windshield promptly fogged. He smeared ineffectively at it with his shirtsleeve, then punched a button, and they pulled onto the highway with the draft from the defroster bouncing off the windshield into their faces. The wipers fought a losing battle against the sluicing rain. Oncoming headlights painted streaks on the rain-slicked blacktop. Thunder cracked. An eighteen-wheeler roared past in the opposite lane, hosing muddy water onto the streaming windshield.

"Eight-hundred-pound gorilla," muttered Gregory. He hadn't buckled his seat belt and he was driving too fast for the wet road. Janet's hands were gripping each other in her lap. She unknotted them, but seconds later found them clenched again.

This was a stupid thing she was doing. So what if the mailing was late? She tried deep breathing.

"I heard you've got something coming from Mr. Hale's will," Gregory said.

"Where'd you hear that?" He'd startled her and tension sharpened her voice.

"Oh, hey," he said. "I didn't mean—I was just making conversation."

"Sorry," she said. "This speed is scary in the rain."

"Don't worry, I have good night vision," he said. But after a moment, the van slowed a bit. "Kevin Emmett heard it from his dad," he said. "What he said was that Mr. Hale left you a land partnership with Charlie, up on Potter Road. Like, part of the Bradford estate?"

"You know the land?"

"Everybody knows the Bradford estate. Kevin said you've got a buyer."

"We're closing Monday."

"That's what he said. He says they want to subdivide it into horse farms."

"That's what I heard."

A little silence was filled with the drumming of rain on the van roof. "I like horses," he said.

"Do you have one?"

"My dad said we couldn't afford it. I used to hire one from a livery stable when I could get the cash together, and then when I was old enough, I got a summer job working in the stable at a dude ranch. I thought I'd died and gone to heaven."

"Colorado's beautiful."

"Yeah, well."

"Not?"

"Oh, sure. It's just, like, I had to move to Boulder when I was thirteen, leave all my friends, you know, and I didn't want to hear about beautiful. My mother'd just died and my dad and I didn't get along. Well, it wasn't all his fault, I was acting like a punk. I was really miserable until I discovered horses."

It sounded like a Disney scenario. Janet considered mentioning water pollution, but the kid was doing her a favor, so she just said, "That's interesting," which must have indicated some failure of enthusiasm, for he didn't answer, and for quite a while they rode without speaking.

The thunder and lightning moved out but the rain barely slackened; it thrummed with an almost musical sound on the outside of the van. Presently Janet jerked herself out of a drowse. Bad; driving at night, a passenger had a responsibility to keep the driver alert. She scrambled for a subject. "Are you ever going to get a horse?" is what she came up with.

"Not until I'm through grad school," he said.

Something she hadn't known. "Grad school where?"

"MIT. Computer science."

The up-to-date ambition. It crossed her mind to ask him about locked files in WordPerfect, but instead, something moved her to say, "What was it you were working on in the studio?"

"A building-permit application."

Building permit? This, she remembered, was the son of the vandal of Big Bear. "What're you building?" she said, although she wasn't sure she wanted to know.

"A house."

"Where's the site?" she asked, in spite of probably not wanting to know.

"You know Oak Hollow Road?"

She didn't want to know. "Yes, sure."

"It's about three miles outside the village limits, on top of that big outcrop by Henley Lane."

She'd known. Shit. "What does an MIT grad student want with a house in New York state?" she said.

"It's something my mother was planning when she died. She left me the land and everything, so I thought, well, why don't I build her house myself? Like a memorial?"

Oh, lord, unresolved mourning. "Are you going to live in it?"

"I don't know. Maybe. I'd like to, summers anyway. What happened, when my mother died, my dad just shoved a lot of her things in storage, her papers and stuff. Now I'm twenty-one, I've got my bachelor's, and I've got control of the money she put in trust for me; I pulled her things all out, and I found the house plans. So I thought, she died before she could build it, so why don't I build it for her?"

A true Disney mind. She said, "I've heard about that house. It sounds to me as if you're planning on blowing up a lot of landscape."

"There's plenty of landscape."

God, the arrogance. "Not if everybody with enough money goes around blowing it up willy-nilly," she said. "It's finite. The earth is our home, and it's finite, and we have to use our big, ar-

rogant human brains to respect it, cherish it, not blow it to bits. It was here for billions of years before us and we owe it our respect."

"It's going to be a beautiful house." His voice had changed timbre, grown tight and stubborn. He hadn't absorbed a word of her harangue. She had only angered him. "Wait till you see it. It's going to be the most beautiful house in the Hudson Valley."

God, she was sick of angry men. What did it take to stop them?

Steep Slopes? The damn house would impinge on one very steep slope. But the Steep Slopes law had been assigned to limbo when Uncle Bud had fallen off the quarry cliff.

The glow from the dashboard picked out curling red hairs on the backs of Gregory's hands—

Uncle Bud, teasing, saying he was going to vote for it. A flash of anger; a shove, as sudden and unplanned as a thundercrack—

She folded her arms across her midriff. She wasn't going to say one more word about that house as long as she was in this van. She'd call Marion and Paul as soon as she got home; maybe they'd be able to stop it with another lawsuit.

Beneath the thrum of rain on the van roof, the silence grew. Presently the turn signal started to click; the van slowed and eased into a right turn and the headlights slid over a street sign too fast for her to read it. "Where are we?" she asked.

"I'm going to drive up to my house for a minute," he said. "There's something I want to show you."

Oh, no. There was that foam mattress in the back; male anger wasn't always expressed with fists. He was strong.

"It's right on the way," he said.

Fear turns them on, so stay calm. "I don't think that's a very good idea," she said. "It's late and I'm tired. Bring it to the office in the morning."

"I don't want to carry it around where somebody might see it," he said.

"I understand," she said, "but I'm beat, it's late, and there are still all those cartons to unload."

"It'll only take a minute," he said. "Honest."

She had no idea where they were. The headlights showed narrow, pitted blacktop, forest, and rain. "Gregory," she said, "read my lips. No."

"Oh, hey—" His voice skidded into an adolescent crack. "I don't mean *that*." The exclamation rang with sincerity. Maybe he didn't mean *that*. And maybe he was just good at managing his voice. Now his voice became earnest. "What it is," he said, "there's this paper I found in my mother's stuff. You really need to see it. It's kind of sensitive information, you know? I don't want to carry it around where somebody might get it. Honest, it'll just take a minute."

He wasn't going to be talked out of it. She started to reach for the door handle but changed her mind; he was taking the road too fast. Once more her hands gripped each other in her lap.

They turned right again and again she missed the street sign. Now they were on a dirt road. After a few minutes, they eased left into a driveway and the headlights picked up a bridge, and all at once she knew where they were. They'd been driving on the little road that she'd reached by bushwhacking out Uncle Bud's overgrown back lane; this was the driveway where she'd turned around; and deep under that bridge was the ravine that paralleled the road. They'd approached it from the opposite direction, disorienting her; from this direction, the bridge looked sort of lopsided.

The wheels crossed onto the bridge with a double bump and rumbled on the planking. She felt an odd, vertiginous swaying and heard a *CRACK* as loud as gunfire.

"Whoa," exclaimed Gregory. The van lurched as he braked. *CRACK*. Too late. *CRACK-CRACK*.

The bridge swayed, the planking dropped away in front of them, and Janet's stomach lurched as they hung in the air for a moment and then, with a down rush like a roller coaster's first drop, plunged nose first into the ravine.

SIXTEEN

Up

THE CRASH OF METAL on rock went on and on, fading and rising and fading as if somebody were playing with the volume dial. At last it died away and the only sound was the rain battering the outside of the van.

Janet couldn't get her breath. Her chest felt crushed, and panic swelled. But by degrees her wits crept back, and she realized that the shoulder harness was binding her chest. The van was nose down and gravity was dragging her weight against it.

She braced her hands on the dashboard to push herself back, and a spike of pain through her right wrist dizzied her. But she held on to her wits and found leverage for her feet, and letting her left wrist take the rest of her weight, she managed to shove herself back an inch or two. Her indrawn breath whined in her throat but the next one came more easily and her eyes began to focus.

Through the windshield, spiderwebbed with fine cracks and spattered with dark blotches, she saw a glistening close-up of wet boulders. The headlights had survived.

Gasoline, she thought. *Fire—*

But what she was smelling wasn't gasoline; it was the warm butcher-shop odor of blood. A retch thrust against the back of her throat. She forced it back and managed to say, "Greg?" But it came out as a quaver, nearly drowned by the drumming of the rain, and she drew breath past the pain in her chest. *"Greg!"*

No response.

Outside was that bright still life of wet rock, but inside, something was blocking the dash light. Where Greg should be sitting was a mass of something she couldn't identify.

Her calf muscles were threatening to cramp with the effort of holding her free of the seat belt. She reached across her body with her left hand and felt down beside the seat for the release, the twist aggravating the pain in her chest. The release wouldn't give at first, and once more panic nudged her, but at last her shifting and poking produced the right angle of pressure and the harness snapped loose. She still had to keep her feet braced, but her breathing was eased and she could, though painfully, turn her body.

Realization came with a rush, and with it a burst of horror. It was a jumble of cartons that was blocking the dash light. The impact that had pitched her against her shoulder harness had shifted the copy-paper load; the heavy cartons had slammed into the back of the driver's seat, breaking it loose and jamming it forward, pinning Greg against the dashboard. The cartons stacked on top had slid the farthest, driving his head against the windshield, spattering that bloody pattern across the glass. As her eyes adjusted to the back glow from the headlights, she made out Greg's right hand gripping a broken-off arc of steering wheel, protruding from behind the forwardmost carton.

Just managing not to retch again, she worked the fingers of her left hand around the exposed wrist, searching for the hollow between tendons where the pulse should beat.

Nothing.

Forcing patience into her movements, she shifted her fingers from spot to spot. Nothing.

Her legs were trembling with the strain of holding her off the dashboard. She let go of Greg's wrist and reached across her body for the door handle. The latch released but the door would open only an inch. Shoving at it sent new pain through her chest, but at last, twisting sideways, shifting her feet to the door and

using the power of her leg muscles, she managed to force it open far enough to squeeze out.

Her stomach heaved again, and this time she made no effort to suppress the nausea. She stumbled a few steps from the van, doubled over, and vomited. She hadn't eaten since lunch; all that came up was the coffee she'd drunk at the mall.

Rain sluicing off her hair and her bare arms set off a trembling fit. She turned back to the van, folded her arms on the roof and rested her head on them, letting her back receive the force of the rain, breathing in and out shallowly past the pain in her chest.

Greg's determination to keep the cartons off the mattress had saved her.

She didn't know how long she stood leaning against the van. Eventually she became aware that the rain was slackening. She smelled wet earth and heard water rushing. She raised her head and looked around.

It was the right headlight that had survived; the left one had smashed. A litter of planks and twisted ironwork lay scattered around—the remains of the bridge, she realized with renewed shock. A few yards beyond where the van had landed, a storm-fed stream rampaged over rocks.

She tried a deeper breath and decided her ribs were all right; the pain was centered in the bone between her breasts, and it was settling into a dull ache. The sternum, she recalled from anatomy class, was a sturdy bone.

Her right wrist was another matter. Every movement jolted it into fresh stabs of pain. It needed something to hold it steady against movement, a splint or a cast—even an Ace bandage, stretchy but firm, would help.

She leaned against the van and hiked up her wet skirt. One-handed, she pulled down her underpants, easing them over her sandals one foot at a time, leaving her bare crotch feeling ridiculously vulnerable. Working left-handed, she wound the fabric around her right wrist as tightly as she could, twisting it and tuck-

ing it under to hold it in place. The improvisation helped; the stabs of pain subsided into a steady, bearable ache.

She was alive; she would mend.

Gregory—

Not now. Don't think about that now. Think about getting help.

It was possible that somebody driving along the road up on the ravine rim would notice the light and stop to investigate. But there weren't a lot of houses on that road; if she remembered correctly, it skirted the wildlife sanctuary for much of its length. It could be a long wait.

Could she climb out?

She'd need light; beyond the headlight's glow, it was full night.

She leaned down and felt in the storage bin on the inside of the van door and found only a ragged, half-empty pack of chewing gum. She stretched inside, pushing past the pain, and popped open the glove compartment. Deep inside, buried under a litter of paper and gum wrappers and a fractured Styrofoam cup, she felt the solid cylinder of a flashlight. She squirmed out and pushed the switch. The batteries were good; a disk of light played on the wet stones at her feet.

She turned her back on the glow from the headlight and waited until her eyes adjusted and she was able to make out the form of the land. The rain had let up; the ever present sky glow from West Point, across the river, was illuminating the bottom of the clouds. Behind the van, a heap of stone rubble, dotted with a few venturesome shrubs and an occasional tree, extended up the base of the ravine wall; above the scree, a rock face rose another twenty-five or thirty feet. Even in daylight, uninjured and with two functioning hands, she wouldn't try to climb that bank without proper boots, ropes, and a partner. Some distance downstream, though, the walls on both sides seemed to gentle a bit. Down there she might be able to bushwhack up to the rim. Not on this side. She had no idea how far she'd have to walk on the road to find an inhabited house. On the opposite side, though,

the driveway that was supposed to cross the ruined bridge must lead to Greg's house.

She was prepared to break in, but a subliminal memory sent her back into the passenger seat. Gritting her teeth against pain and a new thrust of nausea, she shoved at the cartons, an inch one way, an inch the other, until she found the key chain dangling from the ignition. She'd remembered right; it was heavy with extra keys. She switched off the ignition, struggled out of the car, and dropped the keys into her skirt pocket.

She picked her way across stones down to the side of the stream and studied it by the combined light of the headlight and the flashlight. It was rocky and swift, but even swollen from the recent storm, not really deep. The footing would be treacherous; still, with the aid of a stick, she could probably wade it.

A few trees had taken root on the ravine floor and over the years had scattered fallen branches along the side of the stream. The first two she picked up were riddled with rot and broke in her hand, but at last she found one that was thin enough to grasp and sturdy enough to hold her weight. Her right hand, stabilized by the improvised binding, consented to grip the flashlight while her left hand managed the stick.

She prodded the streambed until she found a level patch. Cautiously she stepped in. Pebbles shifted under her sandals and the current tickled her ankles. After two more steps, it twitched at her knees; two more and she was in almost up to her hips, the rushing water plastering her skirt against her thighs on the upstream side and tugging at it on the downstream side. But the stick helped her maintain her balance, and a few more precarious steps brought her past the deepest channel and inching up toward the opposite bank. She had made it nearly to the other side when the stick slipped and she lost her balance. The stick rioted downstream on the racing current, but somehow she kept hold of the flashlight and kept it above water. Three pointed, on her knees and her left hand, impeded by her clinging skirt, she

crawled across stones and up the bank. Her skirt pocket was deep; through the fabric Greg's keys thumped reassuringly against her thigh.

She got to her feet and with her good left hand squeezed what water she could from her skirt. The rain had stopped. Straight above her head, ragged clouds scudded across a glitter of stars.

She switched off the flashlight and let her eyes adjust again. Just downstream, a long tangle of ironwork—part of the bridge structure, she guessed—lay slantwise across the bottom of the ravine, but there seemed to be room to pass. She switched the flashlight on again and started downstream. The scramble across stones and fallen logs and through undergrowth was painful, but at last she came to the place where the slope of the ravine wall eased.

And there she found a path—no more, really, than a thinner stretch of undergrowth—leading up into the trees. Probably a deer path. It switched back and forth, following the contour of the slope, but it was still steep and her heavier breathing aggravated the pain in her chest. No sky light penetrated the thick forest canopy and the pale disk of the flashlight's beam flattened out perspective. Stones that looked solid tilted under her feet. Dead leaves concealed crevices between embedded rocks. Once a vine buried in the leaves entangled her ankles and sent her sprawling. Pain stabbed and the flashlight flew out of her hand, but blessedly it stayed alight and she was able to retrieve it, and after that, she shortened her steps and lifted her feet high. Concentrating on the ground and failing to notice what was at eye level, she blundered into a thicket; a strand of briar whipped across her face and when she put her hand to her cheek, she felt blood.

But at last the ground leveled and she found that she'd reached the top. She turned right and worked back through the forest, keeping her bearings by staying close to the rim of the ravine. The footing was more secure up here on the level and it wasn't long before she came to the driveway, curving uphill through the trees. She followed it up, walking freely at last on the graveled

surface, and just beyond the third bend, she came upon the house. It was set in the middle of a weedy lawn, gabled and clapboard sided, with an old-fashioned front porch, probably, like Uncle Bud's, an old farmhouse. The driveway skirted the lawn and ended at a little graveled space that was big enough to park three or four cars.

She had to try two keys, awkwardly with her left hand, before she found the one that opened the front door. As it turned in the lock, she hoped she was activating an alarm. Nothing would bring help faster. But nothing clanged or howled; if there was an alarm, it was a silent one.

The door opened into a quarry-tiled entryway. She unbuckled her muddy sandals and kicked them off, stepped through onto dark-stained hardwood, and found light switches. She was in a center hall, facing a staircase. Through an arch to her right was the living room, furnished with a worn sofa and matching chairs upholstered in something nubby and brown. To her left through a matching arch was the dining room; a pine table and chairs were centered on a round, braided rug. A swinging door led from the dining room into the kitchen and just inside it was a little built-in desk, and on it was a telephone. It had a row of memory-dial buttons, and one of them was labeled "Sheriff."

SEVENTEEN

Mountain Rescue

JANET STOOD ON THE driveway in the dark a few feet back from the brink of the ravine, cradling her throbbing right wrist between her breasts, drawing deliberate, deep breaths against her stomach's quivering. The Phillips Landing firehouse siren, which had moaned into life while she was on the phone, was still howling in the distance.

Breathe—in...out...in...

The scent of wet leaves soothed the nerve endings where the scent of blood lingered at the back of her throat.

The firehouse siren slid down into silence. Far off, a patrol car screamed; after a moment an ambulance's distinctive *WOW-WOW* joined it. The wails mounted for what seemed like a long time; when they cut out, Janet guessed they had turned into the tangle of dirt roads where there was no traffic to warn.

Insects chirred. At intervals water plopped from motionless leaves to the forest floor. An owl hooted.

Across the ravine, white beams sliced the night and red flickered against the trees. A patrol car inched into view around a curve, its spotlight raking the ravine rim. Janet fished the flashlight from her pocket, switched it on, and waved it. The spotlight found her and she had to put up her hand to shade her eyes. The car turned into the bridge approach and stopped, headlights and spotlight glaring across the gap. The speaker boomed, "DO YOU NEED MEDICAL ATTENTION?"

"I'm okay," she called, her unamplified voice puny in her ears. She pointed down into the ravine. "There's somebody in the van."

The spotlight swiveled down to the wreck. She heard the car door open and saw the deputy get out and edge to the brink.

More lights; the ambulance's square white bulk lurched around the curve. The crew jumped out and she heard their quick, efficient voices without catching the words. The deputy pointed, and one of them looked across the ravine. "Are you injured?" he called.

"I'm okay," she called back. "I just need a way out of here."

"There's a back road to the house," called the deputy, now unamplified. "They've dispatched a car."

She had meant to watch; but never mind what she had shouted across the ravine, she was not okay. Her chest hurt with every breath, her wrist throbbed, and that deep trembling wouldn't be quieted. She turned and trudged back up the curves and went in the front door. Maybe she could find an Ace bandage somewhere in the house. She switched on lights and climbed the stairs.

The house was smaller than it looked from the outside; there were only two bedrooms, front and back, their ceilings sloping under the roof, the bathroom tucked between them. Unlike some bachelor bathrooms Janet had encountered, it was quite decent—shower curtain unmildewed, mirror clear of toothpaste flecks, washbasin free of stubble-studded lather. Only the propped-up toilet seat gave evidence of male occupancy.

It was with a shock that she saw herself in the mirror. A blood-crusted scratch ran down her cheek; leaf fragments were tangled in her hair; her eyes stared, dark circled. She raked the leaves from her hair with her fingers and dropped them in a wastebasket, took a washcloth from the towel rod, wet it and soaped it and dabbed mud and blood from her face, rinsed it and wrung it out and hung it back on the rod. Her tank top and skirt were muddy and there was a ragged tear near the hem of her skirt.

There wasn't an Ace bandage in the medicine cabinet, but there was Tylenol. She downed two tablets with water from her cupped left hand and went back downstairs.

Help would come from the back. She went through the dining room to the kitchen and through it into a small laundry room. A half bath had been partitioned off at one end; there was no Ace bandage there either.

A door in the back of the laundry room led to what had once been a back porch. It had been enclosed and converted into an office: a computer on a desk, a printer on a stand beside it, a two-drawer filing cabinet next to a low bookcase that held a library of computer texts. Three cartons stood in the middle of the floor. One was open; the other two were taped shut. A door in the back wall, when unbolted, opened onto a brick patio.

She flipped a switch by the door and a floodlight came on outside, illuminating four white wrought-iron chairs and a white wrought-iron table under a big umbrella. A weed-grown driveway skirted a stretch of lawn and disappeared into the forest.

She left the light on and turned back into the office. Greg had wanted to show her something he'd found in his mother's old papers. Maybe his mother's old papers were in the cartons. If he'd been telling the truth—and she was more inclined than before to think he had been—maybe what he'd wanted to show her was among them. It obviously wasn't going to be in the sealed ones, and judging form the basic neatness of the house, she guessed that he'd put it away rather than shoving it back into the opened carton. Once more she thumbed the catch on a filing cabinet drawer in a dead man's office.

A pile of folders lay in a heap in the bottom of the top drawer; the other three drawers were empty. She lifted the folders out and put them on the desk, sat down, and leafed left-handed through them.

Movement caught her peripheral vision, setting her heart to hammering again, but it was only a curtain moving in an air cur-

rent. A window must be open. She attended to her breathing until her heart quieted.

Nothing in the folders caught her attention. She had laid them back in the file drawer and was kneeling beside the opened carton when she heard a car approaching. She clambered to her feet and went out the back door to the patio.

The patrol car arrived without siren or flashers, its headlights jerking along a rough track between the trees, then following the drive to the house. It parked where the lawn curved away around the side the house; the lights went off and the deputy climbed out.

They'd sent a woman. It was the officer who had taken their statements at the quarry after Uncle Bud's fall. "Janet Upton," she said, announcing, not inquiring.

Torres, that was her name. Rosa Torres. "Deputy Torres," Janet said. "We meet again."

"We meet again. Do you need medical attention?"

"I'm okay."

"What about that?" Deputy Torres was looking at her bound wrist.

"Just a sprain."

"Sure?"

"Really. I'll see a doctor if it gets worse. I want to stay out of emergency rooms."

"Okay, I hear you." Deputy Torres unhooked a radio from her belt, raised it to her mouth, and said, "Car seven."

Scritch scritch.

"I'm at the house. Contact with Janet Upton. She refuses medical attention."

Scritch scritch.

"Sure."

Scritch-scritch-scritch-scritch.

"Um. Okay. Roger." Amazing; they really did say "Roger." Rosa Torres hooked the radio back on her belt and said, "I'll need you to sign a release."

"Gladly." She tried a deep breath to calm the relentless quivering but the ache in her chest stopped it halfway. "Have they got down to the van yet?" she asked.

A nod.

"Is he—" Why did her voice catch; was *dead* so hard to say?

"Didn't survive. Sorry."

Well, she had known.

Torres said, "No air bag?"

"I guess the van's too old."

"You were lucky."

Indeed. She cradled her throbbing wrist against her aching chest and wondered if even an air bag could have saved Greg from the crushing force of those cartons.

Torres tipped her head toward the white chairs next to the white table. "Why don't we sit down and you can tell me what happened."

They sat down and Rosa Torres took out a notebook and, the pain in her chest somewhat eased by sitting, Janet told her what had happened. When she finished, Torres said, "What do you think? Did he really have something to show you besides his dick?"

The question was not frivolous, and Janet said, "I don't know. Maybe. He said it was something of his mother's that he'd just got out of storage. Some papers. I started to look in some cartons in there, but then you came." With the easing of the pain in her chest, she was more conscious of the pain in her wrist. "You wouldn't happen to carry an Ace bandage, would you?"

"Sorry. What's that, your underpants?"

"I didn't take them off until he was dead." She closed her eyes. "That's gross."

"You're allowed."

Janet wondered what a male deputy would have said. But she probably wouldn't have made her remark to a male deputy. In the presence of Deputy Rosa Torres, this official who was also a woman, Janet was aware of her thoughts widening out, mov-

ing beyond this house, beyond this catastrophic night, acknowledging her wider life. "My camera," she said. "It's in the van. In a padded bag. Maybe it—survived."

"I'll tell them to look for it."

"And my wallet. And my keys." Focused on rescue, she'd thought to retrieve Gregory's keys; only now did she remember her own.

Torres nodded and used her radio again. They'd take care of it; Janet should call the department tomorrow.

Then Rosa Torres turned to look across the lawn, and then Janet heard it too, a motor growling back in the woods, and then she saw headlights flickering between the tree trunks, and then a black Jeep jounced into view. Torres scraped her chair back and said, "Stay here," and went down the patio steps as the Jeep pulled up and parked beside the patrol car. A bearded teddy bear of a man, thick legged and burly shouldered in shorts and T-shirt, climbed down. Janet shoved her own chair back and Paul Willard said, "Hey, babe," and she hurried down the patio steps and into his outstretched arms, and at last, at last, at last she was safe.

EIGHTEEN

Hold

"FIRST UNCLE BUD," said Janet, "then my car, then Greg and his car."

"You," said Paul, "and Greg and his car."

"I don't count," she said. "I'm alive."

She was huddled in an armchair in Paul and Marion's living room. A hot shower, Marion's terry-cloth robe, and a mug of hot milk, all together, barely held off that deep trembling. Paul wanted to lace the milk with rum but Janet said, "No, I'm already out of control."

Paul had been working in the studio when Janet's name came across the emergency-band scanner he was half-listening to. He dropped everything, ran up to the house, and piled into the Jeep. He'd explained all this as they bumped along the rutted track away from Gregory's house. Yes, she could stay at their house; she *must* stay at their house. Marion would be home from the Town Board meeting any minute. Yes, they had Ace bandages.

After an eternity of bumps, the track led to a dirt road, which led to blacktop, on which Paul turned left. It wasn't until then that Janet recognized the terrain. They were on Oak Hollow Road; Big Bear was right above them.

She cradled her wrist and closed her eyes.

"WHAT COULD HAVE BROUGHT that bridge down?" Home from the Board meeting, Marion was sitting on the sofa leaning into the curve of Paul's arm.

"My guess?" said Paul. "All this rain we've been having washed it out. It's got to be a hundred years old, give or take."

"You'd think somebody would have noticed."

"Rental property, absentee owner? I'll bet you a side of beef nobody'd given it a thought since Alta died."

Alta. "I left out Alta," said Janet. "First Alta, *then* Uncle Bud, then my car, then Greg and Greg's car. That's a lot of falling off of cliffs."

"Hudson Highlands," Paul said. "A lot of cliffs to fall off of."

Cliffs. Marion had been at the Town Board meeting. Janet looked at her and said, "Steep Slopes?"

"Tabled," said Marion.

"Greg—" Janet clutched at coherence. "Gregory Ferguson was applying for a building permit."

"I heard," said Marion.

"What?" said Paul.

"For that house," said Janet. "As a memorial to his mother."

"Oh, lord," said Paul. "Here comes Riesbach."

"You couldn't have known," said Marion. "Billy Knox told me at the Board meeting. He just found out this morning."

"No." Janet set the mug on the table beside her and struggled upright. "No, listen. Greg was talking about it in the car. He was like—he was obsessed. But if Uncle Bud had been alive to vote for the Steep Slopes law, Greg wouldn't have been allowed to. And he was up there when Uncle Bud fell."

"Love—"

"Nobody knew how Bud was going to vote," said Paul.

"No, but Greg said—" Janet closed her eyes. It was all clear to her, but getting it said seemed dreadfully intricate. "Greg said he heard him—heard Uncle Bud—telling Schuyler Vanstaat he was going to vote *for* it."

"He could have been teasing," said Marion. "Schuyler was being a perfect pest. I thought at the time the reason Bud went off down that steep trail was to get away from him, but Schuyler followed him anyway."

"What's it to Schuyler?" said Paul. "He doesn't own any mountains."

"Oh, the principle of the thing, I expect," said Marion. "The divine right of property owners. You know the script."

"And then," Janet said, "he said—Greg said—that Schuyler Vanstaat went away and he went over, Greg went over, and Uncle Bud did say he'd just been teasing."

"We'll never know," Marion said.

"But what if Greg didn't believe him? What if he thought Uncle Bud was going to vote for it? He wouldn't have been able to build the house up there, would he?"

"Well, he'd have had to apply for a permit," said Marion. "I'm not sure he'd have got one."

"Never," said Paul. "He couldn't show hardship. There are plenty of buildable sites on that property."

"And he was in the darkroom more than anybody," said Janet.

"The darkroom?" said Marion.

"My film. He had the best chance."

"Love, what are you talking about?"

"My film. Didn't I tell you? Somebody ruined my film, and it was Greg who had the best chance." Struggling for coherence, she told them.

"Good heavens," said Marion.

"Let me get this straight," said Paul. "You think the Ferguson kid pushed Bud over the edge so Steep Slopes would fail, and then wrecked your film on the off chance that you'd shot him doing it."

Hard to believe? Everything was hard to believe. "You didn't hear him going on about that house. He was obsessed."

"But he wouldn't have been able to build it anyway," said Marion. "I don't care what Charlie said, it encroached on the setback, and Billy Knox isn't bribable."

"Doesn't matter," said Paul. "He could move the damn thing back ten feet and get out of the setback. It'd still vandalize Big Bear, and without Steep Slopes, it'd be legal."

"Wait a minute," said Janet. "Charlie?"

"What?" said Marion.

"You said you didn't care what Charlie said. Charlie who?"

"Oh. Charlie Emmett was the building inspector who granted the original building permit. We were suing him along with Alta."

"Charlie Emmett."

"Mm-hm," said Paul.

"My partner."

"The same."

"Did he take bribes?"

"Well," said Marion, "there was never any evidence."

"But the Town Board canned him a couple of years later," said Paul.

"For taking bribes?"

"Not in so many words."

"You didn't tell me."

"Oh, well, bygones," said Paul. "No point in getting you upset when you'd be out of it in a week anyway. Babe, you're awfully spacey. How about tucking you in?"

Afraid of nightmares, she'd resisted earlier, but Paul was right, she was spacey. Too much was coming at her, and all at once, lying down seemed the only activity she could manage. She struggled groggily to her feet, and in the guest room, she let Marion tuck her in.

THERE WERE NO NIGHTMARES, only two or three half rousings when a shift in position stressed her wrist. When she woke at nine-thirty, it was no worse; as long as she kept the Ace bandage firm, the fingers of her right hand would move and grasp. The blue bruise slanting across her chest was less painful and the scratch on her cheek had scabbed over. She examined herself in the mirror and decided she wouldn't frighten dogs and little children. It would be different if she were fair and fluffy like Leora; she'd look like a doll that had been left out in the rain. Her own

angular build, dark coloring, and no-nonsense cropped hair was better able to stand up to a bit of battering.

Leora.

Lowell. Uncle Bud, and now Gregory, and before that, Alta—

It all seemed remote, as if sealed off behind glass, nothing to do with her.

She was hungry.

She found her clothes, clean and ironed, in a neat pile on a chair outside her door. The tear in the skirt had been invisibly mended, for Marion was a needlewoman as well as a working poet and a grant-proposal consultant to not for profits.

The day was heading toward ninety again. Paul was out in the studio. Marion was in her study, at the computer. Janet dressed and went out to the kitchen, found orange juice in the refrigerator, scrambled a couple of eggs, made toast, cleaned up after herself, and interrupted Marion to announce that it was time to go to work.

Not unexpectedly, Marion suggested that she could call in sick, but Janet said that she'd be far better off working than idle.

Marion drove her. Halfway there, Janet said, "Oh, lord, my keys are in my camera bag."

"I've got an office key," Marion said. "It should be on a ring in my purse."

It was.

In the parking lot, Marion got out, peered down the drop-off at the ruin of Janet's car, and said, "Oh, my, that looks final. How are you going to get around?"

"I thought of springing for a bike until the money comes through. I could use the exercise, and it wouldn't pile up as much debt as a four-wheel."

"Take mine," said Marion.

"You'll need it."

"I doubt it. I haven't ridden it since I fell off last spring. Come to dinner tonight and pick it up."

"Well, in that case—okay. Thank you." There'd better be re-incarnation, because it was going to take three or four lifetimes to repay Marion and Paul for everything. "But if you ever want it, say so."

Marion's key let her into the office. She kept a spare key to the inner stairway in a bottom desk drawer. Up in her apartment, the reporter was on her answering machine again. She deleted the message and punched in the sheriff's number.

Deputy Somebody answered on the first ring. She asked about her camera. He said, "Hold on."

Serious, no-music hold.

A new voice said, "Property office."

Her camera case?

"Hold on, please."

Long, serious hold. She visualized Property Office ambling down a hall, pouring a cup of coffee, shooting the breeze while it cooled to drinkable temperature, ambling into another room, looking at a bank of shelves, returning to the desk, drinking half the coffee. *Click*. Would she describe the item, please?

She described the bag with the nametag that said "Janet Upton"; the Nikon F-3 camera and the three lenses she'd been carrying, the polarizing filter, the lens tissues and lens cleaner, the film; the keys and the wallet with her driver's license and a few bucks.

Yes, they had it. She could come in and pick it up during office hours.

The sheriff's office was twenty-five miles away, at the other end of the county.

She had a job, she said, and no car. If it wouldn't violate any laws, could they maybe send it over to Phillips Landing with whoever was patrolling this end of the county? If it wouldn't be too much trouble? Please?

Mm. Well. He'd see what he could do.

She thanked him, hung up, propped her elbows on the table, and rested her face in her hands.

Gregory; Uncle Bud; Alta—The glass barrier was vaporizing.

But life goes on, and after a while she got up from the table and went down to the office, where life presented her with fly-ers to proofread, mailing lists to rationalize, books to balance. Tedious stuff, life. Her wrist hurt, her sternum was going to start hurting as soon as she began to breathe normally, and her brain wanted to go on a cruise.

The portfolio Kristin Vanstaat had found in the closet was still lying on the corner of her desk. The Post-it still advised Janet to look at it. She unzipped it.

Inside was a stack of photographs, mounted and matted black-and-white portraits, six of teenagers and one of an adult woman. They were competently composed and lighted, and the print quality was good. The photographer was a decent craftsman, and might with practice (if interested) become an artist. She turned over the portrait of the woman and found a typed label stuck to the back of the mounting board. With a shock like a punch to the solar plexus, she read:

"Alta"
by Gregory Ferguson
1987

After her breathing settled down, she remembered: he'd been in a photography workshop when he was a kid; there was to be an exhibition. These portraits must have constituted his part of the show. And they were still here because, in the midst of it all, his mother had fallen off Big Bear and broken her neck. Griev-ing, hustled off to Boulder to live with his father, he'd left these behind.

Under the photographs was a manila envelope with "Gregory Ferguson" scrawled across it in pencil. She was starting to undo the metal clasp when, through the window, she saw Charlie Em-mett's pickup pull into the lot and park next to the Dumpster. Char-

lie—who might have taken bribes—climbed out and headed for the office door. She slid everything back into the portfolio and was poking one-handed at computer keys by the time he got there.

"Hey, pard," he said, predictably. "Glad to see you among the living."

"You heard."

"Picked it up on the scanner. You okay?"

"I'll survive."

"Glad to hear it. A shame about the Ferguson kid. I didn't know you had a thing going with him."

"Is that what people are saying?" She should have known. "Not?"

"Not." Whether anybody would believe her was debatable, but she'd better put it on record. "He was just helping the art center out by picking up some copy paper from Office-Rite, and then on the way home, he said there was something he wanted to show me at his house."

"Yeah? What was that?"

"I don't know. I didn't want to go, but he was in the driver's seat, and the way he was driving, jumping out of the car didn't seem like a great idea." She caressed the Ace bandage. "Had I but known."

"He give you a hint?"

"Not really. Something sensitive, he said." Charlie's grin was, predictably, cousin to a leer and she said, "Yes, well, I wondered."

"It was a come-on. Young guy full of hormones, good-looking girl in the car, you can bet on it." He yawned, stretched, and said, "Well, I'd better get to work or the boss'll be on my back. Glad you're among the living, pard."

NINETEEN

Camera Work

HELEN ARRIVED JUST BEFORE noon. "You're here," she said.

"I work here," said Janet.

"I thought maybe you'd be in the hospital."

"You heard."

"Everybody's heard. Everybody's been calling everybody else."

"Oh, lord, and I suppose everybody's assuming I was getting it on with Gregory."

"Only speculating. Were you."

"I do authority figures, not infants. He was kidnapping me."

"Are you serious?"

"I am serious." Once more she told the story. She left out the proposed vandalizing of Big Bear.

"You have some kind of guardian angel." Helen's shoulders hunched as if warding off menace. "And he seemed like such a nice kid."

"Eagle Scout." Janet closed her eyes and rested her head on her left palm. "Our copy paper—"

"Is not important," said Helen. "Take a break. Take the day. I'll deal."

Janet rubbed her eyes, opened them, and pushed her chair back. "Lunch, anyway."

SHE TOOK GREG'S PORTFOLIO upstairs with her. After she ate a tomato sandwich—toasted—and washed her hands, she opened

the manila envelope. Inside was a yellow legal pad, the curled and dog-eared pages covered with adolescent scrawl. The top sheet was headed "History of the Bradford Family."

She blinked. It couldn't say "Bradford"; her obsession with her legacy was creating optical illusions. She squeezed her eyes shut and massaged her lids with her fingertips and opened her eyes again. It took a couple of seconds for them to refocus.

It said "Bradford."

It seemed to be a report for a social studies class, an exercise in historical research. A first draft, judging by the cross outs and misspellings. The kid must have spent hours with the genealogical tables and privately printed family biographies in the local library.

His information expanded on what Marion had told her. An early Bradford had received the land in 1652 by crown grant, whatever that might be. Greg had made a marginal note to look it up. For three centuries, Bradfords had logged it, farmed it, operated a grist mill on a stream that ran through it, prospected its hills for mythical silver and copper and settled for iron to be forged into the cannons of the Civil War. The lode was mined out by the end of the century, but meanwhile, Bradfords had invested cannily. By the first decade of the twentieth century, Bradfords were sitting on the boards of developing industries in Albany and Buffalo and New York City.

The principal recreation of late generations seemed to have been firing guns. From an ancient *Field & Stream,* Greg had copied a catalog of creatures slain by notable hunters of the Northeast; the Bradford tally filled half a page. When wild game birds unaccountably grew scarce, Bradfords purchased captive-bred turkeys and pheasants and doves to be released by the hundreds within shotgun range of themselves and their guests. When the state established hunting seasons, Bradfords built their own skeet range and soon were attending competitions and winning prizes.

Until Thaddeus Bradford came into his inheritance.

An only child born in 1899, Thaddeus served in France during World War I. He returned physically unharmed, only to lose his mother in the flu epidemic of 1918 and his father two years later in what was called in those days a "motoring accident." Thaddeus tore down the skeet houses and began to farm.

Eventually he married and sired four daughters, who married and scattered across the country, producing grandchildren who scattered farther. When he died in 1980, his descendents had no interest in returning to the land of their forebears; by late 1986, when Greg had done his research, all the land was in other hands, including, presumably, the undistinguished flat land that Broderick Hale had bought in partnership with Charlie Emmett.

She turned the pages back to their original order, absently smoothing the curled corners with the flat of her hand.

Was this what Greg had wanted to show her? Not this draft, of course, but a later version? Maybe he had finished the paper and turned it in and got it back with a grade; maybe his mother had stored it among her souvenirs, where Greg had just rediscovered it. There wasn't anything urgent about this stuff that Janet could identify, but something was niggling at the far end of her consciousness. Maybe the final version—if it existed—had information that didn't appear in this draft.

WHEN SHE GOT BACK down to the office, Kristin Vanstaat was sitting in the chair beside her desk, her acne-pocked face blotched and her eyes red. She'd been talking with Helen.

"Sorry," Janet said. "I'm interrupting something."

"No, it's—" Kristin's voice wobbled; she fished a tissue from the box on Janet's desk and blew her nose. "It's okay. It's just— Greg was friends with my brother and I really liked him."

"Oh, Kris, I'm so sorry." Rich had had friends; Janet had really liked one of them. Kristin would have been nine or ten back then. Greg at fourteen, strikingly red haired, could have been the stuff of prepubescent dreams. His mother's sudden death and the

exile to Colorado wouldn't hurt; other people's bereavement could be romantic. "That's rough."

"I left something on your desk."

"Yes, thanks, I found it. He was a good photographer."

"He never even saw the show." Kristin's eyes teared again.

"I'm going to try to get in touch with his father," Janet said. "How about if I ask him if you could have the prints? He might like to leave them with somebody who was Greg's friend. Especially," she added, "an artist who would appreciate them."

"Oh!" Kristin mopped her eyes and blew her nose. "Could you?"

"Absolutely. Did you by any chance look at the stuff in the envelope?"

"Just to see what it was. I remember him talking to my dad about that assignment."

"Your dad?"

Kristin's face brightened with what looked like pride. "My dad has a Ph.D. in history. He works for the County Historical Society. He knows absolutely everything about the history of the Town."

Well. This seemed to be a day for things to fall into her lap. (Fall? Oh, well.) "Actually," she improvised, "I'm interested in the subject myself. Do you think he'd be willing to talk to me?"

"Oh, sure. People consult him all the time." Kristin pulled another tissue from the box, mopped her eyes, blew her nose, and tossed it in the wastebasket with an air of finality. "I've got to go. I just came here because—you know. When you cry at home, everybody gets nosy."

"THAT WAS NICE of you," said Helen.

"My brother had friends," said Janet.

"I know what you mean. I thought I told you to take the day."

"I came down to be nice."

IN THE MIDDLE OF the afternoon—another hot one—a car pulled into the lot and parked next to the office. A man got out, un-

locked the trunk, and lifted out a camera bag. They'd sent it with somebody in plainclothes in an unmarked car—an exceptionally plain somebody in exceptionally plain clothes: khakis and a shirt whose plaid was so muted that it might as well have been unpatterned—

Oh, rats.

Paul's bête noir, Investigator Noel Riesbach, had been assigned to bring back her camera.

But he had more on his mind than simply returning her property. After Janet examined it and clumsily signed a receipt and tucked the bag out of sight behind her desk (the damage was minimal; the padded bag, snug between the back of the passenger seat and the foam pad, had preserved the camera and lenses; the only damage was one cracked filter), he asked for a place where they could talk undisturbed. She took him into the studio and sat across from him at the big table where Gregory Ferguson had only yesterday been working on his building-permit application.

"Last night," Riesbach began, "did you see or hear anybody around the house?"

"No. Well, Deputy Torres, when she got there. And then Paul Willard."

"How did you get in?"

"With a key. I turned off the ignition and the house key was on the chain."

"Which door?"

"The front door."

"Was it locked?"

"Yes, of—" Wait a minute. Had she needed to turn the key back and forth, inadvertently locking and then having to unlock an already unlocked door? To the best of her recollection, it had been a straightforward unlocking. "I think so."

"Not quite sure?"

"Pretty sure."

"And you turned off the alarm."

"No, I didn't. I didn't even know there was an alarm. I was hoping there was one and somebody'd hear it."

"There is one. It was turned off."

"Not by me," she said. Full face at close range, Investigator Riesbach didn't look as ordinary as she had thought. It was his eyes. They were a chilly gray-blue that created the illusion of piercing her skull to the thoughts behind. Catching the force of that shade of blue on film would be an interesting challenge. "I think Greg might not have bothered much with precautions," she said. "He didn't fasten his seat belt. Maybe setting the alarm was too much trouble."

A flicker of the eyes acknowledged the unused seat belt. "Where did you go in the house?"

"When I first got there—the front hall, through the dining room, into the kitchen. That's where I found the phone. Then I went out and down to the bridge. After the ambulance came, I went back. That time I went upstairs." She caressed her bound wrist with her left hand. "My wrist was hurting and I went to see if there was an Ace bandage or something. There wasn't, and I went down and through the dining room and kitchen and laundry room and looked in the half bath, and still didn't find what I needed, so I went into that enclosed porch with the office stuff."

"And spent some time there."

"Yes." She'd told Rosa Torres what she'd done there.

"Did you notice that one of the window screens was slit and the window was broken?"

She started to say no, but then memory delivered a little jolt to her solar plexus. She said, "I do remember that the curtains were blowing a little. I thought Greg had left the window open. I didn't look."

"You told Deputy Torres he wanted to show you something. What do you think it was?"

Another little jolt; if there was really something, had somebody broken in to look for it? She said, "I don't know."

"What did he say about it?"

"Hardly anything. Just—it was sort of urgent. Sensitive, something like that."

"You must have made a guess."

"I was worried he had rape in mind, but I don't know. I didn't know at the time, and I still don't know."

"What were you talking about before he brought up this thing he wanted to show you?"

"Nothing."

"What do you mean?"

"We'd stopped talking. I guess we'd run out of things to talk about. Then he turned off on a road I didn't recognize, and I asked him where he was going and he said he wanted to go up to the house because he had something to show me."

"Before you stopped talking, what were you talking about?"

The house on Big Bear? She wasn't going to discuss that with Investigator Noel Riesbach. She tried to reconstruct their exchanges. "Horses."

"What about horses?"

"He liked them."

"What else?"

"I don't remember all of it. He talked about how bad he felt after his mother died and his father took him to Colorado, and how horses made him feel better. He worked at a dude ranch." She groped for more. "Graduate school—he'd been admitted to MIT."

"Did he talk about a house he was planning to build?"

The eyes knew. "He mentioned it," she said. "But I didn't have any idea what it was he wanted to show me and I still don't. I can tell you this, it made me nervous. I thought about jumping out of the car but he was going too fast."

"Who knew you were going with him to pick up the paper?"

"I don't remember telling anybody."

"Your friends the Willards?"

"They weren't home."

"How did Paul Willard know to come and pick you up?"

"He heard the emergency call on his scanner."

"Last Saturday," he said, "were you on that hike?"

"No, I wasn't." The way he was controlling their exchange annoyed her and she said, "Is there a connection?"

He ignored the question. "But you were on the mountain."

Irritated, she said, "I explained all this to Deputy Torres at the time. I was partway up the trail beside the quarry, on my own, photographing. Specifically, I was working on studies of the light on the rocks. It was technical work, the way musicians do five-finger exercises."

"Was that the film that got spoiled?"

"Yes, and I explained all that to Investigator Youngblood." She tried again: "Did the lab find any fingerprints?"

A pause. "Just yours," he said finally.

Getting an answer—even one that didn't help—seemed a small triumph. "Did Investigator Youngblood tell you there's a supply of latex gloves in the darkroom?"

"He did. You saved all that material but you didn't tell us about it."

"I told Investigator Youngblood."

"Not until he asked." It was an accusation, not a question, and now her anger was full-fledged. She returned the cold stare without speaking until he made it a question. "Why?"

She could have answered. She could have said that there'd been a lot going on. It had been late Tuesday night when she'd finished in the darkroom; the next day, she'd had the appointment with Eric, the funeral in the afternoon, the visit with Paul and Marion in the evening. That night her car went over the edge. She could have said that the ruined film had simply slipped to the back of her mind, and it would have been very close to true. She could have told him all that, but she didn't because to her it sounded like excuses instead of reasons. She said instead, "You think somebody pushed Uncle Bud off the cliff and I caught it on film, don't you?"

"Is that what you think?"

No answers, just more questions. It was like talking to a shrink. "I keep telling you people, from where I was shooting, I couldn't see the place he fell from. If I couldn't see it, the camera couldn't shoot it."

"But the person who ruined the film wouldn't necessarily have known that."

Well, hadn't she been thinking that herself? "No."

"The pictures that didn't come out would have shown where you were, wouldn't they?"

"You could probably work it out from the angles. Do you want me to take you up the trail and show you where I was? I think I could find it again."

"When did you learn about the inheritance?"

First shock: "You think *I*—" Then, furiously, "I never heard of that damn land until Sunday morning, when Finlay Keene called me down to his office and told me. Ask him; he'll tell you how surprised I was. And don't give me any bull about faking it; I'm a photographer, not an actress."

The eyes didn't flicker. "Last night, whose idea was it to pile all those cartons behind the driver's seat?"

Jolted again, she said, "Greg's."

"Is there anybody who can confirm that?"

"Oh, for Pete's sake. It was pouring. Nobody was standing around watching us. Greg said he didn't want to put anything on top of that foam pad. He didn't say why, but I made a guess later. What are you getting at, anyway? You can't think I *planned* to take that dive."

Riesbach surprised her with an answer. "Ms. Upton, I'm not getting at anything. I'm investigating a couple of fatal occurrences and you were at the scene of both of them." He stood up, took a business card from his shirt pocket, and laid it on the table. "Thank you for your cooperation. Call me if anything else occurs to you."

Following him through the office, Janet shook her head at Helen's questioning glance. She waited in the doorway, watching him cross the parking lot to the gap in the fence and peer down the drop-off. Not until he got into the unmarked car and drove away did she turn back into the office.

Helen said, "Police brutality?"

She did feel brutalized; but what, actually, had he done, beyond ask obvious questions? "Just routine, ma'am." She sat down at her desk, flipped her Rolodex, and dialed the Historical Society.

Schuyler Vanstaat was delighted to hear from her. Yes, he did have some rather interesting Bradford material. It was at home, unfortunately; would it be convenient for her to come by his house tomorrow morning—say around ten?

His house. "I don't want to impose," she temporized.

It would be no imposition; his wife would be delighted to see her.

Wife. Okay, she'd trust in the wife. "Ten o'clock's fine," she said. "Thank you."

TWENTY

Stuff Happens

HELEN HAD LEFT FOR the day and Janet was making a desultory attempt to proofread a press release when Paul arrived to take her out to the house for the promised dinner. He backed the Jeep to the office door, jumped out, and opened the rear hatch. Inside was a load of cartons.

"Paul," she said.

"Didn't figure the raccoons had much use for them." He hauled one out. "Where do you want them?"

"Paul—"

"I only brought eleven. The other one was too messed up. Where do you want them?"

She tried not to think about the nature of the mess. "Against the wall, beside the copier. How did you get them?"

"That deer trail you found." He maneuvered the carton through the door, eased it down, and went back for another.

"On foot?"

"Have you priced helicopters lately?" He carried the carton in and set it down beside the first.

"For Pete's sake, how much do those things weigh?"

"Not too much. Fifty pounds, give or take."

Eleven trips up that ravine bank, fifty pounds of paper per trip. "Paul—"

Back at the Jeep, he reached in and took out a contraption of webbing and buckles. "Nothing to it," he said, shaking the thing

into shape and holding it up. "They're compact. With the sling, they ride like a backpack." He tossed the device back in and took out a third carton. "Not like the deadfalls."

For a long time—since well before Janet had run off to Texas—Paul had been hauling downed timber out of the woods. He used winches and pulleys and blocks and tackles to move the heavier pieces, but Janet had also seen him—not always with an assistant—manhandling twelve-foot lengths of maple trunk out of the Jeep and into the studio. "Sure," she said. "Nothing to it."

"Well," he said, "I did knock off for lunch after the seventh."

SHE DIDN'T MENTION Riesbach's visit. After she'd cooled down, she'd begun to suspect that Riesbach himself knew that none of his infuriating innuendos was true. And there was no point in getting Paul riled up. They talked, instead, about an opening that Paul and Marion planned to attend on Sunday. The artist was an acquaintance of Marion, a former dressmaker who had given up the craft when her fabric sculptures began to attract grants. Paul was hoping her current show would resolve his own question as to whether her asymmetrical tents and biomorphic draperies were a stunt or authentic art.

A black van was parked in front of the house. "Who's here?" Janet asked.

"Eric." A sideways glance. "He came up to monitor the Town Board meeting last night and stayed over to take care of some business, so Marion asked him to dinner."

ERIC SWANSON WAS IN the kitchen, establishing his credentials as a male of the nineties by washing spinach leaves. Not looking at his left hand was like not thinking about elephants.

He wasn't wearing the wedding band.

Maybe your memory's going, she told herself; *maybe he wasn't wearing a wedding band after all.*

Bull.

He was wearing a ring, but it wasn't a wedding band.
Unadorned gold; it couldn't be anything but.
He got divorced between Wednesday morning and Friday night.
Please.
He took it off to do something messy, like gardening or fixing his car, and forgot to put it back on.
Possible.
He's a sexual predator who took it off when he learned he was going to have dinner with a divorcée.
Oh, drop it.

WITHOUT FANFARE, Marion had prepared food that didn't need to be cut up with a knife, allowing Janet to manage with only a fork. For the first half of the meal, she concentrated on feeding herself left-handed without dropping food in her lap. Eventually she gained enough mastery to allow her mind to move to more interesting subjects. "Marion," she said, "some stuff of Gregory Ferguson's turned up when we were cleaning out a closet at the center. A portfolio with seven mounted photographs and a yellow pad with a draft of a school report. Do you—"

"Oh, *dear*," said Marion.

"You do."

"I'd forgotten all about it. He had some work in a student show, back before Alta died. *Just* before she died. He was using one of those old lockers in the basement, and when his father came for him, he went off without cleaning it out. There were a couple of library books, I remember, and that portfolio, and some other things. The yellow pad, I suppose. I remember taking the books back to the library, and I must have put the photographs in the portfolio when the show came down. I meant to send it to him, but he left so suddenly I didn't get his address, and then I just plain forgot. And now—oh, isn't it always like that—now it's too late."

"He was writing about the Bradfords," said Janet.

"Speaking of the devil," said Paul.

And it was just then when the notion that had been jabbing at the back of her consciousness burst through into the light. She looked at Eric and said, "Lead shot."

His eyes showed amusement. "In the locker?"

"Sort of. The Bradfords were gun people. It was in Greg's report. They shot everything that moved, and when they'd killed them all, they bought birds and released them and shot them, and when they'd killed all of them, they built a skeet range and shot at clay pigeons."

"On your parcel?"

"I don't know. But if it was—what if it's like that place—" She groped—a wildlife preserve, once a shooting range, that had been so polluted by lead shot that the birds had died—

Eric said, "Blue Mountain Reservation."

That was it. "Could it be?"

"I doubt it. At Blue Mountain, a gun club had been shooting over a wetland for something like twenty-five years. Dozens of members, every day. The shot was so thick on the ground in places, it looked like caviar. I can't believe a single family could have done that kind of damage."

"They had guests."

"Even with guests. Your buyers want horse pasture?"

"That's what Charlie said."

"Then I wouldn't worry. Lead isn't taken up in the vegetation to any significant degree, and horses don't graze down to the roots, so they wouldn't be likely to pick up the shot by accident. Sheep, maybe, but not horses or cattle. At Blue Mountain, apparently the waterfowl thought it was gravel for their gizzards. They swallowed it and wrecked their reproductive systems."

"You wouldn't want to put a day-care center there," said Marion. "Children pick up stuff and put it in their mouths."

"The well's okay, anyway," Janet said. "Finlay Keene mentioned that it tested clean."

"The bank wouldn't have touched it otherwise," Eric said,

"but that wouldn't prove there isn't lead in the water. You only need a test for bacterial contamination to get financing."

She was learning more about buying and selling real estate every day. "So maybe it's there and nobody knows?"

"And maybe it isn't. If I were representing the buyer and knew about a prior use as a shooting range, I'd suggest a test for heavy metals, just to be on the safe side."

"Why doesn't everybody do it? Just to be on the safe side?"

Eric said, "Cost."

She maneuvered two more forkfuls of spinach salad before saying, "I hate being ignorant."

Eric smiled.

"I'm talking to Schuyler Vanstaat tomorrow," she said. "Kristin says he knows a lot about the Town. If I find out it was that land where they did the shooting, shouldn't I tell the buyers? I mean, warn them there might be lead around?"

"Well—you could if you wanted to, but you aren't under any obligation. What's the zoning, residential?"

"I guess so."

"Then even if you were the owner, you wouldn't have a legal obligation to volunteer any information. On commercial property, yes, there are strict notice requirements, but on residential property it's caveat emptor."

"That doesn't seem right."

"It's based on the perception that industrial pollution is several factors of ten worse than anything that might turn up on a residential plot. If a buyer asked a direct question, a seller would be obliged to tell the truth, but he wouldn't have to volunteer anything. And he wouldn't have any obligation to stand on his head to find out anything he didn't already know."

"Let the buyer do the headstand, babe," said Paul. "Take the money and run. And speaking of Schuyler, as we were—I just found out why he was so hot to defeat Son of Steep Slopes. He thinks he's going to sell some property to the land trust."

"Just a conservation easement," said Eric. "He owns a parcel contiguous to one we're interested in. It isn't anything we'd bother with if the law had passed, but since we're going to purchase the scenic piece, we want an easement on his land to serve as a buffer."

"Only an easement?" said Marion. "That can't bring in enough to make him so vehement."

"I guess he thinks if he holds out, we'll buy the whole parcel."

"Will you?"

"Not worth it."

"I suppose an easement's cheaper," said Janet. She did know—more or less—what an easement was.

"About a tenth," said Eric.

AT AROUND TEN, Janet began to yawn uncontrollably. The third time it happened, Eric looked at his watch and said he'd better be heading back to Tarrytown, and since the village was almost on his way but would be a nine-mile round-trip for Paul or Marion, why didn't he drive her home?

Marion's bicycle fit easily in the rear of the van.

As Janet belted herself in and Eric turned the key in the ignition, a shudder surprised her. He paused with his hand still on the key. "Are you okay?"

Embarrassed, she said, "A little flashback, I guess." Damn. She wasn't interested in developing post-traumatic stress disorder.

In the glow from the driveway light, she saw that he was smiling. "Rather ride the bike?"

That made her laugh, and the laugh loosened the back of her neck. "This is fine." And it was. He'd buckled his seat belt, and when they got onto the road, his speed was rational. And it wasn't raining.

As they rounded the curves below Big Bear, she said, "As long as the land trust is saving mountains, why doesn't it buy Big Bear?"

"Tried," Eric said. "Alta wouldn't sell. After she died, we

tried to buy it from the estate. The father was ready to sell, but the kid objected and he backed out."

"The kid's dead now," she said.

"Yes, and we may renew the offer."

"May?"

"It depends on funding priorities. With Steep Slopes in limbo again, we're having to negotiate for a bunch of properties that the law would have protected."

"How's it going?"

"About as usual. Some owners like the idea of getting their investment back without developing, and some still hope they'll make a killing on condos."

"Or horse farms."

"I didn't mean for that to bother you," he said.

"No, that's not—what I mean is, some things are coming together. Last night, coming back from the mall, Greg said he wanted to show me something. He wouldn't say what it was, but he wouldn't drop it. And what I'm remembering now is that we talked about Uncle Bud's legacy and how the buyers wanted to sell the land for horse farms, and he started talking about how much he liked horses." If Investigator Riesbach hadn't irritated her so much, maybe she'd have thought of this while he was questioning her. But he had, and she hadn't, and Eric didn't irritate her at all. "Now I'm wondering if maybe he had a copy of that report at the house, and if maybe he thought he should tell me about all the shooting the Bradfords did. Maybe he thought the shot would harm the horses."

"Why tell you? Why not tell the buyers directly?"

"I don't know. Well, this was the first he'd heard about the horse farms. Maybe it just popped into his mind and out of his mouth. Maybe he was afraid he couldn't locate the buyers in time, and I was sitting there beside him mouthing off about protecting the land. Maybe he thought I had a conscience and would tell them myself."

Eric slanted a glance at her. "And maybe he thought he'd demand half the proceeds or he'd tell the buyers."

Blackmail? Well, it was an idea. But after a moment's consideration, she said, "I don't see how it would work. I couldn't pay him until after probate, and at that point the deal would be done and I could just refuse to pay him."

"He might have demanded that you borrow on your expectations and pay him at once."

"Oh." She caressed her sprained wrist. "Finlay Keene mentioned that I could do that, but I'm phobic about debt. I might even have said to go ahead and tell."

"That is phobic."

"Anyway, I don't see why he'd be trying to get money out of me. From all I hear, he got plenty from his mother."

"That's the word around town." They drove in silence until the houses along the road grew dense and they passed the "Welcome to Phillips Landing" sign and he slowed to the village speed limit. "Could he have been after something else?" he said then.

"You aren't the first to suggest that," she said.

"I suppose the question has arisen."

"It sure crossed my mind. I just don't know. Maybe Marion told you, I'm coming off a rotten marriage, and I'm leery about trusting my instincts."

"Marion didn't," he said. "I'm sorry."

"It's okay. Pretty much. Stuff happens."

"That it does."

Summoning her nerve, she said, "Your turn."

He didn't pretend not to understand. "Fair enough," he said. "Good marriage, then some jerk doing ninety on the Sprain spun out, and she died."

"Oh, God." The Sprain Brook Parkway was notorious; people did ninety on the Sprain and people died. "I'm sorry. I'm really sorry."

"Five months' pregnant," he added.

"That's terrible. Recently?"

"Two years and a bit."

And he could probably recite the weeks, days, and hours in that bit. Not long enough. Long enough to be fading into the past, not long enough to avoid guilt at the fading. So some days it's okay to leave the ring off, and other days you can't deal with the fading or with the guilt and you put the ring on. So she supposed, anyway; the day she'd left Cal, she had sold her wedding ring, and now a wave of relief rolled over her every time she noticed the nakedness of her left hand. "I'm really sorry," she said again.

"Stuff happens," he said. "Life goes on."

HE PARKED CLOSE to the art center and took charge of maneuvering the bicycle out of the rear of the van. The tape across the break in the fence was vivid in the streetlight. "That's where your car went over?"

"Everything's been going over cliffs," she said.

"I've noticed."

"In thunderstorms."

"I'd missed that."

She let him take charge of wheeling the bicycle along the path beside the dark building. She unlocked the door left-handed and reached in and switched on the stairwell light. He bumped the bike over the threshold into the vestibule at the foot of the stairs. There was just room to prop it against the wall. "Thank you very much," she said.

He smiled and said, "My pleasure," and didn't turn back along the path until she'd closed the door behind her. She locked it, went upstairs, and let herself into the apartment, and still in the dark, went through into the bathroom, pushed back the curtain, and watched his taillights disappear down around the turn into Oak Ridge Lane.

TWENTY-ONE

Gus

USUALLY JANET WAITED until Sunday to call her brother, but this weekend she made the call on Saturday morning.

"Hey, sis," he said, "what's up?"

"Wrong direction. It's what's down."

"What *is* down?"

"London Bridge."

"London Bridge isn't down, it's falling down. Watch your verbs."

"Are you a writer or something?"

"Something. What's down?"

She told him.

"My God," he said. "Are you okay?"

"Amazingly, yes. Only a bruised sternum and a sprained wrist and they're mending."

"How about the little old psyche?"

"Okay, I guess. A little more fear of falling, maybe, but no nightmares. Listen, Rich, do you happen to know if there's a program to retrieve a WordPerfect locked file if you've lost the password?"

"Now there's an abrupt transition. No, I don't happen to know, but it seems to me there's a program for everything."

"Point taken."

"It might cost. Is it important?"

"I don't know. I came across a computer disk of Uncle Bud's with locked files on it, but nobody knows the password."

"Did you ask Lee?"

"She didn't know the disk existed."

"I guess she wouldn't." He fell silent.

"Rich?"

"I'm thinking. Are there any other files on the disk?"

"Old Christmas letters and Uncle Bud's poems."

"Uncle Bud's what? Do you mean written by or collected and transcribed by?"

"Written by, as in 'Spring,' by Broderick Hale."

"You're serious."

"Never more."

"How bad are they?"

"Not quite as bad as you think but bad enough. Leora picked one for the minister to read at the funeral. Autumn leaves and farewell."

"And to think I missed it."

"I'll print them out and send them to you."

"Take your time. The reason I asked, I think people sometimes conceal the password in another file."

"That's a thought. The title, maybe?"

"Possible. Maybe that's a little obvious."

"Or maybe like that thing where you read down the first letters to get a message?"

"That *thing* is called an acrostic, and that's a decent idea."

"How will I know which file?"

"Let your artistic imagination run riot."

"Thanks. Listen, I've got to go. I've got a ten o'clock appointment."

"Appointment or date?"

"Stop it. Bro, take care of yourself." So far he had avoided the plague.

"Worry not. I'm making do with survivor's guilt. And listen, baby sis—you stop going for rides with strange men."

After she hung up, she realized that she hadn't told him about Uncle Bud's legacy.

Two things prevented Janet from riding Marion's bike to her appointment with Schuyler Vanstaat: she couldn't find the wrench to raise the seat, and her right wrist couldn't quite control its end of the handlebars. She walked.

The Vanstaats lived in a big turn-of-the-century house with a big lawn on a little maple-shaded street three blocks above Main Street. The lawn needed mowing and tufts of grass were sprouting between the bricks of a walk that curved gently to the front porch.

Schuyler Vanstaat looked a bit seedy as well when he opened the door to her ring. His eyes were pouched and red rimmed, his cheeks sagged in doughy lumps, and his smile seemed forced. But he said, "Good morning," heartily enough as he admitted her from another hot and humid August morning into shaded coolness. The interior—sprigged wallpaper, knobby maple furniture, hooked rugs scattered on hardwood flooring—was dustless and smelled of Lemon Pledge. A stairway with an elegant banister supported by white-painted, lathe-turned spokes led upward from the hall.

"I heard about the accident," Vanstaat said. "Terrible thing. I'm amazed that you're able to get around so soon."

"I was lucky."

"Indeed. It's terribly sad about Gregory. My son, Josh, is quite shaken. They were great friends, they and Charlie Emmett's boy, Kevin. Thick as thieves, to coin a phrase. I can't say I'd have relished trying to teach those three. No harm in them, but you know boys. Oh, hello, dear," he said as Diane Vanstaat, elegant in a flowing blue cotton skirt and blouse, appeared from somewhere in the rear of the house. The Wife, appearing on cue to reassure The Female Visitor. "You know Janet Upton, of course."

Janet had evidently walked in on a family crisis; Diane Vanstaat's eyes too were red rimmed. But like Schuyler, The Wife was determined to put a good face on it. With what Janet's grandmother would have called graciousness—not a word much used

in Janet's circle—she said, "Yes, of course, we've met at the art center. How nice to see you again."

Janet said, "I'm sorry to be intruding on your Saturday morning," then realized that her words might be taken as recognizing what they might prefer to conceal. She made a stab at a little graciousness of her own. "What a lovely house you have."

Diane Vanstaat's chin rose higher. "Thank you so much." With a nod—a gracious nod—she said, "I mustn't keep you; I'm sure you and Schuyler have serious business to transact," and, her task of reassurance completed, vanished once more into the rear of the house.

"All the material is upstairs in my study," Schuyler said, adding as Janet followed him up the elegant stairway, "You'll have to forgive the mess." The study was a small corner room full of leather, walnut, and books, and only someone unsympathetic to the nature of intellectual work could apply the word "mess" to the litter of scribbled-on papers and splayed-open books on the desk. He waved her to an easy chair beneath an old floor lamp, seated himself behind the desk, propped his elbows among the papers, and said, "You're curious about the Bradford land. Anything in particular?"

She had resolved not to ask point-blank about the skeet range. The question might put the notion of lead-shot pollution into somebody's mind, and in spite of her uneasiness, she really wasn't sure she was ready to risk half a million dollars. She said, "Maybe you know I've inherited sort of an interest in a piece of it?"

"So I've heard. And I believe you're fortunate enough to have found a buyer."

"And I just thought I'd like to know more about it. Kristin said you're the person to ask."

He smiled. "A loyal daughter. You know, I find it a bit eerie, your showing up with this question just after Gregory's death. He consulted me about the Bradfords for a school project many years ago."

"Actually," Janet said, "I ran across a draft of his paper yesterday. I mentioned it to Kristin and that's when she sent me to you."

"Is that a fact? You know, that project only lasted the one year. Somebody decided it was too strenuous for freshmen, and the teacher who conceived of it moved on to a more academically rigorous environment. Well—where to begin? The Bradfords go back a long way."

"Actually," she hastened to say, "I picked up quite a lot about the first couple of centuries from Greg's paper, but his information got a little thin around the time of the First World War."

"That must have been an early draft. My goodness, yes, Thaddeus and the Great War. Nineteen-Fourteen marked the beginning of the end of many things, not just the Bradfords. When Thaddeus passed away in nineteen-eighty, it was the end of an era. A microcosm of our time, really." He opened a drawer and took out a small tape recorder. "I dug this out of the files after you phoned yesterday. It will give you some of the picture. It's an interview I had in nineteen eighty-five with an old-timer named Gustave Becker. He worked for Thaddeus's father before he went off to war, and again after he came back from the trenches. He was living in a nursing home in Peekskill when I interviewed him. Wonderful character. His short-term memory was shot, but he remembered the Bradfords in detail." He pushed buttons, produced squawks, pushed another. "Here we are."

Off mike, a voice that was recognizably Schuyler Vanstaat's said, "How long did you work for them, Gus?"

Gustave Becker's voice came through thin and whiny. "Not near as long as I wanted to, I'll tell you that. I started working for the old man before the war, not much more than a kid, and I went right back after the Armistice. He was a real old-time gentleman. But nothing was ever the same after the war. Thaddeus come back with his ideas, and after the old man died, he just up and done away with my job. Nineteen twenty, that was."

"What was it you did for the old man?"

"Gamekeeper is how I started, age fifteen. Keeping the poachers off the land. I wasn't ever a big fellow, but I was strong for my size and the best shot in town too, and everybody knew it. Nobody messed with the game on the old man's land when I was patrolling. After that, he made me master of guns."

Schuyler interrupted the tape. "it sounds grandiose," he said, "but I expect it was serious work. The Bradfords were big-time hunters."

"So I'd heard."

Schuyler turned the tape recorder back on.

"…beautiful guns," Gus Becker said, "and me oh my, could they shoot. You never caught them buying butchers' birds. Bagged their own, you name it, goose, duck, turkey, Thanksgiving and Christmas, year in and year out…."

Come *on!*

"…cooking them wild birds takes some know-how too. Holiday time, you should have smelled that kitchen. Nothing like it, ever. Great days. Oh, could they shoot. You should have seen the trophy room…."

Janet listened through tedious catalogs of the guns Gus Becker had cared for and the shooting matches the Bradfords had taken part in and the prizes they had won. Gus chuckled. "The old man said it's like what they say about getting to Carnegie Hall. Practice, practice, practice. They had themselves a full-fledged skeet range, you know."

Ah.

Gus had reached the life and character of Thaddeus and his whine intensified. "What he said, the war give him enough shooting to last the rest of his life. It never took me that way, but Thaddeus didn't have a lot of grit to him. He come back home in one piece, but he wouldn't pick up a gun. Shell shock, we called it back then. His mother passed away in the flu epidemic of 'eighteen, died the day he got home, like she'd been waiting for him. He wasn't ever the man he started out to be. The day after the

old man's funeral, nineteen twenty that was, he went out and tore down the skeet house, every board of it, pretty near with his bare hands."

"Is that when he took up farming? Nineteen twenty?"

"No, he was farming before then. He come back after the Armistice and said he was going back to his forebears, something like that. The old man didn't mind. The missus passing on like that, I think that give him a touch of shell shock too. He was so glad to have Thaddeus home safe and sound, he give him the run of them scrubby old fields as soon as he asked for them. Thaddeus hogged out all the scrub and got him a couple pretty good crops of hay before the old man died—"

There it was! Janet leaned forward.

"Not that the old man cared about hay," Gus was saying. "He was just glad to see Thaddeus taking some kind of an interest in life."

There it was. Thaddeus Bradford has started farming while the skeet range was still in operation. Logically, then, the farmland couldn't have been the skeet range.

Gustave Becker was saying, "Thaddeus said I was welcome to stay on after the old man died." A wheezy chuckle. "I told him, I wanted to drive a team behind a plow, I'd haul my butt out to Iowa. My dad's uncle hauled up stakes and homesteaded out there in the eighteen-eighties. Plowed up the prairie and built himself a house and never come back to all this rock and scrub. But Thaddeus said his forebears farmed this land and he was going to farm this land. I told him, his forebears give up fighting the rocks and the scrub a long time ago, but it wasn't any good trying to tell Thaddeus anything. He never made a nickel off that farm, but the Bradfords had enough money, they could play any games they felt like. So he tore down the skeet house and sold the guns. I got to say, he was decent enough about it. Give me first pick, free and gratis, and sold the rest. Give me the old man's dog too. She already thought she was mine, anyway. Lady, her name was. Yellow Lab bitch, nice soft mouth. She dropped

some good litters in her day. Don't get me wrong, Thaddeus was all right. He had his ideas, but hell, the Bradfords all had their ideas. When he saw he wasn't going to make a farmer out of me, he give me a good reference, and I went off to work at the rod and gun club."

Vanstaat punched the Off button. "Is that any help?"

Any *help?* It only meant she could let Finlay Keene sell that damn land with a clear conscience. "It's very interesting," she said. "Thank you. How long did Thaddeus go on farming, do you know?"

"Until nineteen seventy-nine. He was eighty when he stopped."

"You're kidding."

"He used hired help, of course, but it was his farm, no question about that. He didn't ride the tractor much in the later years, but he was out in the fields just about every day from planting through harvest. He was still pretty active when we moved here in nineteen seventy-three. I enjoyed talking with him. He liked to experiment. He started with hay, as Gus said, but he grew corn for a good many years, and I believe he tried soybeans when they first came in as a cash crop, and he even tried some truck farming—potatoes, I remember, and sweet corn, and cabbage for a while. But that's labor intensive, and as time went on, local hand labor just wasn't available. He wouldn't employ migrants. On the day he turned eighty, he just walked off that land and let it go back to scrub. And died the next year."

"And the skeet range?" she ventured. "Is any trace of that left?"

Vanstaat shook his head. "I could show you the site, but I doubt if you'd be able to tell it from the rest of the woods. The forest has had over seventy years to reestablish itself."

TWENTY-TWO

The Father

KRISTIN WAS SITTING on the office doorstep when Janet trudged into the parking lot. The Vanstaat crisis was apparently inescapable; her eyes were teary and her face was blotched.

Ignoring her distress was impossible. "Anything I can help with?" said Janet.

"Yeah." Kristin got to her feet and swiped the back of her hand over her nose. "Adopt me."

It was cooler inside, so Janet closed the door behind them. "Interesting thought," she said, "but the last time I looked, you had parents."

"I'm divorcing them." Kristin plumped down in the chair beside Janet's desk, took a tissue from the box on Janet's desk, and blew her nose. "If anybody says 'investment' to me one more time, I'm going to kill them."

"What's wrong?"

"We have to move. To Poughkeepsie. I don't know a living soul in Poughkeepsie."

"How come?"

"Because my dad's a—" Her eyes teared again. "I hate my mom when she says it, but he's a failure."

"Kris—"

"He is. I hate my mom, but she's right. What's a man with a Ph.D. doing scrounging part-time jobs and trying to make up for it by wheeler-dealering in real estate?" She sniffed. "He bought

this stupid little house in Poughkeepsie. As an *investment*. He was buying land and houses all over the place. I was only like eight years old, but I remember him talking about how real estate was such a hot *investment*. And then the market crashed and he couldn't sell half of it and he's sitting there with all the taxes and the mortgages and now the money he got for the good stuff he did sell is all gone paying for the rotten things he couldn't."

"Kris—"

"He's been renting out that stupid little house, but the kind of people who'd live there are the kind of people who trash the place, and it's costing more to keep it up than the rent brings in and nobody wants to buy it and I don't blame them. It's a stupid little dump on a poky little lot, with the neighbors, like, right on the other side of the window. *Nobody* wants it." Her voice wavered. She fished out another tissue and scrubbed at her eyes. "He can't sell *it,* but he can sure as hell sell my *home,* and don't tell me I shouldn't swear. It isn't fair. It's my senior year and I don't know a living *soul* in Poughkeepsie and it's a horrible house and if anybody says 'investment' to me one more time I'll kill them."

"Bummer," said Janet.

Kristin wadded the tissue and dropped it into the wastebasket. "It was going to be all right, the land trust was going to buy one of the parcels—another one of my dad's great *investments*— and we wouldn't have to sell the house, but then they went back on it."

Not quite Eric's version. The phone rescued Janet from the need to formulate an appropriate response. She picked it up and said, "Art center, Janet Upton."

A male voice said, "Yes, hello, Ms. Upton. This is Don Ferguson." She blanked for a moment. "Gregory's father."

Oh, God. "Yes, of course," she said. "Mr. Ferguson, I'm terribly sorry about Greg."

Kristin's face came alert.

"Thank you," said Ferguson. "The reason I'm calling, I'm in

town for a couple of days and I was hoping we could get together and talk a little, touch base before I have to go back home. I'm tied up all day today, but I wonder if I could buy you dinner tonight."

Her wrist hurt, her chest ached, and she was bone weary; but the man's son was dead and she was the last person to have seen the kid alive. And he was paying. "Yes, all right," she said.

"I hear the Station Stop is pretty good," he said. "We could meet there."

The Station Stop, a converted railroad depot just down the hill, was Phillips Landing's closest approach to a steak house—perhaps a natural choice for a Coloradan.

"Fine," she said, though "barely tolerable" would have been more accurate.

"Seven o'clock? I expect we won't have any trouble identifying each other."

"Just look for the Ace bandage on my wrist."

"His dad, right?" said Kristin when Janet had hung up. "He sure isn't hanging around. He only got here last night and he's going back tomorrow."

"I expect he has responsibilities."

"The guys tried to talk to him about a funeral, but he said it'll be in Colorado. That's wrong. Greg never wanted to go to Colorado in the first place." A sigh. "Parents just don't get it."

Groping for control of her fraying nerves, Janet said, "Kris, I know you feel bad. Moving to another school your senior year is a definite bummer. But you're stuck with it, and I want to tell you the most important thing anybody ever said to me in art school."

Kristin blinked.

"Are you ready?"

"What?"

"It was a photography teacher, but it applies across the board. She said, 'Photograph what troubles you.'"

Kristin blinked again.

"I'm passing it on to you. Kristin Vanstaat, sculpt what troubles you most."

"Parents?"

"If that's what's troubling you. You're a sculptor and you've got a shot at being a good one. So cry if you have to, but get your fanny in the studio and sculpt."

"Parents?" Kristin's eyes went remote. Almost whispering, she repeated, "Parents."

DONALD FERGUSON WAS WAITING in the bar, a stein of beer in his hand, his khakis still creased from packing. He bore no physical resemblance to his stocky, freckled, red-haired son; he was tallish, thinnish, tanned, and balding, with sun-country crow's-feet at the corners of his eyes. Always susceptible to older men, Janet found him not unattractive.

His first words were an inquiry about her injuries. He sounded genuinely concerned, and of course he was; the more serious her injuries, the greater his liability. "I'll live," she said.

"Well, that's one blessing," he said. "What'll you have to drink?"

She'd better keep her wits about her. She asked for iced coffee; then the hostess bustled up with a handful of menus and led them to a booth.

"My engineer has been doing her best to stave off my guilt," said Ferguson when they had ordered, "but I was the trustee of that property until this past May." He tasted his beer and set it down. "What's so maddening is that I had that bridge inspected before I rented the property in eighty-seven and it checked out sound."

"What happened to it?"

"Subsurface erosion, apparently." He unrolled a paper napkin from the silverware in front of him and felt in his shirt pocket for a pen. "Something you couldn't see without taking a backhoe to the whole structure. The ends of the bridge are anchored

in rock and concrete and they're still intact, and the planking was sound. You could probably have driven over it for another fifty years." Uncapping the pen, he began to sketch. "You've had a lot of heavy rain."

"You could say so."

Turning the napkin so that she could see it the right way up, he said, "The problem was the center support. I don't know if you looked at the structure."

"It was dark."

"Yes. Well, there's this steel center support"—two quick vertical lines extending down from the middle of the horizontal line that was the bridge itself—"set in a three-by-three-by-three-foot block of concrete in the bottom of the gulch"—the pen sketched a square—"and that was supported"—a bigger rectangle under the square—"by a six-by-six-by-two concrete footing. It was sixty years old, but the design would qualify for a permit today."

"But it fell down," she said.

"What happened"—he drew wiggly lines under the big rectangle at the bottom—"is that the concrete for the footing was poured on earth, not bedrock, and it got undermined."

"That's okay?"

"My engineer tells me it's done all the time. What she thinks is that it was originally on dry land, but over the years the stream moved, so that by now, it was actually flowing around the footing during high water." He had another taste of beer and said, "I hadn't thought about it, but of course streams don't stay put. Debris falls in and blocks the flow and the water moves to where the going is easier. In this case, it moved right over against the footing, until every time there was high water, the earth underneath got saturated. Then, when you had all those heavy storms one after another this summer, the saturated soil washed out from underneath the whole structure. In the end, it was so undermined that the support was basically just hanging from the bridge

itself. When the van drove onto it, its weight shifted the balance enough to pull the whole thing down."

Janet's stomach tightened with the memory. "Didn't anybody notice?"

"I sure wish somebody had. If you weren't watching it over time, I guess you'd assume the footing had always been in the floodplain." He bunched up the napkin as their first course arrived.

Don Ferguson had ordered clam chowder. Janet discovered at once that she should have too; what the menu called a tossed salad consisted of hard, pale disks that were barely recognizable as tomato, bedded on the bitter inner white leaves of iceberg lettuce. Where did they find this stuff in August, she wondered, when all up and down the valley, crimson globes bursting with juice were dragging down the vines? She picked at it left-handed, looking for green bits of lettuce. "You never lived there?" she said.

"I never saw the property until Alta died. My first wife," he thought it necessary to explain, "Greg's mother."

Janet nodded.

"We lived on Long Island," he said. "When we split, I hit the road for a new life in the golden west and she moved up here with Greg." His tone changed, and when Janet glanced up she saw his jaw muscles tighten. "Greg was only seven when I took off. We'd sure have had an easier time of it after Alta died if I'd stayed closer to the situation."

At least, thought Janet, I didn't run out on a child. But Don Ferguson had regrets enough, so after a few more unsatisfactory mouthfuls of salad she said, "He talked a little about the transition while we were driving back from the mall. He said it wasn't all your fault."

.   Ferguson's spoon stopped halfway back to the bowl. "Greg said that?"

"Yes, he did." She gave up on the salad and laid her fork on the plate. "He said he'd acted like a punk."

"Well, I'll be darned." The spoon finished its journey and

sought out the last fragments of clam. "I guess you must have got to know him pretty well this summer," he said.

"Actually," she said, "I didn't. We'd only met two or three times. He was just doing me a favor, hauling some cartons of copy paper back from the mall after my car was wrecked. The only reason I was going up to the house is that he said he had something to show me." She hesitated, then decided it would be best for Don Ferguson to hear it all right now. "I told him I wanted to get home, but he insisted."

"Oh boy." He leaned back to let the soup bowl and salad plate be bussed away.

"I'd have had to jump out of the van," she added.

"Oh boy. That sounds like him. He had a stubborn streak a mile wide."

The main course was put in front of them. Janet had hesitated over her order. By now, her right wrist was probably strong enough to hold a fork steady while her left hand cut steak; there was no point, however, in overdoing independence or letting Don Ferguson know how quickly she was recovering. She'd ordered shrimp; shrimp appeared before her; she picked up her fork left-handed, speared one, and conveyed it to her mouth. It was better than the salad. She chewed, swallowed, and said, "Naturally, I've been wondering what it was he wanted to show me."

"Beats me."

She ate another shrimp. *Much* better than the salad. After probate, she was going to have shrimp once a week. At least once a week. "I remember we were talking about horses."

"I'll bet you were," said Ferguson. "My wife said, 'Well, he's finally found something to like, for heaven's sake, don't get in the way.' He spent, I don't remember, four or five summers mucking out the stables at a dude ranch. Loved it."

"So he said. And he was talking about the house his mother was going to build. He said he wanted to build it as a memorial to her."

"Oh, that house. I hate that damn house and it hasn't even been built. The cops were on me about it. I told them I didn't know or care about the house, it was Greg's mania." He drank another mouthful of his beer, set down the mug, attacked the steak. It looked tender. She'd have steak once a week too. "Real estate," he said. "If you know what you're doing, I guess it beats Vegas, but if you don't, it'll put you in the poorhouse. Alta knew what she was doing, I'll say that for her, and that damn house was going to be her trophy, show what a genius she was to be able to afford to put up a house like that, and by God, she was going to stick it in everybody's face." More beer. "Myself, I never could see treating God's green earth as a commodity." More steak; then, considerably calmed, he said, "Do you think that mysterious something of Greg's had to do with that house?"

"I don't have any idea. He said he'd been looking through her papers. Have you looked at them?"

"Alta's papers? Not personally, no. After she died, the lawyer sorted out what I needed to administer the trust. He told me I could junk the rest, but Greg threw one of his famous fits, so I just had it boxed up and stored."

"He said he'd got them all out of storage."

"He would." Ferguson ate steak, drank beer, wiped his mouth. "Tell you what, Janet. I have to fly back to Boulder tomorrow. I haven't had time to do much of anything with the house. I've hired a caretaker to keep things under control. I'll be back here in a couple of months to finish up, but you don't want to wait that long. Why don't I just loan you a key and you can take a look for yourself?"

TWENTY-THREE

Mail Drop

JANET STOOD ON THE curb and considered how to occupy the rest of the evening. The key and the house-alarm code were in her shoulder bag, and the meal—three times as much as she normally ate in a day—lay heavily in her stomach. While drinking decaf. and watching Don Ferguson down a wedge of glutinous cherry pie, she had mentioned Kristin's interest in Gregory's photographs. "Sure," he said, "let her have them. I'm glad somebody cared."

A cold front had moved in, inviting her to walk. Two hours later, she'd completed a circuitous six miles through the village, climbed the hill to the art center in the dark, and let herself into the apartment.

She wasn't sleepy and she suspected that horrors lurked behind the scrim of consciousness for a cue to enter her dreams. She fished the Stuff disk copy out from under her bras and panties and took it down to the office. Computer humming, disk in the drive, she studied the list of files.

Interesting. Maybe Rich had been on to something. (It wouldn't be the first time.) There were twelve poems and twelve locked files, and furthermore, each poem had been entered on the same date as one of the locked files.

Where to start? Well, the system for locating passwords must be a simple one, because if it were too complicated, you'd risk forgetting it as well as the password. She printed out the poems

and penciled the date on each. "Spring," "Tulips," and "Daffo-
dils" had been entered on May 1, 1987, and so had the first three
locked files. She'd have to play with the permutations to find out
which poem went with which file—assuming any poem went
with any file.

"Spring" was the shortest. She had read it for sense; now she
studied it as a puzzle.

Spring
by
Broderick Hale

In the merry month of May,
Everything is bright, nothing is dull,
Everything grows, nothing decays,
In May everything seems possible.

In the merry month of May,
Lilacs are blooming but not goldenrod.
Spring is the time when it's easy to pray.
Spring is when it's easy to believe in God.

She ordered the computer to retrieve file 01. The screen
flashed Enter Password. She entered "Spring."

ERROR—File is locked.

All caps? SPRING. ERROR. spring. ERROR. The same se-
quences on 02 and 03 produced ERROR, ERROR, ERROR.

Rich had said titles might be too simple. Try an acrostic. She
returned to 01 and to SPRING and entered IEEIILSS.

ERROR.

ieeiilss. ERROR.

Maybe the stanza break was significant. IEEI ILSS.

Chunk muttered the computer. *Chunk chunk chunk-chunk
chunk chunk.* File 01 materialized. It said: *PIN checking 3962.*

Oh, great. Fantastic. The mystery was solved, and when she broke into 02 she'd find the Visa PIN number, and 03 would have his Social Security number. By the time she cracked 12, she'd have learned twelve secret numbers.

Twelve secret numbers?

The list of files showed how many characters each one used. The two words and four digits in 01, for instance, used 589 characters. 02 and 03 were comparably short. The rest, though, were ten to fifteen times as long.

File 04 and the poem entitled "Snow" were a pair. She entered the acrostic, all caps, spacing at the stanza breaks.

ERROR—File is locked.

Damn.

She tried every variant she could think of. 04 remained locked. The other locked files, as well, refused to respond to acrostics from their corresponding poems.

After an hour and a half, she switched off the computer, pulled out the Stuff disk, took it upstairs with the printouts of the poems, and tucked them back in the drawer under her underwear. It took a while to drop off, but she concentrated on slow, deep breathing—ONE...TWO...THREE...and at last fatigue displaced irritation and she slid off the ledge of wakefulness into sleep.

The cold front departed during the night. She awoke at nine-thirty in a swamp of sweat, her head feeling like a clogged drain. But coffee helped, and when she undid the Ace bandage, she found that her wrist would flex a little and even bear a little weight. She rewrapped it and rummaged around, found a wrench, and went down and wheeled the bicycle out and leaned it against a tree. After a certain amount of fumbling, she succeeded in raising the seat to a comfortable height. She went back up and showered and at noon went down to open up.

Sunday, as usual, was a good day for visitors, and she spent most of the afternoon in the gallery. Kristin Vanstaat showed up

just before closing time. "We're having a service for Greg next Sunday," she said, plopping into the chair beside Janet's desk.

"We tried to talk to his dad about it, but he couldn't be bothered, so we're putting it together ourselves. He can do his thing in Boulder and we'll do ours here, even if we're the only ones who come."

"I'll come," said Janet. She slid Greg's portfolio across the desk to Kristin. "His dad said you should have it."

"Oh!" Kristin unzipped it, peered in at the photographs, zipped it again. "Thanks."

"Thank Greg's father. He liked the idea."

"Did he?"

"Take it easy on the man. He did his best in a difficult situation. Who's the we planning the service?"

"My brother and Kevin Emmett and me." Kristin cradled the portfolio on her lap. "They used to call themselves the three musketeers. I thought they were so cool. I was, like, nine years old and they were fourteen and their voices were starting to change. Greg's started first. It was, like, you know, the first real guy thing?"

"Mysterious, intriguing, and scary."

"You got it. It seems so young now. I mean, right now I'm three years older than they were then. I got the book out of the library, *The Three Musketeers,* and I read it straight through three times. Nine years old. The librarian couldn't believe it. I was looking for a girl I could be, but the girls in guys' books are such wimps. What I did find out, there were actually four musketeers. Athos, Porthos, and Aramis were the three in the title, but D'Artagnan teamed up with them and he was the real hero. The librarian told me how to pronounce it, *Dart-an-yon.* So I just pretended I was D'Artagnan."

"What did the guys think of that?"

"Oh, I didn't *tell* them, I just hung around. If my mom had ever found out I was riding my bike on the roads, tagging along

after them, she'd have locked me up and thrown away the key. Josh used to threaten to tell her, like to get me to take out the garbage when it was his turn and things like that. Actually, it was pretty boring, but I couldn't let them run me off. I mean, they didn't actually *do* anything like in the book. Josh didn't even read it. It was just something to call themselves because there were three of them. I mean, they wouldn't want to be the three blind mice or the three little pigs."

"Or the three Stooges," said Janet. "So now the survivors are letting D'Artagnan help plan the service."

"I guess they've mellowed with age."

"Where will it be held?"

"We're working on it. Outdoors someplace is what we'd like. What the guys really wanted to do was put his ashes in a secret place they used to have, but his dad's taking the ashes back to Colorado."

Secret place?

"Charlie—Mr. Emmett—said anything to do with ashes was ghoulish and he was glad Greg's dad was taking them away," said Kristin.

"Charlie's helping with the plans?"

"Not really. It's just, he was around when Josh and I went over to talk to Kevin. Then he went to Stewart to meet Mrs. Emmett's plane and I came here. My mom has this ridiculous thing about me hanging out with the guys. I mean, for gosh sake, Josh is my brother and Kevin's got a girlfriend."

"Parents," said Janet.

"You got it. Say, that was sort of a good idea you had. I've been making sketches."

"I'm looking forward to seeing the finished product."

"It's going to take a long time."

"You don't need ashes to remember a friend," said Janet. "What is that secret place, some kind of clubhouse?"

"No, it's a little hole in a stone wall, like a space between the stones. It was their secret mailbox. They used to leave notes for

each other. Guy stuff, really gross. They about killed me when they found out I was reading it."

"Do you still know where it is?"

"Oh, sure, I've got a photographic memory. How come you're so interested?"

Well, there wasn't any reason to make a secret of it; she'd already told half the world. "The night of the accident," Janet said, "Greg said he had something he wanted to show me. He wouldn't say what it was. I said to wait until the next day, but he was being stubborn. That's why I was in the van when the bridge collapsed. I was afraid to jump out."

"Oh." Kristin's face reddened; obviously she'd thought what half the town thought.

"I expect half the town thinks we had something going," said Janet. "Actually, he was too young for me."

"Oh." The blush faded. "You think maybe he put it there? Whatever it was?"

"I expect it's a wild idea, but I do sort of wonder. Have the guys been out to look at it?"

"No, they couldn't remember where it was. I had to tell them. Listen, do you want to go and look? I could ride along and show you."

The offer had its appeal. "I'm riding a bike," said Janet.

"Oh. Oh, right, your car's wrecked." Kristin made a face. "So's my bike. How about if I ask Josh to drive us?"

"Well—I don't know, Kris. Greg said it was sensitive material and he didn't want people to know about it."

"Just you."

"I'm sorry. I'd be glad to have you along, but—"

"But not a crowd. It's okay."

"Do you think you could tell me how to find it? If it's there, and if I can talk about it, you'll be the first to know."

Kristin stroked the portfolio. "I'll do better than tell you," she said. "I'll draw you a map. Give me a piece of paper."

TWENTY-FOUR

Search and Destroy

A BAND OF THUNDERSTORMS was scheduled to pass across the Hudson Valley later in the evening, but it was supposed to stay north of the Highlands. Janet decided to gamble. She wasn't eager to put off her search for the mail drop; the surviving musketeers might get there first. She ate a peach—it was a good year for peaches—changed into jeans, shoved Kristin's sketch, her wallet, and her keys into a butt pack, strapped on Marion's helmet, and set out on Marion's bicycle.

In spite of the excellent gear ratio, she puffed a good deal pumping up the hilly roads, and as always she suffered a few incipient panic attacks when the slipstream from the occasional passing car seemed about to blow her off balance. But her wrist bore up, and it was with mild euphoria that she found herself at the intersection where Henley Lane entered Oak Hollow Road, just short of the hill that was crowned by Big Bear.

If she proceeded a quarter of a mile farther along Oak Hollow Road, she'd reach the driveway to Uncle Bud's place. About the same distance beyond that was Paul and Marion's house. Maybe there'd still be enough light when she finished this errand to pedal on over and say hello; maybe, if dark were imminent, she'd even cadge a lift home.

She turned onto Henley Lane's dirt surface and pumped up three switchbacks to the shoulder of a ridge. Ahead, the dirt road skirted several miles of the wildlife sanctuary boundary. To the

right, an overgrown set of tire tracks led to the abandoned house site on top of Big Bear; the track that led to the back of the Ferguson house branched off a few feet beyond and plunged into deep forest.

Janet turned right and labored along the ruts. Presently the track became too rough to ride. She dismounted and pushed the bike. She had just about decided that the track had no end when it turned a corner and the forest opened into lawn, the track became a graveled drive, the house struck straight lines across the curves of the landscape, and an unexpected fit of the shakes twisted her stomach.

Drawing a breath to quell the quivering, she remounted and pedaled along the gravel to the back of the house. She dismounted and bumped the bike up two steps onto the patio, wheeled it around the side of the house on a flagstone walk, got back on, and coasted down the curves of the front drive.

A dry-stone wall bordered the right side of the driveway down to a point ten or fifteen feet short of the ravine, where it turned away from the drive and ran off through the woods. The musketeers' secret mail drop was over in there, behind a removable stone in the wall. Kristin had mapped the location at the top of the sheet of paper and at the bottom had sketched in detail the movable stone and its neighbors.

Janet did not immediately follow the wall into the woods. She coasted slowly on down to a yellow police-line tape strung across the drive. A short length of bridge, still attached to the rim of the ravine, reached into nothingness. Trying to ignore the quivering in her midsection, she leaned the bike against a tree, stepped over the tape, and inched forward until she could see down to the bottom.

The red van, its driver's-side door open, rested close to the stream, which had shrunk to no more than a large trickle, among the litter of planks and metal beams. The bridge's center support still lay angled across the stream, still attached to the concrete base. A muddy puddle filled the hole the base had left when it had torn out of the ground.

She should have brought her camera.

She stepped back over the warning tape, retrieved the bike, and wheeled it back up the driveway to the angle where the stone wall emerged from the forest and turned to edge the driveway. She propped it against another tree, fished Kristin's sketch from the butt pack, and followed the wall into the woods. Where it bordered the driveway, it had been maintained in reasonably good repair, but back here among the trees, freeze and thaw had tumbled the stones and stretches were overgrown with tangles of greenbrier.

But by golly, the girl did have a photographic memory. There it was, in an untumbled stretch: a triangular stone, just larger than Janet's fist, filling a triangular space between larger stones. It came out easily when she pulled. She picked up a twig and poked into the cavity. Nothing growled, hissed, or snapped. She put the twig down and reached in cautiously. She felt nothing but damp leaf mold and some hard fragments that proved, when she pulled them out, to be broken acorn shells.

So much for the musketeers' mail drop.

And after all, how likely was it that Greg would have stashed something of importance out in the woods, subject to rain and rodents? Even a rainproof plastic bag wouldn't withstand teeth that could shell acorns.

She tucked the stone back into its hole, stood up, dusted leaf mold off her jeans knees, and made her way back to the driveway and up to the house. She bumped the bike up three steps and onto the front porch and leaned it against the wall beside the door. She fished her key chain from the butt pack, unlocked the door, let herself in, found the keypad inside a coat closet where Don Ferguson had told her it would be, deactivated the alarm, and tucked the keys away again.

The interior looked much as it had on the night of the accident. But Don Ferguson had taken some action: nothing happened when she flicked a light switch, and when she put the telephone to her ear, she heard the flat silence of a disconnected line.

She had no clue as to where Greg might have hidden It—if It even existed. The refrigerator door stood open on emptiness; the cupboards held nothing but nonperishables. In the laundry room, the hamper, the washer, and the dryer were empty and a wall cabinet held only detergent and fabric softener. She had already discovered that the half bath held nothing but bathroom things; nothing had been added. A door beside the laundry room opened on a steep staircase leading down to a cellar that smelled of mildew and mice. She was willing to gamble that Greg wouldn't have stored anything of importance down there.

She went through into the back-porch office. It took about fifteen minutes to examine the papers in the opened carton. None of them had anything to do with her.

A dusty assortment of glasses in the dining-room hutch; nothing but the nubby brown furniture in the living room. She went back to the hall and climbed the stairs.

The back room had obviously not been in use. A faded plaid bedspread covered a bare mattress; under the bed were dust fuzzies. The closet held only a few wire hangers. The chest of drawers was empty. She pulled out the drawers and found nothing under them or stuck to their bottoms. She went along the hall to the front bedroom.

A sense of trespass froze her in the doorway. It was the room Greg had been using, and Don Ferguson had obviously left it as he had found it. Rumpled khaki shorts, jockeys, and a T-shirt lay where Greg had tossed them on the queen-size bed; sandals lay tumbled beside it. Entering seemed an impossibly crude intrusion.

Ridiculous. Don Ferguson had granted her—had even volunteered—the right of entry. She entered.

It was large and light, newly painted, curtained and carpeted in spring colors, with a double window facing the front and a dormer in the side wall that looked out on to treetops and a wedge of sky. She started with the nightstand. On top were a box of Kleenex, the current issue of a science fiction magazine,

and a digital alarm clock that kicked over from 6:41 to 6:42 as she looked at it. Nothing was tucked between the tissues or the pages of the magazine. In the drawer, she found a sealed packet of condoms—waiting for anybody in particular?—several issues of *Penthouse* and *Playboy,* and a manual of computer design. She shook the magazines and the book; nothing tumbled from between the pages. Nothing under the drawer or attached to the bottom.

The sunlight paled as she was reinserting the drawer, and through the dormer she saw a bank of clouds piling up above the trees. The forecast of thunderstorms to the north might have been off by a few miles. She ought not stay too much longer.

In the top drawers of the dresser, she found socks, jockey shorts, T-shirts, dress shirts still wrapped from the laundry. She felt under the piles and found nothing. In the bottom drawer, sweatpants, sweatshirts, sweaters—

—and under the sweaters, an envelope.

A business-size window envelope, addressed to "Ms. Alta Ferguson." In the upper-left corner, the return address: "KILLIAN LABORATORIES—Environmental and Medical Testing"; an address in White Plains. Postmarked August 1987.

The top was slit open. She was slipping her fingers in to fish out the contents when from the back of the house she heard a motor and the gravelly scrunch of tires.

She unzipped the butt pack, doubled the envelope, jammed it in next to the keys, and zipped the pack shut. She went out into the hall and along to the back bedroom. Standing a few feet back from the window that overlooked the backyard, she saw a big blue pickup pulling up, and after a moment, a foreshortened Charlie Emmett climbing down from the cab and starting toward the house.

Charlie Emmett?

When he got too close for her to see from where she stood, she followed his progress by the clump of his boots on the patio

and then on the flagstone path around the side. She returned to the front bedroom, stood back from the window, and presently saw Charlie heading down the driveway, away from the house.

Charlie Emmett?

She didn't want to encounter him. In truth, she didn't want to encounter anybody; she couldn't rid herself of that ridiculous sense of trespass. It even crossed her mind to try to sneak away; but Charlie might already have seen the bike on the front porch, and even if she could retrieve it without being seen, the only way out was along that rough track to the road. If Charlie drove back out and overtook her, she'd be hard pressed to explain her secretiveness.

Anyway, this reluctance was unreasonable. She was there with permission, and there wasn't any reason to suppose that Charlie didn't have adequate reason to be there too. Therefore, her mind told her quivering stomach, there wasn't any reason to hide or sneak away. The obvious, normal thing to do was to acknowledge that they were both there on legitimate business; to go out and meet him, say, *Hey, Charlie, what's up? I didn't expect to see you here.*

All the same, it took an effort to go downstairs and out onto the front porch. She locked the door behind her, bumped the bike down the porch steps, climbed on, and coasted slowly down around the curves.

Charlie was no longer on the driveway. The rustle of dead leaves told her that he had gone off into the woods, and as she coasted nearer, she saw him squatting beside the stone wall.

Her progress was no more silent than Charlie's. He turned his head at about the same time she spotted him. He scrambled upright and said, "Where the hell did you come from?"

"Oh, it *is* you," she said. "I thought that might be your truck. What's up?"

He started back toward her. "You got business out here?"

The truth: "Remember I told you Greg wanted to show me something? I saw Don Ferguson last night and he gave me the

house key to come out and have a look. I was just heading back home. What brings you out this way?"

"You been in the house?"

"Just finished."

"Any luck?"

The truth, yes; not necessarily, though, the whole truth. "It's hard to find something when you don't know what it is. To tell you the truth, Charlie, I'm afraid I know what Greg wanted to show me."

"Hormones, huh?"

"Looks like it. What's with you?"

"Oh, drumming up business. Ferguson's going to have to do some work on the place if he wants to sell it, and I figured it wouldn't hurt my chances any to find out what needs doing and crunch some figures."

A reasonable explanation. Except that Charlie didn't do dry-stonework; in this part of the Highlands, stonework was just about monopolized by an Italian craftsman up the road. But, of course, if stonework was part of a bigger refurbishing, Charlie would be subcontracting it. "Smart," she said, and turned to wheel the bike back up the drive.

Thunder muttered in the distance. "Holy moley," Charlie said, "haven't we had enough of that?"

"It was supposed to pass by to the north." Janet swung her leg over the bicycle seat. "I'd better get going. Good luck with the contract."

"I'll give you a lift," said Charlie.

"Thanks," she said, "but I'm just going on up the road to the Willards'."

Thunder mumbled again. Charlie said, "That's quite a haul on a bike. Come on, we'll put it in the truck and I'll run you up there. Keep you out of the rain."

There was no denying him. Tension held Janet rigid in the passenger seat until they stopped on the Willards' driveway. While

Charlie lowered the tailgate to take out the bike, she climbed the steps to the front deck and tried the door.

It was locked.

They never locked the doors before bedtime when they were at home, so they had to be out. She went back down to the drive-way where Charlie was lifting the bike out of the truck bed. "Nobody home?" he said.

Oh, of course they were out. This was Sunday; they'd gone into the city to that opening and, after that, dinner with the art-ist. They wouldn't be back until late.

But she was—probably unreasonably—unwilling to ride back to the empty art center with Charlie Emmett, so she said, "It can't be for long. I've got a key. I'll wait for them."

The keys were in the butt pack, which at the moment was a belly pack, since she had slid it around to her front when she got into Charlie's truck. She unzipped it. The key chain, obedient to the law of gravity, had worked its way down to the bottom.

Charlie held the bike with one hand, watching as she groped. She got hold of the key chain and eased it past the wallet, only to have it catch on a corner of the envelope. Fumbling with her weakened right hand, she tried to work the chain free, but as the keys cleared the zipper on the pack, the envelope, still caught on the chain, came out with them. Once past the zipper, it fluttered loose and landed on the ground at Charlie's feet.

She snatched for it, but it had landed on the other side of the bike and it was Charlie who, still holding the bike one-handed, bent and picked it up.

He thumbed the fold open and read the face of the envelope, and his grin faded. "Thought you said you didn't find anything," he said.

His unsmiling face scared her. Struggling to maintain an ex-pression of naiveté, she said the only thing she could dredge up: "I don't know what it is."

"Yeah, well. Nothing you have to bother with." Charlie re-

folded the envelope one-handed and tucked it into his shirt pocket.

Protest and lack of protest seemed equally inadvisable; what she really wanted was a locked door between her and Charlie. Clutching the keys that had betrayed her, she turned toward the house, but before she could take a step, Charlie lifted the bicycle with both hands and shoved it broadside at her, catching her across the midsection. She kept her balance only by grabbing the handlebars. Charlie gave the bike another shove and she staggered backward another step. He turned toward the truck; for an instant she thought he meant to slam the tailgate up, but then, past the bulk of his shoulder, she saw his hand move inside the truck bed and close on something—a bar of some sort, metal, narrow and rigid.

She slewed the bike to head down the drive, flung her leg over the seat, and pushed off. Her feet found the pedals, and with all her strength she pumped down the driveway and out onto the blacktop surface of Oak Hollow Road.

As soon as she turned, she realized her mistake. A homing instinct had turned her toward the village, but that was wrong. There were houses in the other direction, less than a quarter of a mile beyond Paul and Marion's. In the direction she was going, there was nothing until one was nearly to the village limits except Uncle Bud's empty house and then Henley Lane, empty of dwellings for miles.

Then the pickup's tailgate did slam up; she heard it through the rush of wind in her ears, and then she heard the growl of the engine, the changes in its pitch as Charlie reversed and shifted and headed down the drive. It was too late to turn back. He'd catch her before she got back past the driveway entrance. Crouching over the handlebars, she down-shifted and pedaled furiously up a grade, the wind whistling in her ears. Her helmet, she realized, was still in the pickup bed.

Killian Laboratories.

It meant something to Charlie. Something serious. She musn't forget. Pumping at the limit of her strength, she gasped the words aloud, grooving them into her memory: *Killian Laboratories. White Plains. August 1987.* The grade slackened and she shifted up to cover more road with each pump of the pedals.

Some distance behind her, a horn blared. Tires squealed; the howl of a souped-up engine drowned the pickup's roar, and the horn blared again, closer.

Traffic, thank God. She fought the urge to pull to the side. Holding to the middle of the lane, she raised one hand from the handlebars, trying to make the gesture look like an SOS.

The car blasted up beside her, horn still blaring. As it came even, she screamed, *"Help!,"* and risked a glance sideways. But there was no help to be had; as the car swept past her, a bearded, ponytailed fellow in the passenger seat gave her the finger, and then it was past and cutting back into the lane, just missing her. The howl diminished as the car raced down the road and vanished around a curve, riding high on oversize wheels, and once more she could hear the pickup, its roar growing.

The bike was a mistake. She'd jumped on reflexively, responding only to the need to put distance between herself and Charlie, between herself and whatever it was he'd been reaching for in the truck bed. What she should have done was scramble into the forest that grew right up to the edge of the driveway. Among the trees, they'd be on even terms at worst; at best, smaller and lighter, she might even have an advantage. Here on the road, she had only the bike's gear ratio and her own legs, while Charlie had whatever horsepower was built into that big blue truck.

A concrete-lined drainage ditch separated her from the line of trees on the right; on the left, a rail guarded a steep dropoff.

She'd have to take her chances. She gritted her teeth, braked, and swung to the right.

She did it too fast. The bike slewed onto the shoulder and hit

loose gravel and she went over in a tangle of handlebars and spokes. Her right side scraped down the concrete and she saw the bottom of the ditch coming up at her—

coming up at her—

coming up at her—

coming up at her—

TWENTY-FIVE

Truck

ONE—TWO—THREE—

Her head hurt. God, how her head hurt. Her futon had never felt so hard, and it was behaving weirdly, jolting up and down, each jar sending a fresh spike of pain through her head. Where the blazes was her pillow?

—*four—five—*

God, how her head hurt, and somebody kept counting and she couldn't figure out how to make them stop. Her eyes were shut. Opening them took a conscious effort.

She saw blobs. Dark green blobs. She had opened her eyes and dark green blobs were moving across her field of vision. She was lying on her back and the dark green blobs were high above her. And she wasn't in bed. She was lying on something hard that was jolting.

A memory of panic fluttered in her chest. She'd been afraid of hitting her head. She must have hit it, because it was hurting and she was dazed.

Wasn't it odd to be in a daze but know you were in a daze?

No, drop that; no time for philosophy, something was wrong and she had to pull herself out of this damn daze. Take charge—

—*six—seven—*

Stop it. For God's sake, stop that damn counting.

Trees. Those green blobs she was looking up at were treetops, and if she got her head off this hard, jolting surface, it wouldn't

hurt as much. She started to roll to her right, but a new pain, harsher than the throbbing in her head, arrested her. Her right elbow was scraped raw; contact with the hard surface under her was agony. She rolled to her left and raised up on her elbow. The pain in her head swelled like a balloon, but she held the position and the pain shrank until it settled in a spot somewhere above and behind her right ear.

She was lying in the truck bed of a pickup, next to the side panel, jolting along what must be an extraordinarily rough road, through a forest. She had been riding a bike. Concrete had come up at her. A ditch—the concrete bottom of a ditch. She had run off the road into a concrete ditch. That's how she had hit her head and scraped her elbow.

She twisted to bring her scraped right arm around in front of her face. The movement brought a twinge from her wrist and she remembered that a while ago she had sprained it and it wasn't yet completely healed. She must have hurt it again in the fall. The elbow was scraped from midforearm up, bloody, the lower part only oozing droplets, but the elbow was scraped deeply enough to drip slowly onto her shirt. Pain where her jeans touched her right leg told her she had another scrape there.

Scrapes and sprains heal. The pain in her head frightened her. She had been riding without a helmet. That was stupid, and not like her.

She twisted to look back over her shoulder. The bike was in the pickup with her. It was a wreck, the handlebars twisted and the front wheel bent like a Dali watch. The helmet was rocking back and forth in the corner beyond it.

Thunder rumbled beyond the treetops.

Killian Laboratories, said her own voice inside her head, and a dam broke and memory flooded back.

She'd found the Killian Laboratories envelope hidden under Greg's sweaters. She'd dropped it on the Willards' driveway—

The flood crested, foamed into terror. Charlie Emmett. She

was in Charlie's big blue truck. She'd been trying to get her key chain out of her butt pack—

She felt for the butt pack with her free right hand and found it still buckled around her waist; it had worked around to rest on her right hip.

The Killian Laboratories envelope had caught on the key chain and fallen on the driveway, and Charlie had picked it up and looked at it, and his face had changed. He'd shoved her off balance with the bike and reached into the truck bed for something to hit her with—

Now, wait a minute, said a motherly voice from a sanctuary somewhere inside her head but outside her terror. *Wait. Calm down.* Her helmet had still been in the truck bed; he could have been reaching for the helmet.

No. She'd seen what Charlie had been reaching for and it wasn't the helmet. It was something straight and metal, a couple of feet long—not quite a jack handle or a wrench, but something like that. She'd run away on the bike and he'd followed in his truck to run her down on the road—

Wait. Wait. Slow down. He hadn't run her down. She'd crashed under her own steam.

Then why was she in his truck, jolting along this terrible road?

Slow down, slow down. Couldn't he have picked her up to drive her to the nearest doctor?

No. If he'd been trying to help, he wouldn't have dumped her into the hard truck bed, where every bump banged her injured head.

Wait, wait, wait. He might have thought it was better to let her lie down in the truck bed than to jam her upright into the passenger seat.

No. No, no, no. She had seen his face, and she had seen what he was reaching for, and the way to a doctor was on paved roads, not a rough track through deep forest—

The Ferguson track?

What was he bringing her in here for?

Telephone? Call for an ambulance?

But the motherly voice had lost its assurance, and she ordered it to stop maundering. Nobody would drive in a back track to an uninhabited house for a telephone. He'd expect the phone to be disconnected. It was disconnected. If he'd been looking for help, he'd head for somewhere closer and more certain.

Thunder rumbled again.

Above her, the treetops slid away. Beyond them, the sky was mottled, the color of pewter. The jolting smoothed. She raised herself high enough to see over the side panel, and yes, it was the Ferguson place. They were rolling along the drive beside the back lawn. It ended at the back of the house. Then what?

Panic reminded her of the rearview mirror; instinct warned her not to let Charlie know she was conscious. She eased herself back down on her back, cushioning her head with her left arm.

…one…two…three…

Stop it. Whoever's doing that damn counting, just stop it.

The drive ended, but the truck didn't stop. It lurched and swung to the left and she heard the motor change pitch as the gears shifted down. White clapboards and dark windows jolted past on the right. Charlie had turned off the gravel and was driving across the side lawn, around the house, to the front—

Terror hit her like a fist in the stomach. The front, where the driveway snaked down the curves to the ravine.

The comforting motherly voice was silent.

The truck lurched up onto the front driveway and the motion smoothed to a sway as it rounded the curves.

She had to get out. She must get into the woods, where the truck couldn't go. She must jump.

She inched closer to the side and reached for the top of the side panel.

The truck stopped. She dropped back to the floor, her heart hammering. She heard the driver's-side door open.

She needed a weapon. A toolbox was bolted to the back of

the cab, but it was padlocked. Whatever it was that Charlie had been reaching for was nowhere in sight.

Over the idling engine, she heard his footsteps on the dirt, not coming back to the truck bed but—good!—walking forward, away from the truck and toward the bridge.

Now, while the truck was between them.

She closed her fingers over the top of the side panel, but before her sluggish muscles could haul her upright, she heard Charlie's steps crossing in front of the truck, crossing to her side. She dropped back down to the truck bed. If she tried to climb over now, he'd hear her and look back and see her, and even if she could land squarely, which she couldn't count on, she wouldn't have more than a ten-foot start. Her body wasn't responding normally; she was far from sure that she'd be able to outrun him.

Her mind strained but failed to make sense of scufflings and scrapings in front of the truck. After a little time she heard his footsteps returning. He had crossed back to the driver's side. But he didn't get into the cab; he walked on back to the truck bed. She kept her head turned away, praying that he wouldn't notice the tension in her muscles, grateful for the tangle of bike between them.

He paused for a moment; then he made a satisfied sort of noise in his throat and crunched on to the front. The truck rocked as he climbed in and slammed the door.

Okay, now, this wasn't too bad. The truck was heading down the driveway and Charlie was inside the cab. If she jumped over the side as soon as it started to move, she could be into the woods before he could stop and get out. In the woods, the odds would be shortened. She got up to her knees and grasped the side panel, ready to swing herself over. But instead of moving forward, the truck reversed and cut to one side, shifted and jerked forward once more—

Oh, shit, he was making a K-turn. If she jumped now, she'd risk falling under the wheels, and if she avoided that danger, she'd risk Charlie's seeing her as the cab passed her.

He completed the turn, and now the truck was facing back up the drive, not toward the ravine, but up toward the curves and the house.

Okay, as soon as it started moving forward up the drive, she'd jump out and get into the woods down here. Not as good, but still better than waiting for whatever Charlie had in mind.

But the truck didn't move forward; it backed, down toward the edge of the ravine. Down toward the broken bridge.

It was then that she realized what Charlie had been doing while he was out of the truck. He'd taken down the warning tape, and now he was backing the last few yards to where the stub of bridge extended out over the ravine.

Cliffs. She was supposed to fall off another cliff. For a stomach-wrenching instant, she envisioned the truck bed canting up and dumping her over the edge.

Reason returned. It wasn't a dump truck, so unless Charlie planned to back off the end of the broken bridge—that wouldn't make any sense, but nothing made any sense and her heart was hammering out of control—unless he was going to back the truck itself over the edge, he was going to have to stop and get out and come around to the back and let down the tailgate and reach for her.

A weapon—

Oh, for Pete's sake. Of course.

Hoping the motion of the truck would mask her movements, she rolled onto her stomach, biting back a cry as her scraped elbow hit the bottom of the truck bed. She hitched the butt pack around to her butt and inched behind the bicycle on her stomach. Her left hand found a grip on the twisted handlebar while her right hand grasped the edge of the seat. She wasn't sure how much force her sprained wrist would be able to exert, but with her feet braced against the toolbox, she'd be able to use leg strength. She drew her knees up under her and braced her feet.

The truck stopped short of the bridge and relief washed her.

Thunder rumbled, closer than before.

Up front, the driver's door opened. The truck rocked as Charlie climbed down.

She shouldn't let him know she was conscious. She released her grip on the bike, closed her eyes, and tried to go limp. A lot of the light had gone; she doubted if he'd be able to see much.

She heard his footsteps and then his breathing as he looked over the side panel. "Cargo shifted a little, huh?" he muttered. His footsteps moved to the tailgate. Bolts rattled. The truck bed jarred as the tailgate came down, rocked as Charlie's weight leaned in.

She opened her eyes, braced her feet, eased to her knees, and tightened her grasp on the bike.

"Okay, out you come, girlie," he said. "It's time to dissolve this goddamn partnership."

The bike shifted in her grip as he started to move it out of the way. Uncoiling all the force of her braced legs, she lunged, shoving the bike in front of her. The impact rode up the tangled metal to her arms. Charlie yelled and stumbled backward. She kept her grip, got her feet under her, and shoved the bike ahead of her all the way to the tailgate. One final shove, and then her balance tilted and she let go and managed to convert her fall into a twisting jump. She hit the ground on her feet, barely missing the tangle of man and bike. The landing jarred her head, and dizziness nearly pitched her off balance, but some instinct of equilibrium kept her on her feet and then she was running, past the truck and up the driveway, away from the broken bridge, running up and away from that godawful drop into the ravine.

On her feet, she felt how much her injuries had sapped her. Her legs felt as sluggish as if she were running underwater and each footfall sent a thump of pain through her head. But the curses and clatters behind her heartened her. She was more than halfway to the first curve; if the bike tangled Charlie up long enough, she might get out of sight before he came after her.

She heard the truck door slam. She ran. The motor roared. She ran. Headlights raked the trees beside the drive, but she was nearly around the first curve and the lights, slanting away to the right, didn't pick her up. She plunged off the drive to the left and nearly ran into the stone wall.

You could break an ankle climbing over a dry-stone wall. Paul had shown her a safer way. She spread-eagled herself on top of the stones and wormed around until she could edge off onto the ground on the other side, barely aware of pain as the stone rasped her scrapes. Just as she slid off, the headlights lit the trees above her. She lay flat behind the wall and heard the truck pass.

Her body wanted to stay where it was, full-length on the ground, sheltered behind the wall. But she was too close to the driveway, and even if Charlie hadn't seen her going over the wall, surely he'd be back when he didn't find her up ahead. She had to move, get away from the wall and in among the trees, where now it was nearly dark.

She pushed herself to her knees, staggered to her feet. She could see the forms of the trees, but darkness hid what lay underfoot. She should travel diagonally up the grade, bisecting the angle between the driveway and the ravine; that way, she could skirt the house and yard and then move out through woods, keeping her route parallel to Henley Lane when she got to it, on out to Oak Hollow Road, keeping to the woods until she reached people. Reliable people.

If her rubbery muscles would carry her that far.

Don't think about that. Think about the next step—*one*—and the next—*two*—

She heard the truck stop. It ground into reverse, and through the trees she saw the headlights move backward down the driveway. But she was too deep in the trees for the beam to pick her up, and she kept moving, her feet swishing on the leaves *one…two…three…*

The truck stopped just about where she'd gone over the wall.

Maybe he'd seen movement when she went over. The motor died; the headlights went off; the door opened.

If she could hear all that, Charlie could hear her footsteps stirring the leaves. But she had a head start and she doubted if he could move through the woods in the increasing dark any faster than she could. Her eyes had accustomed themselves to the dimness and now she could make out the unevenness in the ground, the occasional tangled strand of greenbrier, the long, low shapes of fallen trees.

Above the treetops, lightning gleamed for a moment. Behind her, stones rattled. Charlie, climbing over the wall. She kept going. Off to her left, light flickered low down, on tree trunks. She glanced back and saw the bright disk of a flashlight. She stepped sideways to put trees between her and the light and kept moving. . Thunder thrummed. When it died, she heard Charlie's footsteps rustling the leaves, still well behind her. A brighter gleam lit the sky, and another just after it. The storm was on its way.

In front of her, the forest thinned; she was coming to a clearing. When she reached it, she saw that it wasn't a glade in the woods; it was a lawn, and beyond it was the house. In dodging the flashlight, she had moved too far to her right and had failed to skirt the house. On the lawn, the darkness was less deep, and just in front of her was another tumbling stone wall that marked the boundary between forest and lawn. Beyond the house, clouds loomed against deep purple sky. Lightning lit them from within; thunder played an extended drumroll.

If she weren't hurt, she'd go over the wall, onto the lawn, and run; with good footing and a halfway level surface, she didn't doubt her ability to outrun Charlie Emmett. But not with her head hurting and her muscles feeling as flaccid as wet string.

BOOM, BOOM, BOO-OOOM.

She looked back. The flashlight was perhaps a hundred yards behind her. It disappeared for a second behind a tree, reappeared, swaying back and forth.

He didn't know where she was.

Lightning, this time a streak against the clouds. She went down on hands and knees, lowering her silhouette to blend with the wall.

CRACK BOOM-BOOM-BOOM-rumble rumble.

She groped along the base of the wall, closed her fingers over a fist-size stone; found another.

FLASH. A gust swished the branches over her head. *CRACK-BOOMBOOMBOOM*.

She rose to her knees and flung the stone along the line of the wall. Somewhere beyond her vision it clattered on stone. She threw the second stone after the first and dropped to hands and knees as it clattered. Back in the woods, the flashlight beam turned toward the sound. The wind gusted again, the swish of the heavy summer leaves not quite covering the rustle of Charlie's hurried stride.

FLASH. FLASH-FLASH-FLASH. *BOOM-BOOM-BOO-OO-OOM*.

Still on hands and knees, she crept back along the base of the wall, toward the driveway. When she glanced back again, she could no longer see the flashlight's disk, only the beam striking the trees as Charlie moved away from her, looking for the place the hurled stones had fallen, the place he thought she'd gone over the wall and onto the lawn. Now she was closer to the driveway than he was.

And now the storm was nearly upon them, and thunder and wind drowned all lesser sounds. The lightning was nearly continuous, lighting her way as she clambered to her feet, no longer afraid of the noise she was making. She headed back toward the driveway. The first raindrops spattered just as she reached the stone wall. She scrambled across, got to her feet, and sprinted downhill, around the curves, to where Charlie had left the pickup.

The driver's-side door hung open, just as he'd left it in his

haste. She ran, reached the cab, scrambled in; she slammed the door, fumbled for the door locks, and locked herself in. As she had prayed, Charlie in his hurry had left the keys dangling from the ignition. Perched sideways, she slid the butt pack around to her stomach.

She found the seat release and hitched it forward until her feet reached the pedals; she turned the key and rejoiced as the motor roared. It was too dark to drive without lights so she turned them on, shifted into Drive, and eased her foot down.

The storm hit as the truck began to move. She found the wiper switch, and as the rain slashed the windshield and drummed on the cab roof, she drove up the driveway to the house. At the top, she steered off the drive and plowed across the side lawn to the back, heading out as Charlie had come in, accelerated on the gravel of the back drive, and plunged into the woods, her heart pounding with panic and exhilaration.

It wasn't until she was halfway out the track that the rush died away. The back-and-forth sweep of the windshield wipers set up a rhythmic throb—*one—two—three—four*—and the track in front of her kept blurring out of focus. Keeping her grip on the steering wheel as the truck lurched in and out of the water-filled ruts took all her strength.

One step at a time. She wasn't walking. One second at a time, then—

—five—six—

Twin beams of light swept the sheets of rain from a source around a bend. Her heart banged and a new adrenaline surge cleared her vision. The lights crept into view; dazzled, she just made out the dark form of the car behind them. There wasn't room to pass. She cut right and braked and the other car stopped, facing the truck. Janet switched off her headlights, leaving the parking lights on, rolled down her window, and leaned into the downpour. "Hey!" she shouted. "Can you help me?"

The other car's headlights went off. The driver's-side door

opened and a figure leaned out into the rain, craning to see over the top of the door. "Janet?" shouted Kristin Vanstaat's voice. "What are you doing in Charlie's truck?"

TWENTY-SIX

TLC

SHE DIDN'T WASTE TIME answering Kristin; she switched off the lights and the motor and, leaving the key dangling, clambered down from the cab and scurried through the rain to the car. Kristin leaned across and popped the lock; Janet slid into the passenger seat, relocked the door, and said, "Get us out of here."

It wasn't until Kristin had got the car turned around and bucking back along the track that she said, "What's going on? You look awful."

Janet folded her arms across her midriff in an effort to stop shaking. The whole story, just then, was just too much. "I had a bicycle accident," she said. "What are you doing here?"

"I got worried about you. Where's Charlie? How come you were driving the truck?"

"What got you worried?"

Kristin slanted a glance at her. "Well, after I talked to you, I went home to work on my parents thing, and a while after that Josh comes in, and he goes, 'Boy, Charlie Emmett is sure interested in that old hiding place.'"

Janet drew in a breath.

"What?"

"Later. I promise."

"You'd better. Anyway, so I go, 'What do you mean?' and Josh says Charlie—Mr. Emmett—"

"Call him Charlie, it's fine with me."

"Right, okay, so Charlie comes back from picking up Mrs. Emmett at the airport and the guys are still talking, like what music to play at the service, and would people have a fit if there was a band, and like that, and Charlie starts asking them about the secret place, where it is and how you find it. So they tell him. What I told them, you know, but by that time they remembered. So Josh says Charlie listens to all that, and then all of a sudden he goes out and takes off in his truck, and Josh thinks that's weird because Mrs. Emmett just got home from being gone for a week. I said to him that I don't think it's so weird, they fight a lot, and Josh says well, yes, like just today she went out for groceries when she got back and she locked the keys in the car and Charlie had to go down in the truck to get the car open and they were fighting about that. But anyway, Josh figured maybe he came out here to look for it, and he was wondering why Charlie was so interested, and I'm thinking, Greg wanted to show you something and maybe Charlie knows something about it and he's looking for it too. And I got worried. Because, you know, weird is weird. So, what happened?"

Killian Laboratories? No. Not until she knew more. "He came out here and—he was acting weird."

"Did he, like, do anything to you? You look really banged up."

"That's from the bike accident. You and Josh guessed right. He was looking in the wall where you said. Your sketch was accurate, by the way."

"Yeah, well, I knew that. Did he find anything?"

"No. I'd already looked and there wasn't anything in it but acorn shells."

"So where is he now? How come you were driving the truck?"

"He was acting so weird, I got scared. I tried to get away on the bike but I fell off, so I hijacked the truck. Kris, do your parents know what you're doing?"

"My *parents* are in Poughkeepsie cleaning up that dumb little house so we can move in."

"How did you get hold of a car?"

"It's Josh's. I told him I'd go for pizza and he gave me the keys."

"And you rode off to the rescue? Kris—" Tears pushed at Janet's eyelids. "Kris, that was crazy."

"No, listen, I locked the doors." They had reached Oak Hollow Road. Rain was bouncing off the blacktop. Kristin braked at the stop sign and looked at Janet again. "So, you know, I think you should go to a doctor. You really don't look too good."

Janet didn't know any doctors in Phillips Landing. Marion and Paul would, but they weren't home. Who—"Do you know Leora Lamont?"

"Oh, sure. I babysit the girls sometimes."

"She's my cousin. Take me there, and then go pick up your pizza. Your brother's going to wonder what happened to you."

"No, he won't. He'll think I'm cruising for the fun of driving his car."

LOWELL TOOK ONE LOOK at Janet in the glow of the porch light, said, "Holy shit," and let her in. Her battered condition activated the practiced mother; while Lowell worked the phone, Leora sat Janet down in the bathroom, gently sponged the blood from her scrapes, and sprayed them with something that stung for a few seconds and then soothed.

The Lamonts' doctor—a pediatrician—was unavailable. The answering service offered a pediatric referral twenty miles north. Lowell said, "That's crazy," and said he'd drive her twelve miles south to an emergency room.

He was stone cold sober. Janet said, "Thanks."

Leora tried to lend her a pair of jeans, but they were so baggy on Janet's angular frame that she decided to stick with her own, pointing out that blood and torn clothing were entirely appropriate for a visit to an emergency room. She did, however, accept the loan of a shirt.

IT TOOK A WHILE; an accident on the wet roads had filled three ambulances. But a rumple-haired resident finally got around to her. He shone lights in her eyes and asked who she was and where she was and where she lived and what day and month and year it was and who the president of the United States was. She had no problem answering, but he finally declared that, just to be on the safe side, she should be admitted for observation.

All night, people kept waking her from confused and unpleasant dreams, shining lights in her eyes, and asking ridiculous questions that she thought prudent to answer straightforwardly. The sixth time they woke her, daylight was graying the window across the room, and she knew she was awake for good. After her interrogator left, she sat up and swung her legs over the side of the bed. She took her butt pack from the drawer of the nightstand and, holding the knee-length, tied-in-the-back hospital gown around her, tiptoed past her snoring roommate and retrieved her clothes from the closet where an aide had stored them. She took them into the bathroom, scrubbed her teeth with one finger, and combed her hair with all ten. The lump above her right ear was sore to the touch, but her head had stopped aching. She dressed in yesterday's underwear, her torn jeans, and the borrowed blouse; she strapped on her watch, buckled on the butt pack, and looked in a full-length mirror on the back of the door.

She looked like someone who'd fallen into a concrete ditch. The scrapes on her forehead and elbow had scabbed over, and now a bruise had developed, spreading down across her temple, discoloring the skin around her right eye in a first-class shiner.

She decided she looked worse than she felt.

SHE HAD DISCOVERED that her keys were missing when she fished her wallet from her butt pack to dig out her medical insurance card. She must have dropped them during the scuffle on

the Willards' driveway. Charlie might have picked them up. Charlie Emmett might have the key to her apartment.

She scouted the corridors until she located a pay phone next to the elevators. Her watch told her it was six-fifteen, so she found a room fitted up as a lounge and skimmed back issues of *Reader's Digest* until the breakfast cart rattled along the corridor. She went back to her room and sat in the chair beside her bed to eat tepid Cream of Wheat, hear more than she cared to about her roommate's appendectomy, and give half-true answers to half-interested questions about her accident. At a few minutes past nine, a nurse and a resident on rounds looked at her chart, asked a few questions, mumbled together, and finally agreed that she could be discharged as soon as transport got up to the floor with a wheelchair. She said she could walk perfectly well; they shook their heads. Liability and lawsuits, she realized. She signed papers, and when they left she went back out to the phone, rummaged in her wallet for Eric Swanson's business card, slotted in a quarter, punched in the number, and asked to speak to Mr. Swanson.

Hold please. Elevator music. Eric's voice: "Janet, how are you?"

She said, "Alive, which is more unusual than you might think. I'm calling because I want to retain you as my attorney. It's a long story and I'm on a pay phone."

No hesitation. "Read me the number and hang up. I'll call you back."

In less than thirty seconds, the phone rang, she picked up, and Eric said, "What's the story?"

"The closing. It's this afternoon and I want to be there, but I don't want to go alone. Weird things have been happening. If you're free, and if you'll let me pay in installments, I want to retain you to represent me."

"Where and what time?"

"Three-thirty at Finlay Keene's office in Phillips Landing. I know it's short notice—"

"Actually, today's pretty good. Tell me about the weird things."

Turning her back on the corridor behind her and trying to keep her voice both quiet and distinct, she began with Greg's having something to show her, continued with Donald Ferguson's loan of the key, went on to finding the Killian Laboratories envelope under Greg's sweaters.

"I know Killian," Eric said. "Big outfit, reliable. Sorry, go on." She went on.

When she finished, he said, "When you say weird, you mean weird. Have you told any of this to the police?"

"Nobody but you, just now. I told people I had a bike accident."

"Which you did. How're you feeling?"

"Passable. Only—Eric, I'm scared."

"I can understand that. Where are you now?"

"The hospital." Out of the corner of her eye, she saw someone pushing a wheelchair down the corridor. "I think they're about to let me out."

"Do you have transportation?"

"I was going to call a cab."

"I don't think you should go back to Phillips Landing at the moment," he said. "If it's okay with you, I'll send somebody to bring you down to my office, and then I'll drive you up in time for the closing."

It was supremely okay with her. "Can we stop at my apartment and let me get into some decent clothes?"

"We will. Hold on a minute, would you?" Elevator music. "Janet? Laura Whitson is going to pick you up. She should be there in forty or forty-five minutes if the traffic's okay. Long-haired blonde in a yellow hatchback. She'll have a note from me on letterhead."

"Fine," she said. "Meanwhile, is there any way you can find out what was in that Killian Laboratories envelope?"

He was quiet for a moment, then, "Possibly. I can call some-

body I know at Killian and see what he can tell me. Are you instructing me to do that?"

"Yes, I am, and if that doesn't work, I'm instructing you to do anything else you can think of to find out why Charlie turned into a homicidal maniac. If you want me to, I'll sign it in blood when I get there."

"Ink's fine. Okay, I'll see what I can do. And—Janet? Don't wander around while you're waiting for Laura. Stay close to people. Security-type people if possible."

TWENTY-SEVEN

Potatoes

WHEN THE LONG-HAIRED blonde—a summer intern who spent much of the drive talking about how good Eric was to work for—ushered Janet into his office, Eric was muttering a series of mm-hms into the telephone and scribbling on a legal pad. He waved at a chair; Janet sat in it; the blonde said, "Nice to have met you," and left.

After a few more mm-hms, Eric said, "Very interesting. Would you fax it to me, please? Many thanks." He hung up. "My God, you did take a beating," he said. "How are you feeling?"

"Not as bad as I look."

"Concussion under control?"

"It must be. They let me out."

He intertwined his fingers and stretched his arms above his head, lowered them and rested his hands on the yellow pad. He wasn't wearing the wedding band. "I was just talking with somebody I know at Killian," he said. "He read me a copy of a well-test report they did for Alta Ferguson in nineteen eighty-seven."

He paused, waiting for her to ask. She asked. "Lead?"

"Aldicarb."

"What's aldicarb?"

"An organic pesticide."

"That sounds bad."

"You have a good ear. It's effective in controlling"—he looked at his yellow pad—"colorado potato beetle and golden nematode.

It was heavily used on Long Island potato farms in the seventies, until they found out it was contaminating the groundwater." He turned over a sheet on the pad. "In June of nineteen eighty-seven, Alta Ferguson ordered a test of a water sample from a well on a property that we can identify as the land Broderick Hale owned in partnership with Charlie Emmett. She asked them to test for organics. She actually named aldicarb. They looked for it and they found it. Thirty-eight ppb."

"Ppb?"

"Parts per billion."

"Per *billion?*"

"Doesn't sound like much, does it? The EPA's acceptable level is ten and New York State's is seven."

She'd known there had to be bad news in that envelope. *Thirty-eight,* and the acceptable level is seven; seven into thirty-eight—"Five times as much as there should be. More than five."

He read from the legal pad again. "High mammalian toxicity. Clinical signs in humans are gastrointestinal disturbances, unconsciousness, blurred vision, excessive salivation, seizures, disorientation, and possibly death."

"They use it on *food?*"

"On the plants, not the tubers. At recommended levels, it's safe for produce."

"Who says?"

"Well, I eat potatoes without having seizures. The real problem is that it accumulates in the groundwater. Suffolk County wells had serious trouble in the late seventies."

"Potatoes," she said.

"And vineyards upstate."

She shook her head. "Thaddeus grew potatoes."

"Who's Thaddeus?"

"The last of the Bradfords. He farmed that land. Schuyler Vanstaat told me he grew potatoes."

"You don't say. How long ago?"

"A while. He quit farming in"—she strained her memory—"nineteen seventy-nine?"

"That's about when New York banned aldicarb. Maybe that's why he quit."

"Or maybe because he was eighty."

"Multiple causes. Was Alta thinking of buying that land?"

"Not that I ever heard."

"It's odd that she'd be the one to order the test."

Janet had spent last night's enforced wakefulness constructing hypotheses to fit the craziness. "What if she was looking for something to blackmail Charlie Emmett with?" she said.

Eric's face went still.

"Big Bear," she said.

"I'm with you."

"Charlie knew what was in that envelope."

"I'm with you. We thought she'd bribed him, but blackmail makes more sense."

"Sense? Something makes sense?"

"Well, in context. Charlie stood to make a bundle from the sale. He wouldn't have needed to risk accepting a bribe just to pick up a few more dollars. But if Alta threatened to tell the buyer about the aldicarb, they were likely to lose the sale, and the future prospects wouldn't be all that good either."

"Only—couldn't they just dig another well?"

"Sand-and-gravel aquifer. A lot like Long Island, actually. In sand and gravel, contaminants spread in all directions from the source. If aldicarb showed up in one well, it'd show up in any well drawing on the same groundwater."

"Don Ferguson said they lived on Long Island before they were divorced," said Janet. "If she was a real estate broker back then, she must have known about the well problems."

"If she lived on Long Island, she knew. Could she have known that the last of the Bradfords grew potatoes? I guess it wasn't any secret."

"I'll bet she did. Remember that old school report of Greg's I found in the art center? The yellow pad in the portfolio? That draft didn't say what Thaddeus was growing, but Greg talked to Schuyler Vanstaat when he was writing the report. Schuyler's the one who told me about the potatoes, so what if he mentioned potato farming to Greg and Greg mentioned it to his mother?"

"Not unreasonable." He didn't seem to be dismissing her middle-of-the-night hypothesis out of hand. "How does this play out? Alta applies for a building permit for the house on Big Bear. Charlie Emmett makes a field visit and finds an error in measurement; as drawn, the house would encroach on the setback. The plans could be redrawn and resubmitted, but the Town Board is about to vote on the Steep Slopes law, and if they pass it before she has time to fix the plans, she won't be able to get the building permit."

"Were they going to pass it?"

"I expected them to. Councilman Hale was playing it cute, but he dropped a confidential hint or two. I think he'd have cast a yes vote just to spite Alta. He didn't like her."

"I found something about a boundary lawsuit in his files."

"Common practice between neighbors. Okay, Alta knows Charlie and his partner are about to sell that old farmland. She finds out about the potatoes, possibly from Schuyler Vanstaat via Greg. She knows about Suffolk's trouble with aldicarb, so she makes a midnight raid; she takes a sample from the well and sends it to the lab. To her delight, but not entirely to her surprise, they find aldicarb."

"A lot of aldicarb."

"Correct. Either Thaddeus was using amounts in excess of recommendation or he had a bad spill. She shows the report to Charlie and says she won't tell the buyers if he issues the building permit before the Town Board votes on Steep Slopes. He issues the building permit."

"And Paul and Marion sue."

"And Alta breaks her neck. Fast forward: eight years later Greg comes back to town, digs up the report, and figures out what it means. Do you think that's what he wanted to show you?"

"I thought so when I found it," she said. "At first. But why? He didn't need the money, he'd inherited a bundle from Alta, and I don't have anything to do with building permits."

"Let's assume the best of the kid," he said. "What if he just wanted to save the horses?"

"Then why me? Why not the buyers?"

"We've already had this conversation," he said. "He'd just learned from you that they were going to graze horses on that land, and the buyers weren't there but you were."

"That was my theory, wasn't it? Is it plausible?"

"I didn't know him, you did, and since it occurred to you, you must not have felt it was completely off the wall."

"Oh, you just don't know the kinds of things that occur to me."

"If you say so. What *would* you have done if he had shown that well report to you? Just shown it to you, told you what bad stuff aldicarb was, made no demands?"

"We've already had this conversation too."

"Not quite. The lead was hypothetical."

And the aldicarb wasn't. "You're really asking me what I'm going to do now, aren't you?"

"I guess I am."

Unicorns. She closed her eyes and sighed. "Why didn't those stupid buyers test for that junk in the first place?"

"Cost. Testing for every conceivable contaminant would be prohibitively expensive. You wouldn't think of aldicarb unless you knew about Thaddeus's potato farm."

"Well, why didn't they know about it? If a fourteen-year-old kid could learn about the potato farm, why didn't they?"

"Maybe they did. We don't know how much aldicarb is in the well now. They might already have had it tested and found that it had biodegraded to a harmless level."

"Can that happen?"

"It biodegrades. The rate depends on a bunch of variables—soil chemistry, average temperature, that kind of thing."

"Eight years after Thaddeus stopped farming, there was still five times as much of this junk as there should be. How much difference would another eight years make?"

"That depends on how much there was to start with."

"Charlie didn't think it was harmless. He was ready to kill me—my God, he was going to *kill* me—to keep me from—doing what I'm doing."

"And what are you doing?"

She drew in a breath and blew it out. "Eric, I don't see how I could sleep nights if I let somebody start using that well without knowing its history."

"Are you sure?"

She nodded.

"Half a million dollars."

"Blood money."

"Did Charlie Emmett know you'd feel this way?"

"Of course he did. He attacked me as soon as he saw I had the envelope."

"You're sure he did attack you?"

The question caught her off guard. When she recovered her voice, she said, "Of course I'm sure. For Pete's sake, I just spent the night in the hospital."

"You said you ran the bike off the road under your own steam."

"He was chasing me in the truck." She heard her voice begin to rise and tried to bring it back under control. "He was trying to run me down and I was trying to get away."

"He was behind you in the truck. That he was chasing you is your inference."

She stopped trying to control her anger. "You're damn right that's my inference. I saw his face when he picked up the envel-

ope. He was furious, and right after that, he shoved the bike at me, and he reached in the truck bed for a—a blunt instrument. A metal rod. I saw it. I could draw you a picture of it, for Pete's sake."

"Noted."

"I'm not done. When we got to the Ferguson place, he backed the truck down to the bridge, and he came around to the back and said something like, 'Okay, it's time to end this partnership.' And trust me, he wasn't holding any legal papers for me to sign."

Eric smiled. "And you were never partners in the first place."

"He kept calling me 'pard.'" Her anger began to ebb. "Are you preparing me for cross-examination or something?"

"Testing."

She blew out a breath. "Lawyers."

"Right. Okay, understanding that you aren't obliged to do anything but keep your mouth shut and collect your half million, what do you want to do?"

It was easier than she would have supposed. "I want to tell the buyers about that well report and let them decide whether they want to go through with the deal."

"Sure?"

"Positive."

"It could cost you half a million."

"You think I'm crazy."

"I'm a lawyer, not a shrink."

"I don't think it's crazy to want to be able to live with myself."

For perhaps five seconds—long enough for her once more to become conscious of how battered she appeared—he simply looked at her. Then he said, "Okay, now what I want you to do is go out and take a walk. Eat something. Drink a cup of coffee. When you come back, we'll talk again."

She spent ten minutes walking, twenty minutes sitting at a lunch counter. When she got back, the taste of raisin Danish and coffee lingering on her tongue, the receptionist sent her in. She sat where she had sat before and said, "No change."

He didn't ask her if she was sure. He slid papers across the desk. "Check them out, make sure they say what you mean."

The first paper was a retainer. She, Janet Upton, hereby retained Eric L. Swanson, Attorney at Law, to represent her in matters relating to her inheritance from Broderick Hale…et cetera. The next was an identical copy.

She nodded. He handed a pen across the desk and she signed both.

The second paper and its copy instructed her attorney, Eric L. Swanson, to inform the purchasers of real property, et cetera et cetera, of the existence of a well test report…et cetera.

"Covering my rear end," he said, "in case you develop second thoughts down the road and decide to sue me for letting the aldicarb out of the bag."

She nodded and signed and pushed the papers and the pen back across the desk. He separated out the copies, folded them and slipped them into an envelope, and slid them back to her; then he opened a folder and shuffled papers. She recognized the contract of sale. He checked a phone number at the bottom, picked up his phone, punched in a number, and after the briefest of waits said, "Eric Swanson here. Is George Goldman available? Yes, thanks, I'll hold." He looked across the desk at her and said, "Given the state of Charlie's temper, we'd better be a little devious. Yes, George, good to talk to you…. Not bad, and yourself?…George, I'm calling about a closing you've got on some old farmland today…. No, the land trust doesn't want it. Hale's legatee has retained me to sit in, and the reason I'm calling is that my client has just found out something your client may or may not know, and being afflicted with an inconvenient ethical streak, she wants to make full disclosure. It seems that in nineteen eighty-seven, a well test turned up an unacceptable concentration of a pesticide called aldicarb…. Yes, George, I most certainly do remember Suffolk…. Doug Zenzer at Killian…. Nineteen eighty-seven, right, and their client was named Alta Ferguson….

You're quite welcome. And, George, if you're able, we'd be grateful if you'd keep the source of this tip under wraps. There's likely to be a little tension with the surviving partner.... How should I know where you learned it? Maybe you were interested in agrarian history and asked the county historian what was grown on that land just before it went out of cultivation in nineteen seventy-nine, and he told you potatoes, so, bright and careful counselor that you are, you decided to check.... Schuyler Vanstaat.... You understand, this will be news to us, so we may have to put up some token resistance if you need time to check it out.... No problem, always glad to be of service."

TWENTY-EIGHT

Late

"WHAT HAPPENED TO YOU?" said Helen, addressing Janet while examining Eric.

"Fell off a bike, and it's nice to see you too," said Janet. "Helen Ives, this is Eric Swanson." Rummaging in her bottom desk drawer for the spare key to the inner stairs, she said over her shoulder, "Did Charlie do any work this morning?"

"Didn't show," said Helen. "He should take on some help."

"Can we talk?" She exchanged a glance with Eric.

UPSTAIRS IN HER stifling apartment, her answering machine was blinking. She punched Play and turned up the volume, leaving the bathroom door open while she pulled off her torn jeans and Leora's shirt and the underwear she'd put on some thirty hours before. "Janet, love," said Marion's voice—oh, *God,* Marion's bike! What was she doing, throwing away half a million dollars?—"we found your keys on the drive. They're safe and sound. Are you? Give us a call." *Beep; click.* She stuffed the clothes into the hamper and reached behind the shower curtain to turn on the water. *Beep.* "Ms. Upton" an unfamiliar female voice—"I'm calling from the law firm of Kinsey and Wells in Denver. Mr. Howard Wells would like you to return his call, collect." A number with a 303 area code. "Thank you."

Denver?

She showered under tepid water at low pressure and patted

the scabbed-over scrapes dry with gingerly care. Finlay Keene's violent air-conditioning would permit a long-sleeved blouse; a below-the-calf skirt would conceal the leg. She checked the mirror, wet her hairbrush, and did what she could about her forehead, but only one of those 1940s draped pageboys would hide that shiner.

Tough. She pulled her wallet out of her butt pack, stuffed it into her shoulder bag, and went back down.

The parking lot was blistering. Eric retrieved a jacket and tie from the backseat of his van, slid the tie under his unbuttoned shirt collar but left it untied, and slung the jacket over his shoulder, holding it with one finger. Trudging down the steep slope of Oak Ridge Lane to Main Street, she said, "I'm nervous."

"Understandable."

"What's Charlie doing?"

"Expecting to collect half a million."

"Oh, God."

"Second thoughts?"

"Too late for that." She wasn't sorry. "Just nervous."

"Let me do the talking unless I give you the nod." In front of Finlay Keene's office, he stopped, buttoned his collar, tied his tie, and put on his jacket.

It was cold inside. They were almost fifteen minutes late; the conference room was well populated, but a rapid glance established that Charlie Emmett wasn't yet part of the population. Finlay Keene presided at the head of the carved-oak table; Janet answered his startled look with, "Fell off a bike."

A woman who was ten years older than her makeup faced Keene from the opposite end of the table. Ranged along one side, half rising as Janet entered, were three middle-aged men in suits; one fit, one fat, and one in between. Three chairs along the opposite side were empty. A flurry of handshaking established that the fat man was George Goldman, the buyer's lawyer; the fit man was from the bank, and the in-between man was the buyer. The

woman was the real estate broker. Keene and the broker were looking sour.

Eric pulled out the chair nearest to Keene's end of the table and held it for Janet, then took the one next to it. "Sorry," he said. "Traffic." With unhurried ease, he laid his briefcase on the table, unsnapped the clasps, took out a folder, snapped the case shut, and stood it on the floor beside his chair. It was a few seconds before she realized how smoothly he had shielded her from the position that Charlie would occupy.

By golly, she thought, *I have got myself a lawyer.*

"I got your fax," said Keene. "No problem with conflict of interest?"

"The land trust has no interest in this transaction," said Eric. "I'll get you an affidavit if you like. Where's your client?"

"On his way, I assume," said Keene. "I wish he'd get here. We've got a little problem."

"Oh?"

"Our buyer wants more time."

Eric looked across the table. "What's the problem?"

George-the-lawyer said, "We've just learned something about the condition of the property that might make it unusable for our purposes. We need time to check it out."

"What about the condition of the property?"

"There might be a problem with contamination of the water supply."

"Surely you tested."

"For coliform," said the man from the bank. "This is something else."

"Isn't it a little late for second thoughts?"

"I only found out this morning," said George-the-lawyer. "I was talking to the county historian, and he let it slip that the land was a potato farm for a good many years. Maybe you remember that mess in Suffolk County in the seventies?"

"Some kind of pesticide, wasn't it?" said Eric. "Got into the groundwater?"

"Stuff called aldicarb. Highly toxic. We can't use the property if we can't use the water."

"That's pretty speculative," said Finlay Keene. "Just because the old man grew a few potatoes for a couple of years."

George-the-lawyer shrugged. "So we check it out. No contamination, no problem."

Finlay Keene said, "Assuming we were to agree to a delay, which we haven't yet, how much time would we be talking about?"

"Three months," said the buyer.

"Too long. It isn't in your interests anyway. If you wait until November, you're going to have a hard time getting your machines in before spring. I can't commit Emmett, but maybe he could live with a month."

The buyer shook his head. "We may need some test wells."

"Two months," said George-the-lawyer. "We'll nudge the lab." He looked at Eric. "Just to check it out. It may turn out to be nothing."

Eric looked at Janet. She shrugged and said nothing.

Keene looked at his watch, got up, and opened the door to the outer office. "Marge," he said, "would you call Mr. Emmett's house and find out what's holding him up?" Still looking sour, he closed the door and returned to his chair. A few minutes of small talk about unusual real estate transactions followed; then the door opened and all heads swiveled.

"Nobody's at home," said the secretary, "but I got Mrs. Emmett at work. She doesn't know if he remembered."

"Mm," said Finlay Keene. "Thanks, Marge."

"Can't close without him, anyway," said George-the-lawyer.

"Give it another fifteen minutes," said Keene.

More small talk; the peccadillos of local judges this time. Marge tried the phone again; no answer at the Emmett house. Fi-

nally George-the-lawyer said, "This is long enough. Silence gives assent." He looked at his wrist. "This is the fourteenth of August. We'll get back to you by October fourteenth."

"Or before," said Eric.

George nodded. "Or before."

Keene, sour faced, nodded.

"HE WOULDN'T FORGET," said Janet.

"It doesn't seem likely." They were clear of Finlay Keene's office; once more Eric's coat was slung over his shoulder and his collar and tie were undone.

"I don't know what I should do."

For a few steps, Eric was silent.

She said, "Whether I should talk to the police."

Eric said, "Did you notice something? Keene's secretary didn't say his wife had actually seen him."

Janet hadn't noticed. "You think maybe he never came back last night?"

"You have to wonder where he is."

He wouldn't forget; he might be on his way at that very moment. Janet looked up the street, a qualm tightening her stomach. "I don't know what I should do."

Another silence, shorter; then, "How about driving out and seeing if his truck is still there?"

"Out to the Ferguson house?" Fear battled with curiosity. "Why?"

"To see—" He broke off and looked at her. "I don't doubt anything you've said, but concussion can affect memory. Before you talk to anybody, I'd feel better if we checked out the lay of the land to see if it tallies with what you remember."

"Oh," she said.

"Okay?"

"*We*," she said.

"That's if you want me in the picture."

She jammed her fists into her skirt pockets. "Oh, yes. Yes, I most certainly want you in the picture."

EVERYTHING LOOKED DIFFERENT with the sun shining. Janet hung her head out the van window searching for tire tracks, but the rain had washed out whatever traces there might have been. They drove all the way to the house without seeing the truck.

The ground beside the house was plowed up where first Charlie and then Janet had driven across the lawn. Eric studied the tracks out the window; then he put the van in gear and drove slowly across the lawn to the front, keeping well to one side of the earlier tracks. The heat of the day had dried the ground; only mashed-down grass marked their passage.

They followed the driveway all the way down to where the crumpled warning tape lay in a heap. A little way beyond, the wrecked bicycle lay in the middle of the drive.

"Mm-hm," said Eric.

"It checks out."

"Very nicely." He set the hand brake and climbed down.

Residual fear bound her to her seat; through the windshield she watched him pass the tape and the bicycle and stop just short of the broken stub of bridge that extended out over the drop.

Something in the set of his shoulders stirred her into motion. She opened the door and climbed down. He glanced back and held up his hand in a stop gesture, but she didn't stop, and he dropped his hand and waited for her. Arriving at his side, she had to make an effort to look down.

Charlie Emmett's big blue pickup was lodged halfway down, at the top of the scree slope. The driver's-side door hung open, and down at the very bottom, just across the stream from Gregory Ferguson's toy-size red van, something that looked like a discarded rag doll lay sprawled among the stones.

Flecks of light spun behind her closed lids; white noise roared in her ears. She barely felt Eric's hand on her arm, drawing her

back. But eventually things stopped spinning; she raised her face from his chest—how had that happened?—and opened her eyes and said, "Now I talk to the sheriff."

"There's a phone in the van," he said.

TWENTY-NINE

Déjà Vu

SIRENS AGAIN, DISTANT and faint—firehouse, sheriff's patrol, ambulance. "Déjà vu all over again," said Janet.

They were waiting on the patio, Janet perched on the step down to the back lawn, Eric pacing. He was pale under his tan. Déjà vu all over again; he'd seen Uncle Bud up close; he'd be imagining what Charlie might look like. "Are you okay?" he said.

"I'm fine," she said. The plate glass was in place again. "Are you?"

Half a smile. "I think so."

She wasn't so sure. She should find a neutral subject. But none came to mind and she gave up. "Why did he do it?"

He came over and sat on the step beside her and said, his voice unusually tentative, "Suicide?"

"Just because that well report turned up?"

"Those land gamblers dug themselves into some deep holes."

"But to kill himself? It's so drastic."

"More drastic than trying to kill you?"

Yes, well. "'Kill'?" she said, testing the word, trying to regain the certainty of last night. "Kill me. Kill *me*." No, she hadn't dreamed it. It might have been her lifeless body down there on those rocks. "It happened. It really did happen. He saw the envelope and he went berserk. But to—just deliberately take that plunge—"

"He can't have been quite rational." Eric got up and paced

again. "When you got away—when he realized you'd got away—the hole got deeper. Now he was in for an assault charge."

"You believe me."

Briefly, the half smile returned. "Oh, sure."

FIRST THE DEPUTY in the patrol car; then the ambulance, the crew leaping out, scrambling down the deer trail with a furled stretcher. After a little while, a plainclothes investigator. It was Investigator Noel Ricsbach, of course; did he never go off duty? She talked to the cold gray-blue eyes, interrupted once when the ambulance crew reached the top with an immobilized Charlie Emmett strapped to a mountain-rescue stretcher, a second time when a medivac helicopter clattered down on the back lawn.

For Charlie wasn't dead. The head injury that had blotted out his consciousness had apparently spared the centers that kept his heart beating and the breath going in and out of his lungs.

Riesbach said, "This should be on tape. I want you to come into the office."

"Voluntarily," said Eric.

"Of course," said Riesbach.

Eric drove her over.

"YOU TAKE YOUR TIME getting around to telling us things," said Riesbach when she'd said everything all over again in a small room with a video camera high in a corner. She hadn't seen any reason to ask Eric to stay with her; he was off in some other room, talking with some other investigator.

"I was concussed," she said.

"Not too concussed to call your lawyer."

"That was for the closing. I thought Charlie would be there and I wanted somebody on my side."

"If you left the truck on the carry road, how did it get back to the gulch?"

Stick to what you know firsthand, Eric had advised her. *Don't speculate or guess.* "I don't know."

"Why did he drive off the bridge?"

"I don't know."

"*Did* he drive off the bridge?"

"I don't know. I never saw Charlie or the truck after I got in Kristin's car. Ask her. Ask Kristin Vanstaat what happened after I got out of the truck."

"Oh, we will," said Riesbach.

ON THE WAY BACK OUT to the sheriff's parking lot, she said, "I think he wanted me to have driven Charlie over the edge."

"That won't last after they fingerprint the truck."

"Why? I did drive it. My fingerprints will be on the wheel."

"And Charlie's will be on top of them."

Oh.

"They aren't planning to railroad you," Eric said. "Did he tell you they found the well report in Charlie's shirt pocket?"

"He didn't tell me anything."

"Everything is going to check out. You may be harassed by the media for a while."

"Oh, God."

"Don't try to avoid them. Stick to facts, don't speculate about anything, and don't sign any book contracts without talking to an intellectual property lawyer."

"Oh, *God!*"

"I'm hungry," he said. "How about you?"

Having just—probably—thrown away half a million dollars, she hesitated. Possibly he read her mind, for he said, "My treat."

Damsel in distress, knight to the rescue? Recipe for a royal mess.

Clairvoyant again, he said, "There's no ethical bar to a lawyer's taking a client to dinner."

Oh. A professional relationship. "Thanks," she said, aware that disappointment was irrational.

With three tables within earshot, they avoided the subject of the day. (After the first glance at Janet's battered face, the other diners avoided staring.) Janet steered the conversation to Eric's career choice—an obvious one, he pointed out, for a tree-hugging ecofreak with an analytic mind—and after a paragraph or two, he steered it back to her goals as a photographer. She admitted to vagueness; he claimed to understand.

A MILE OR TWO into the return trip, Eric said, "It has been occurring to me that maybe Charlie was in for more than an assault charge."

"Mm?"

"This whole mess started in nineteen eighty-seven when Alta ordered that well report, Charlie issued the building permit, and the Willards sued."

"Okay. Yes."

"Well, Charlie could have mooted the case by claiming he'd made an honest mistake and canceling the building permit. We hoped the town attorney would pressure him to take that line and save the Town the cost of litigation. Then the Town Board would pass Steep Slopes before Alta had time to modify her plans and get a new building permit, and the house would be down the tubes."

"I didn't know that," she said. "Paul said the lawsuit was a Hail Mary."

"Well, legally, it was. It was your basic nuisance suit."

"Should I be shocked?"

"It's an option. If I'd been admitted, I might have hesitated to put my name on it. As a mere third-year law student, I just told them what the possibilities were and they proceeded *pro se*."

"And then Steep Slopes didn't get passed after all. Was that Uncle Bud again? Was he on the Board back then?"

"Oh, indeed. Déjà vu. My point is, nobody knew it wouldn't pass, so what if Charlie told Alta he planned to take a dive and

she threatened to make the well report public if he did? He'd have been in a box."

"So he got out of it by pushing her off Big Bear."

"And spent eight years thinking he'd dodged a murder charge. Then you turned up with the report and all bets were off."

"I guess it would explain the berserk."

"Except," he said, "for a little matter of evidence. We don't know whether Charlie was up on Big Bear that afternoon, and I'm sure everybody's whereabouts were exhaustively investigated."

"Lawyers," she said.

"Right. Okay, want to try another theory?"

"Why not."

"He drove off the bridge by accident."

"Oh, come on."

"No, think about it. It was dark, it was raining, the warning tape was down, and he misjudged where the edge was."

"But why would he be driving down there at all? The truck was all the way out on that back road."

"But you were alive and loose. Let's suppose that when he found the truck, he drove all the way out to Oak Hollow Road looking for you. He didn't know Kristin had picked you up on the carry road, so when he didn't find you, he thought you'd hoofed it out and picked up a ride on Oak Hollow Road. You might at the very moment be complaining of his assaultive behavior to the authorities."

"Why wouldn't I have driven all the way?"

"Details. Okay, he knew you had a head injury, so maybe you got too woozy to drive. Anyway, he decided to go back and get the bike, take it out, and dump it on Oak Hollow Road where you had the accident. Then whatever you said, he'd say you must have hallucinated everything you claimed happened after you crashed. But on the way back to pick up the bike, he misjudged and went over."

"Do you write thrillers in your spare time?" she asked.

"Tell me why it couldn't have happened."

"Anything could have happened," she said. "Could we please stop at Paul and Marion's? They have my keys."

"That's another thing," he said. "You should stop keeping your key in that desk drawer."

Authority figure. No wonder he attracted her. "Yes, sir," she said.

"AND YOUR BIKE is wrecked," Janet finished.

"It's insured," said Paul.

"As if it matters." Marion folded her arms and shuddered. "Oh, love, what a week." She hugged herself tighter. "Can you imagine just—driving over the edge like that?"

"After what he'd already done, yes," said Paul.

They urged her to stay over, but she needed her own time and space; and when Eric had seen her to her door and she'd unlocked it and locked it behind her with her own key, she didn't hurry to the window to watch him drive away.

There was bound to be an ethical bar against a lawyer's making a pass at a client.

THIRTY

One, Two, Three…

"MATT INCIARDI'S BID was the next lowest," said Helen. She'd heard, of course. "Do we call him or wait to see if Charlie recovers?"

Charlie wasn't going to recover anytime soon, if at all. "We'll recommend Matt to the Board," said Janet.

IT WAS INVESTIGATOR YOUNGBLOOD who telephoned in the middle of the afternoon; he had something he wanted her to look at over at headquarters. He'd pick her up.

What he wanted her to look at was a sort of lineup: a dozen metal bars laid out on a table, ranging from a little six-inch hex wrench to a four-foot pry bar that would move boulders. Would she look them over and see if any of them resembled the one she'd seen Charlie reaching for?

She saw it at once, about a third of the way in from the end: a thin steel bar, an inch wide and about eighteen inches long, flat like a venetian blind slat, with a hook cut into one end.

"Sure?" said Youngblood.

"I'm not likely to forget it."

"Okay."

"Is that any help?"

He smiled. *Catch Riesbach ever smiling.* "That item was found on the ledge just below the truck door. It has Emmett's fingerprints on it."

"I told you so."

Another smile.

"What is it?"

"A slim-jim."

She'd heard of slim-jims; they unlocked car doors. "Is it legal to have one of those?"

"Depends on whether you're carrying it with criminal intent. One thing bothers me, though. He had a locked tool chest in the back of the truck, but according to your statement, this was loose in the truck bed."

Slim-jim—locks—there was something—yes! "Kristin said his wife had locked the keys in her car," she said. "That same afternoon. He had to drive down to the IGA to open it. Kris said he was mad, so maybe he just threw it in the truck instead of putting it away."

"Mm," said Youngblood.

Something else was tickling the back of her consciousness, but she couldn't get hold of it.

"Well, thanks," said Youngblood. "A few things are getting cleared up."

THAT REPORTER WAS ON her answering machine again. She didn't delete this message, but first she returned the Denver call. Mr. Howard Wells of the law firm of Kinsey & Wells accepted the charge and in a hearty mountain-west voice asked how she was doing.

"Banged up," she said cautiously.

Sorry to hear that. And how was the weather in the state of New York? Still having those torrential thunderstorms?

It was his phone bill. She murmured "Mm-hm" and "Well—" and after what must have been a predetermined interval, he came to the point. Kinsey & Wells represented Donald Ferguson, who had been named administrator of his son's estate. Terrible tragedy, nobody's fault of course, act of God—

Hey, it wasn't God driving me onto that bridge.

But she didn't need to say it; the lawyers were obviously of the same opinion, for they were offering her twenty thousand dollars to release Gregory Ferguson's estate from liability—

She said she'd get back to him.

THE REPORTER AT the other end of the county was only the advance guard; the next day, their attention caught by the extraordinary number of falls off Hudson Highlands cliffs, camera crews from the city invaded Phillips Landing. Janet recited an abridged version of what she'd told Riesbach and referred all their invitations to speculate to the sheriff. The sheriff declined all invitations to speculate, characterized it as a complex case, and expressed confidence in his investigative staff.

TWENTY GRAND WOULD pay off the Visa and leave enough for a serviceable secondhand car. Not a Jeep; unicorns are mythical beasts. She rejected the notion of consulting Eric; it wasn't his field, and anyway, she wasn't about to continue the lawyer-client relationship any longer than it took to clear up the aldicarb question. And even if he gave her a referral, she didn't want to spend the next twenty years involved in a lawsuit, pitting her word against a dead kid and a lot of innuendo. Besides, Don Ferguson was a decent man and that property had given him enough grief.

THE SLIM-JIM NIGGLE finally broke through to the surface.

She remembered that just the day before her car went off the cliff, she'd been mouthing off to Charlie about horses and water pollution. (A real tree-hugging ecofreak, yes, indeed.) What if he'd been afraid she'd find some way to queer the sale? (And that wasn't such a wild idea after all, was it?) What if, when her car slipped its gear and its brakes and went over the cliff, it hadn't, in fact, slipped at all? What if Charlie had opened the door with that slim-jim thing, put the gearshift in neutral, re-

leased the brake a little, and then locked the door again and pushed the car over? Wrecked her car so she'd have to borrow against the legacy to buy a new one? Then she'd be—so to speak—locked in.

What if. Anything could have happened. She didn't bother to mention this speculation to anybody.

PLANS FOR Gregory Ferguson's memorial service were sidetracked by the uproar surrounding Charlie Emmett's fall into the ravine. Maybe next year, Kristin said, like on the anniversary.

"JANNIE!" LEORA'S VOICE WAS hushed, as if she were crouching over the phone in a corner. "Did you tell anybody?"

No need to ask about what. "Of course not."

"It's out. I knew it would get out."

"What happened?"

"Sunday night, after softball, one of the guys in the bar heard something and he started to devil Lowell about his wife—you know—and Lowell punched him, and there was a fight—"

"Was Lowell arrested?"

"Not yet."

"Lee—" God, what a mess. "You can't really think Lowell pushed your dad."

"Jannie, I don't—no, I don't. He was lost. He really was lost all that time. But they aren't going to believe that when they find out about me—"

"Lee, nobody's going to arrest Lowell on the basis of barroom gossip. If you don't go around talking about it, nobody's going to find out anything."

"But—oh, Jannie, it's so awful."

Well, yes. It was.

THE CHECK CAME. Janet signed the release, paid off the Visa bill, and went car shopping. She was picky, so it took a while.

THE MENTOR-MENTEE SHOW came down on the Sunday before Labor Day. Kristin came by for her pieces and Janet, openly playing favorites, helped her pack them into cartons. When they had tucked in the flaps, Kristin said, "Well—I guess this is good-bye."

"You aren't going to be that far away," said Janet. "Come back and visit. Let me see your new work."

"You come and see me," Kristin said. "I don't think anybody in my family is ever going to set foot in this county ever again."

"That sounds extreme."

"Listen, do you know what the sheriff has been doing? He's been hounding my dad about Mr. Hale falling off the quarry. Like he *pushed* him off. *My dad,* for God's sake, and don't tell me I shouldn't swear. You know my dad, he has a hard time slapping a mosquito. Just because Mr. Hale said he was going to vote for that Steep Slopes law, this jerk thinks—oh, it's too stupid."

"Any particular jerk?"

"Riceman, Reeser, something like that."

"Riesbach."

"Whatever. I mean, for God's sake, my dad never *bought* any steep slopes. If he had, he'd have sold them. Even my klutz of a dad would have been able to sell land like that, and we wouldn't have to be moving to Poughkeepsie. But anyway, this jerk, Reesman, whatever—he's just a *Putnam* County sheriff, so he can't come hounding us up in Dutchess County."

Schuyler Vanstaat? God, what a mess. And don't tell me not to swear. "Kris," she said, "call me when you finish a piece and I'll come."

"You'd better." A horn honked in the lot. "I've got to go." She blinked; she stepped forward; Janet opened her arms and they hugged. "Listen," Kristin said, stooping to pick up a carton, "after everything he did to you, if anybody went pushing anybody off any cliffs, I'll bet it was Charlie Emmett."

Others had speculated similarly. Charlie had, after all, been up there on the mountain, and he had shown a certain interest in

dropping people off cliffs. The problem with the theory was that Charlie Emmett was far worse off with Bud Hale dead.

AT NIGHT, in the twilight zone between waking and sleeping, that maddening counting started up again: *One, two, three, four—seven, ten—* It was like that jingle that, once heard, couldn't be gotten rid of: *Punch, conductor, punch with care / Punch in the presence of the passengaire*—Mark Twain, was it? *A pink trip ticket for a five-cent fare—*

    One two...

ON THE SATURDAY AFTERNOON of Phillips Landing High School's first home football game, Janet took possession of a six-year-old Civic wagon with four-wheel drive and a five-speed stick shift. (*Four, five, six—*) Forty-five thousand miles. A little fender rust, not serious. A retired widower had driven it to the IGA twice a week. The salesman said Honda had stopped making them because they never wore out.

A WEEK LATER, Eric called. Thaddeus Bradford's old well still contained twenty-eight ppb of aldicarb—down from 1987's thirty-eight, but still four times New York state's acceptable level of seven and almost three times the EPA's standard of ten. That wasn't quite the end of it, though; now they would drill a test well as far from the original well as they could get and still stay on the property. Maybe, that far away, the numbers would be acceptable.

    Numbers seemed to be governing her life: seven times as much, ten times as much—twenty-eight, thirty-eight—*punch, brother, punch with care—*

CHARLIE HUNG ON, breathing without mechanical assistance, his eyelids fluttering now and then when questions were put to him.

THREE DAYS BEFORE the October fourteenth deadline, the sale of Thaddeus's old farm fell through. The new well tests showed aldicarb all over the place. Under the place, actually. Twenty-one ppb in the new test well. "Old Thaddeus must have had a major spill," said Eric.

She'd have been surprised by any other result. The trust fund would run out in February; after that the bank could have the place, for all she cared. Charlie certainly didn't have the income to keep up the payments and Finlay Keene couldn't in good conscience bleed the estate. Certainly not in a lost cause. "Unicorns don't exist," she said.

"Well, the broker is going to beat the bushes. A buyer might still turn up."

"Oh, sure," she said, "and tomorrow the sun might rise over the Hudson." Phillips Landing was on the east bank.

"Well, you have a point. And speaking of the river—how would you like to go over to Minnewaska next Sunday and hike around in the Shawangunks."

Surprised, she caught herself stalling. "There are a lot of cliffs in the Gunks," she said.

"Well—"

"No, I'm kidding," she said. "Thanks, Eric, I'd like that." Hanging up, she decided he must regard the attorney-client relationship as finished.

DON FERGUSON PHONED ON Saturday morning. He'd come back to Phillips Landing to clear out the house and put it on the market. Would it be all right if he dropped by the art center to pick up the key she'd borrowed?

He showed up late, just as Helen was leaving. Janet hadn't remembered how deep the lines in his face were. "You look beat," she said. "All this must be hard."

"Not exactly a day at the beach. Janet, I've got to ask you.

Have you heard any talk about Greg and that Hale fellow who fell off the cliff? The town councilman?"

"What kind of talk?"

"Well, an investigator from the sheriff's office called me at home a week or two ago. He got wind of Greg's plan to build that damn house of Alta's, and he got the idea that this Hale fellow was going to cast some vote that would make it impossible, so Greg pushed him off the mountain. He was at me about Greg—how serious he was about the house, what kind of trouble he'd been in before." He ran his hand over his face. "Greg had a couple of run-ins with the local cops in high school—the kind of impulsive crap kids'll pull when they're trying to figure out what it takes to be a man." He rubbed his face again. "Janet, there was a lot about my son I didn't understand, but I can't believe he'd—" He stalled, unable to get the word out.

A decent fellow, Don Ferguson. She hadn't heard of this development, and there was no way on this earth that she was going to tell him what *she* had thought. "No," she said. "No, I haven't heard anything of the sort."

"I can't get out of this place soon enough. Did you hear what else they're saying? The sheriff's people got an engineer down there where the bridge went out, and he says that footing probably couldn't have washed out without help. Somebody probably had to go down there while the stream was running high and shovel a shitload of dirt out from around it. Nobody would have noticed. It would have just washed downstream."

"My God," she said.

"They're saying somebody may have killed my son." He rubbed his face again. "I can't get out of this place soon enough. Do you know anything about some outfit called the Hudson Land Trust?"

"I've heard of it," she said. "I know somebody who works for them."

"Reliable people?"

"I never heard otherwise. They buy scenic land to preserve it from development."

"Well, they've made an offer for that goddamn outcrop that killed Alta. I've got a good mind to take them up on it."

"It would make a lot of people happy," she said.

"Good people?"

"Well—me for one."

"Well, Janet," he said, "I guess I owe you one, after my son nearly got you killed."

THE HIKE WAS a success, as hikes go. The air was a crisp sixty-five degrees; the fall color was near its peak; the improbable cliffs of the Shawangunks gleamed in the sun; they avoided all talk of death and destruction. At the end of the day, for the third time in two months, Eric saw Janet to her door and drove away. Except for giving her a hand up a couple of ledges, he'd made no move that even remotely resembled a pass.

She'd heard from her grandmother about the three-date rule; maybe the first two hadn't been dates.

And really, it was just as well.

ONE TWO THREE—

God*damn* it.

It shifted to computer talk: *Oh one, oh two, oh three—*

Hey! Maybe her cockeyed unconscious was trying to tell her something.

She scrambled off the futon, flicked on the light, fished the Stuff disk and the poems from under her bras and panties, and went downstairs to the office.

The last locked file, number twelve, had been entered on August fourth, the night before Uncle Bud's fall. She found the poem that had been entered on the same day and carefully counted the characters in each line, including the spaces, and when she came to the twelfth, she underlined it. When she had

finished, she summoned file twelve, and when the screen said
Enter Password, she entered the underlined letters.

Chunk, muttered the computer; *chunk chunk chunk-chunk—*

PART THREE

October 1995
Paul

PART THREE

THIRTY-ONE

Printout

IT WAS THE SORT of day that brought out the leaf-tour buses: maples flaring gold and scarlet against enamel blue sky, crimson dogwood and dusty rose viburnum anchoring the understory, goldenrod and asters and Queen Anne's lace splashed in every open space. Paul Willard sat on the stone bench beside the studio door, taking a break after a steady morning's work, inhaling the dry spice of October air and resting his eyes on the distant form of Big Bear that he'd framed by pruning an opening in the trees.

Beyond the bit of forest that hid the house, he heard a car turn into the driveway. The motor died; a door slammed; and presently footsteps rustled along the path. Janet appeared around the bend, her camera bag hanging from one shoulder, her tripod from the other.

She'd called this morning to ask if he'd mind if she followed him around the studio with her camera for an afternoon. "Portrait of artist as an old man," he'd said, immoderately pleased. Only later did apprehension creep in.

Janet stood the tripod against the wall and sat down beside him. "Marion out ringing doorbells?"

"Dawn to dark." Marion really was running for the vacancy on the Town Board.

"How's it going?"

"A crapshoot. No nationwide polls in the Town of Claysburgh."

"But people do trust her." She opened her camera case. "Stay there. I like the way you look on that bench."

Presently they moved inside. Paul went back to work with drill and chisel while Janet prowled with the camera. Between flashes, they talked about light and form.

Marion would give him no peace unless he asked, so finally, keeping his face averted while he painted glue on a join, he said, "You seeing Eric, by any chance?"

After another couple of flashes, she said, "We went hiking in the Gunks yesterday." Another shot. "But don't get Marion's hopes up."

"Ghosts?" He stood the glue brush in the pot and picked up a clamp.

She moved in and shot his hands fitting it around a join. "Know any exorcists?" Two more flashes. "Actually, I'm afraid he does damsels in distress."

"Common male failing."

"Can we talk? I don't want to get locked into the role." She flicked the film advance twice, said, "That does it for this roll. Don't do anything picturesque while I'm changing film." She crossed the studio to sit on the bench where she'd left her camera bag.

He tightened the last clamp and went over to perch on the stool beside the drafting table. "Babe?"

She looked up.

"Photograph what troubles you?"

She looked down and busied herself with the camera.

"What is it, babe?"

She finished threading the film, snapped the camera shut, and looked up. Tension lines ringed her mouth. "Remember I told you I found some locked files on a computer disk of Uncle Bud's?"

"Seems to me you did."

"I got curious."

"Naturally."

"And I finally figured out the passwords. A few of the files were PIN numbers and stuff like that, but most of them were sort of a diary. He didn't make entries every day; they were months apart. There was something about a boundary dispute he had with Alta, and another one about the first go-round of the Steep Slopes law. There was a while when he was planning to vote for it. It was mainly to spite Alta, so when she died, he changed his mind. Some stuff about Leora marrying Lowell. He was glad; the way she kept turning down dates, he was afraid she'd never hook up with a guy."

"Knowing Bud, I'll bet he was afraid he'd raised a lesbian."

She looked up, clearly startled. Good lord, he'd been joking. Many a true word—?

"He didn't say that," she said. "There was a sad little piece about Aunt Irene's cancer, and then there was a long break, and then something about why he saddled me with that Bradford white elephant."

"Why did he?"

"Teasing. A double tease. Number one, it was like leaving me a lottery ticket; get me all excited over something that probably wouldn't come to anything. He made that will before the buyer turned up. Number two, by leaving something to me and nothing to Rich, he was sticking his thumb in Rich's eye."

"Ingenious."

"One word for it. I'm almost sorry I threw the damn money away. I could have given it to Rich."

"Would he have taken it?"

"I doubt it. Or he'd have given it to AIDS research or Act Up or something."

"And we could all have gone out to Bud's grave site to watch the earthquake."

Her smile didn't last long. She pulled a couple of folded sheets of paper from a pocket of her camera case. "This one is from the night before he died. I want you to read it." She crossed

the studio and put the papers in Paul's hand and went back and sat down again.

Bud's curmudgeonly rasp was audible through the anonymous typeface:

Friday night, August 4
Well, I haven't had much to put in here for a while, but last night things got a little hairy. It's three in the morning and I sure got something to think about.

Alta Ferguson's boy called up. He came back to town a couple of months ago, twenty-one, full of himself, got control of some trust his mom set up for him. He gave the tenants notice and moved into that old house of Alta's on Ewing Road. He's his mother's kid all right, redheaded and freckled, and got her morals too, maybe worse.

He said he had something to show me and could he come by the house when he got off work. Nine-thirty. A little late, but I said okay, come on up. Well, he sure did have something to show me. He was digging around in Alta's old papers and he found a well-test report from 1987. It was addressed to Alta, but the sample was from that damn Bradford tract I let Charlie talk me into buying. It looks like Alta trespassed in there and took a sample. I don't know what gave her the idea, but it's bad news. The well was full of something called aldicarb. I told the kid I don't know aldicarb from Alka-Seltzer, but he had an article he found at the library. It's something they used to kill potato beetles twenty-some-odd years ago until the state banned it. Old Thaddeus must have been using it on that damn hobby farm. According to that article, it gets into the groundwater and enough of it could kill a person. That test of Alta's showed up enough the state would close down the well if they knew about it.

The kid says this report could kill the deal if our buyer happened to see it, as if I couldn't figure that out for myself. Well, I gave him an argument. That was then, this is now, it could have all dissipated by now. But he gives me an argument right back. Thaddeus stopped farming in '79, he says, and eight years later, in '87, when the well was tested, there was still this high concentration and this is only another eight years after that test. I say big deal, they can dig another well, and he says if this well is contaminated it could of spread through the whole aquifer.

So I said to the kid what is it you want from me, and I might have known. It's that damn Steep Slopes law again. Seems he got a bee in his bonnet about building that house Alta was about to slap up on that outcrop Paul took such a liking to, but the old building permit expired, and if we pass the law he won't be able to get a new one. So what it comes down to is, if I vote no he'll hand over the well report and forget he ever saw it.

Well, that got my back up. I told him my vote isn't for sale and never was. I said he'll find out where I stand when the Board is polled Thursday night, and if it turns out I vote yes, he can do what he has to do. He pushed, but I'm a stubborn old coot and I don't push easy and finally I just about threw him out.

Well, I didn't get a lot of sleep after that. I was talking it out with Irene in my head all night, and what it comes down to is, if I'm going to have any chance of meeting her at the pearly gates, I have to tell the buyer. It may not kill the deal. It'll put off the closing until they can run their own well tests, but maybe the stuff is gone. Even if it isn't and we lose the sale, at least I'll be able to sleep nights.

I have to tell Charlie. Better call him first thing, before I lose my nerve.

Paul looked up. Janet was perched on the edge of the bench, as tense as a deer in the headlights. "Charlie," he said.

"I thought it was Greg," she said. "After I found out how he wanted to build the house, I thought it was him."

"I don't know that this changes that."

"No." She shook her head. "It was Charlie. He was on the hike."

"Well, that's true." And now he was remembering. "Tell you something else, babe. Before we started up the mountain, he was sitting in Bud's car, and they were jawing away. Went on a long time."

"He was telling him."

"Could be. Irene and the pearly gates. Who'd have guessed?"

"And Charlie was up there at the top of the quarry. He said so himself. It was all Charlie. Uncle Bud, my car, Greg. Then me. Charlie all the way."

"Greg?"

"Don Ferguson says that bridge didn't fall down by itself. Somebody undermined it. Charlie. His wife was away all week, he had his nights to himself. Charlie knew Greg had the well report because Uncle Bud told him, so first he killed Uncle Bud to keep him from telling the buyer, and then he broke into Greg's house to look for it, and when he couldn't find it, he killed Greg, and then when he knew I'd seen it, he tried to kill me. It was all Charlie, all to keep that well report under wraps and get that poisoned land into somebody else's hands and the money in his own pocket. *And*"—her voice rose—"he had access to my film. Charlie knew I was shooting at the quarry, but he didn't know where, so he could have thought I caught him pushing Uncle Bud, and he had access to the darkroom key. And he knew how to ruin film. Greg was telling about one time with Kevin—"

"Greg had access and he knew how to ruin film."

"But Greg didn't break into his own house and he didn't undermine his own bridge. Paul—the sheriff's office isn't accept-

ing accident. About Uncle Bud. They're still questioning people. Riesbach is, anyway."

"I know."

"Everybody who wasn't with Marion on the way down. You, I'll bet, and Lowell, and Schuyler Vanstaat, and they've been calling Don Ferguson about Greg and that damn house."

"Schuyler too? I can't see Schuyler and violence in the same picture."

"Of course not. Paul, they didn't do it. Charlie did it." Her fists were clenched in her lap. "They don't know Charlie had a motive, or he'd be at the top of the list."

"This doesn't prove much, babe."

"But it makes things fit."

"That it does."

"They're harassing innocent people."

He sighed. "Can't let that go on, can we? Seems to me you'd better give that printout to the sheriff."

"That won't be enough," she said. "They'll want the disk and the passwords."

"So hand it all over."

"Only—Paul, that isn't all that's in those locked files."

He hadn't thought it was. It had been a long time coming. "Which is why you're photographing me." She was hesitating. "It can't be as bad as that," he said. "Come on, babe, stop havering."

This one was only a single sheet. She crossed the studio, handed it to him, and went back to the bench.

The date was November 5, 1987. Yep, this would be it. Again he heard Bud's voice:

Praise the Lord, Alta Ferguson is dead. The bitch fell off that rock face where she was going to build her monstrosity and broke her neck. I guess you could call it poetic justice, only I wonder if she really did fall. They say it must have happened around four-thirty or five when

it was getting dark, and it wasn't much before that when
I saw Paul Willard crossing over my land from his place,
toward Alta's. I was out on the carry trail picking up fire-
wood and I don't think he saw me. I figured he was out
on one of his log-hunting excursions. Now I'm not so
sure. He sure didn't want that house in his viewshed.

Well, they're calling it an accident and I don't plan
to tell anybody any different. Paul is worth a good deal
more than Alta Ferguson ever was or would have been.
If he did help her along the way to the Bad Place, he was
doing the world a favor. I don't feel sorry for her nearest and dearest either. That boy of hers is going to be
better off without her. I talked to his dad at the funeral.
Seems okay. Makes you wonder how he ever hooked up
with Alta in the first place.

There it was. Why on earth he'd expected to get away with
lying to Riesbach in the first place was a mystery. Well, panic,
of course, and he hadn't known Riesbach was a human lie de-
tector.

Janet's arms were folded, her hands clenched on her upper
arms. She'd have been going through hell.

He said, "The Fergusons didn't have a monopoly on blackmail."

"Uncle Bud was blackmailing you?"

"He didn't want much. Just for Marion not to run for his
Town Board seat until he was ready to retire."

"That's all?"

"The man didn't need money, but the status meant a lot to him.
He knew he could beat most people, but he wasn't sure he could
beat Marion."

"And you kept her from running?"

"I just told her what happened. She decided."

"Marion knew?"

"Babe, there wasn't that much to know. Bud was right, I was

out log hunting. Serving those papers on Alta was stressful, and you know what artists do to relieve stress."

"Drink, smoke, snort, shoot up, fuck, or run off at the mouth for a month of Sundays."

"And for the temperate, monogamous, and taciturn—?"

"Work."

"You got it. And when I'm prospecting for a likely piece of timber, I cross property lines at will. Bud was used to that."

"And that's all? You just crossed Bud's land onto Alta's?"

"Not quite. If that had been all, I probably wouldn't have lied to Riesbach. What happened was, when I realized where I'd got to, I decided to hike on up to the building site and visit the Bear. That lawsuit was a Hail Mary and I thought I might be paying a last fond farewell. I went up the backside of the hill as far as the edge of the construction site. The sun was just going down. I was about to cross over the cleared space when I saw Alta standing right out on the edge beside the Bear."

"Like Uncle Bud at the lookout."

"Those wide-open viewpoints are a temptation. I don't know if she was gloating because she expected to win the lawsuit or if she was paying her own farewell visit. Whatever it was, I sure wasn't going to include her in my last rites. I was just about to turn around and come home when rocks started clattering and she gave a yelp and disappeared."

"She just—fell? All by herself?"

"I was fifty yards away. Later they said the rock gave way. There isn't any direct way down from the top of the Bear, so I went down the driveway cut to Henley Lane and out onto Oak Hollow Road. There were already a couple of cars stopped just under the Bear and somebody was bending over something, so I knew she was being looked after, and that's when I panicked. I started to think about what it would look like if anybody knew I was in the vicinity, so I waited until the ambulance came and

took her away and the road was clear, and then I hiked home and said I'd never been there. Very stupid."

"But Riesbach hassled you anyway."

"He knew I was lying. The man's a human polygraph. But once I'd started, I couldn't seem to find a good time to retract."

"If he sees this entry—"

"It'll be a good time to retract."

"He'll go on harassing you."

"For a while, but eventually he'll know I've stopped lying."

"The first cliff," she said. "Eric had a theory that Charlie could have pushed her off. He thinks she used the well report to blackmail Charlie into approving the building permit and your lawsuit put him in a box."

"Charlie wasn't there."

"But it got him off the hook. At least it could have stuck in his mind how convenient it was for people to fall off cliffs."

"It would have been an impulse," he said. "Seeing Bud out there on the edge of nothing, and knowing what a stubborn old coot he was."

"The rest of it wasn't any impulse," she said.

"No. Once he started—" He eased off the stool and crossed to look out the window that framed Big Bear. "The stuff we give importance to."

She got up and came over to stand by him. "Beauty's important," she said. "All on its own."

"Not just a construct of our piddling little egos?"

"All on its own."

He put his arm across her shoulders. "You know, babe, they said the drilling must have weakened that rock where Alta was standing, but I never thought that was the whole story."

She turned her head to look up at him.

"Earth," he said, "has its own way of punishing blasphemers."